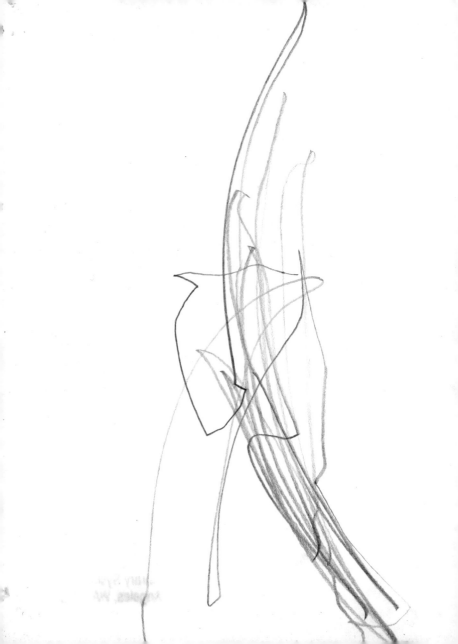

Dragonslayer

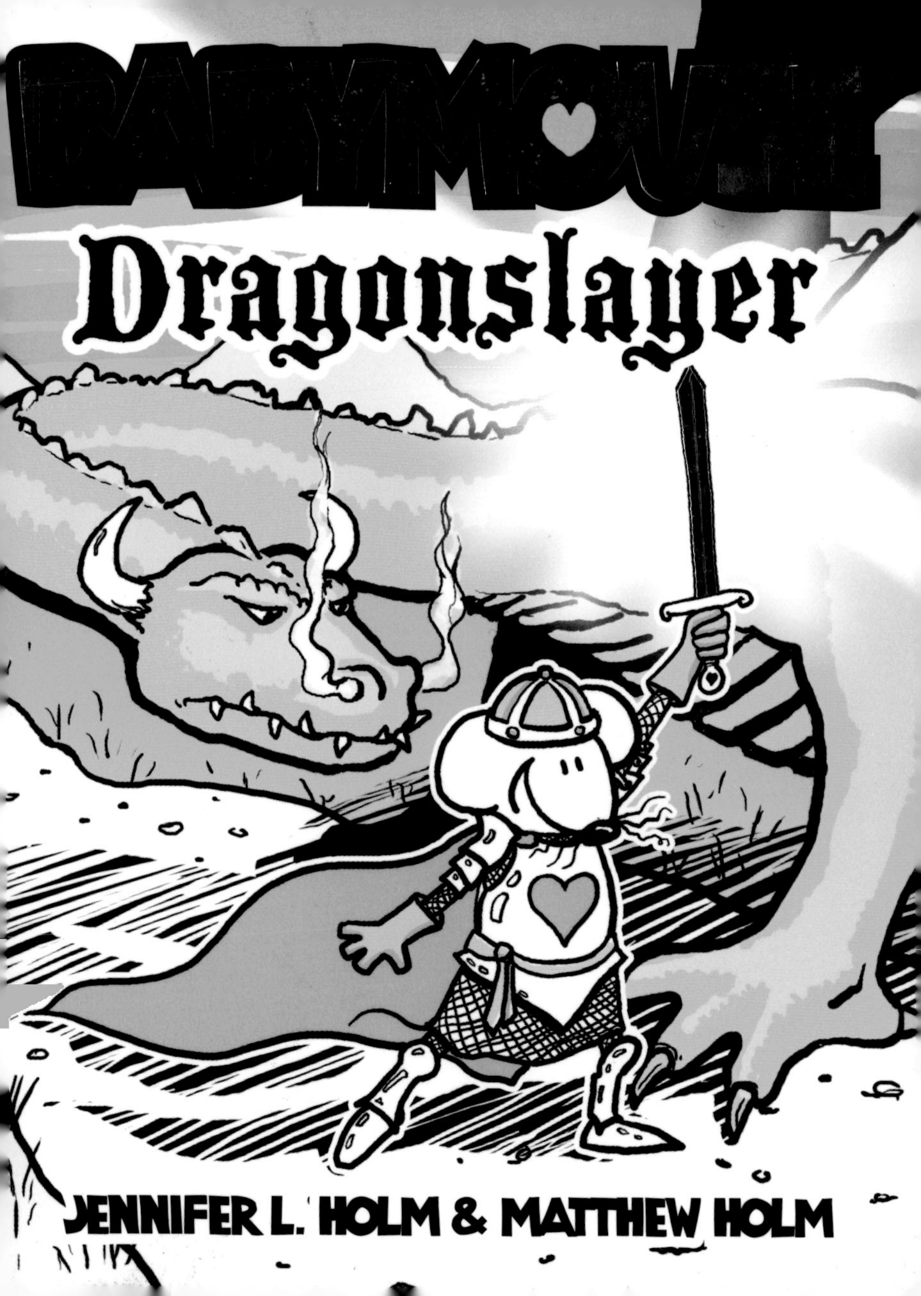

JENNIFER L. HOLM & MATTHEW HOLM

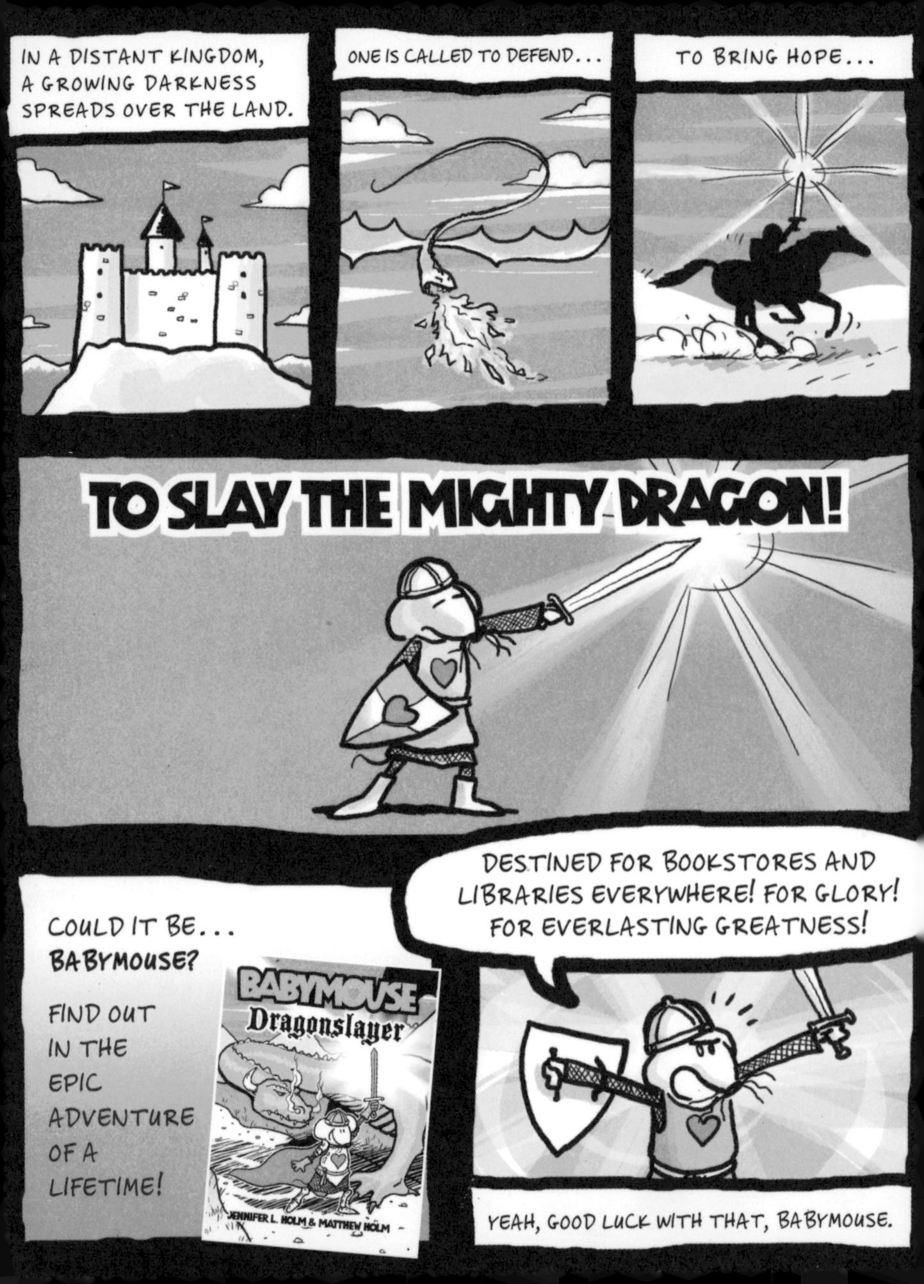
IN A DISTANT KINGDOM, A GROWING DARKNESS SPREADS OVER THE LAND.
ONE IS CALLED TO DEFEND...
TO BRING HOPE...
TO SLAY THE MIGHTY DRAGON!
COULD IT BE... BABYMOUSE?
FIND OUT IN THE EPIC ADVENTURE OF A LIFETIME!
BABYMOUSE
Dragonslayer
JENNIFER L. HOLM & MATTHEW HOLM
DESTINED FOR BOOKSTORES AND LIBRARIES EVERYWHERE! FOR GLORY! FOR EVERLASTING GREATNESS!
YEAH, GOOD LUCK WITH THAT, BABYMOUSE.

MORE PRAISE FOR BABYMOUSE!

"Sassy, smart . . .
Babymouse is here
to stay."
—The Horn Book Magazine

"Young readers
will happily
fall in line."
—Kirkus Reviews

"The brother-sister creative team hits the mark
with humor, sweetness, and characters so genuine
they can pass for real kids." —Booklist

"Babymouse is spunky, ambitious,
and, at times, a total dweeb."
—School Library Journal

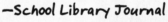

Be sure to read **all** the **BABYMOUSE** books:

#1 BABYMOUSE: Queen of the World!
#2 BABYMOUSE: Our Hero
#3 BABYMOUSE: Beach Babe
#4 BABYMOUSE: Rock Star
#5 BABYMOUSE: Heartbreaker
#6 CAMP BABYMOUSE
#7 BABYMOUSE: Skater Girl
#8 BABYMOUSE: Puppy Love
#9 BABYMOUSE: Monster Mash
#10 BABYMOUSE: The Musical
#11 BABYMOUSE: Dragonslayer

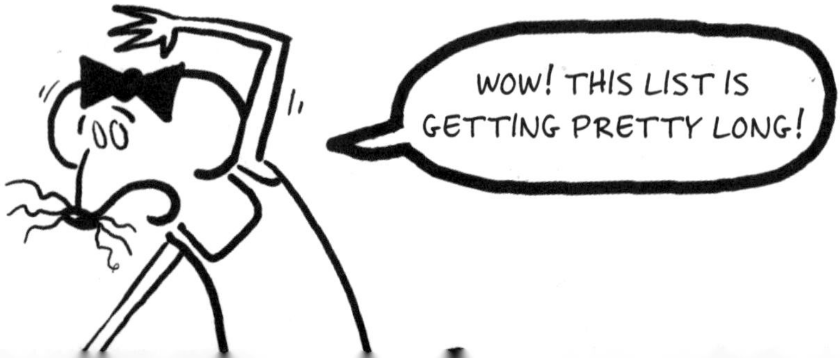
WOW! THIS LIST IS GETTING PRETTY LONG!

BABYMOUSE
Dragonslayer

BY JENNIFER L. HOLM & MATTHEW HOLM

RANDOM HOUSE 🏠 NEW YORK

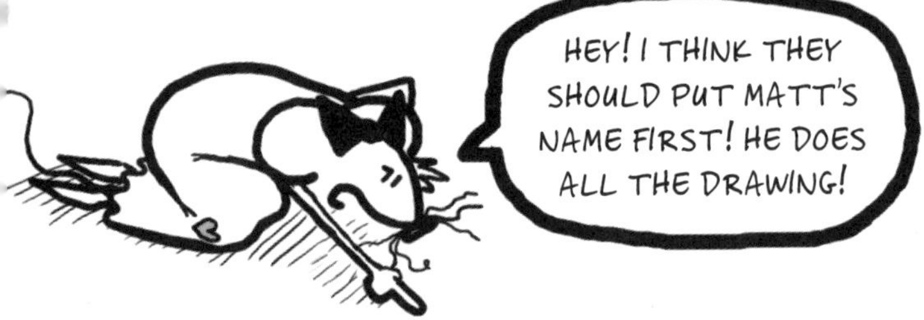
HEY! I THINK THEY SHOULD PUT MATT'S NAME FIRST! HE DOES ALL THE DRAWING!

This is a work of fiction. Names, characters, places, and incidents either are the product of the authors' imagination or are used fictitiously. Any resemblance to actual persons, living or dead, events, or locales is entirely coincidental.

Published in the United States by Random House Children's Books,
a division of Random House, Inc., New York.

Random House and the colophon are registered trademarks of Random House, Inc.

Visit us on the Web! www.randomhouse.com/kids
www.babymouse.com

Educators and librarians, for a variety of teaching tools,
visit us at www.randomhouse.com/teachers

Library of Congress Cataloging-in-Publication Data
Holm, Jennifer L.
Babymouse : dragonslayer / by Jennifer L. Holm & Matthew Holm. — 1st ed.
p. cm. — (Babymouse ; 11)
Summary: An imaginative mouse who likes to read heroic fantasy novels finds herself on the school math team as it prepares to compete for the coveted Golden Slide Rule.
ISBN 978-0-375-85712-6 (trade) — ISBN 978-0-375-95712-3 (lib. bdg.)
1. Graphic novels. [1. Graphic novels. 2. Imagination—Fiction. 3. Mathematics—Fiction. 4. Contests—Fiction. 5. Schools—Fiction. 6. Mice—Fiction. 7. Animals—Fiction.]
I. Holm, Matthew. II. Title. III. Title: Dragonslayer.
PZ7.7.H65Baf 2009 741.5'973—dc22 2008051110

MANUFACTURED IN MALAYSIA 10 9 8 7 6 5 4 3 2 1 First Edition

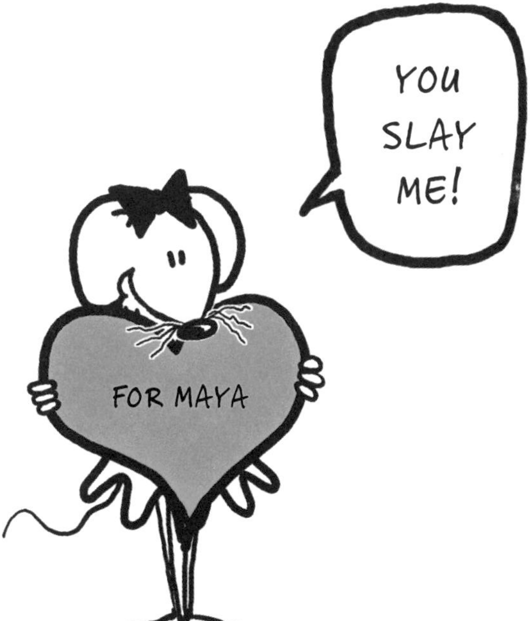
YOU SLAY ME!
FOR MAYA

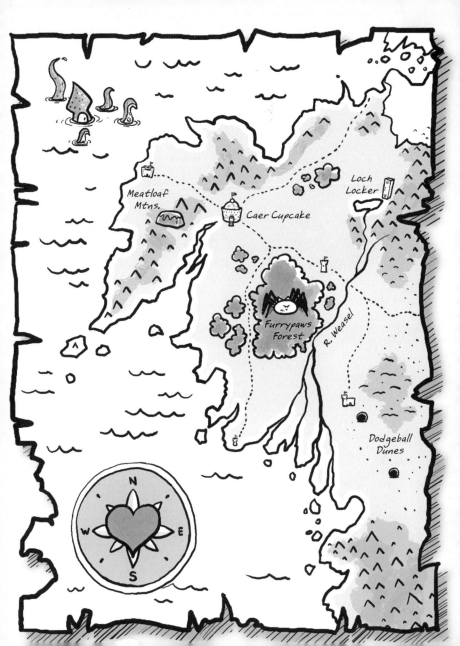

Meatloaf
Mtns.

Caer Cupcake

Loch
Locker

Furrypaws
Forest

R. Weasel

Dodgeball
Dunes

N
W E
S

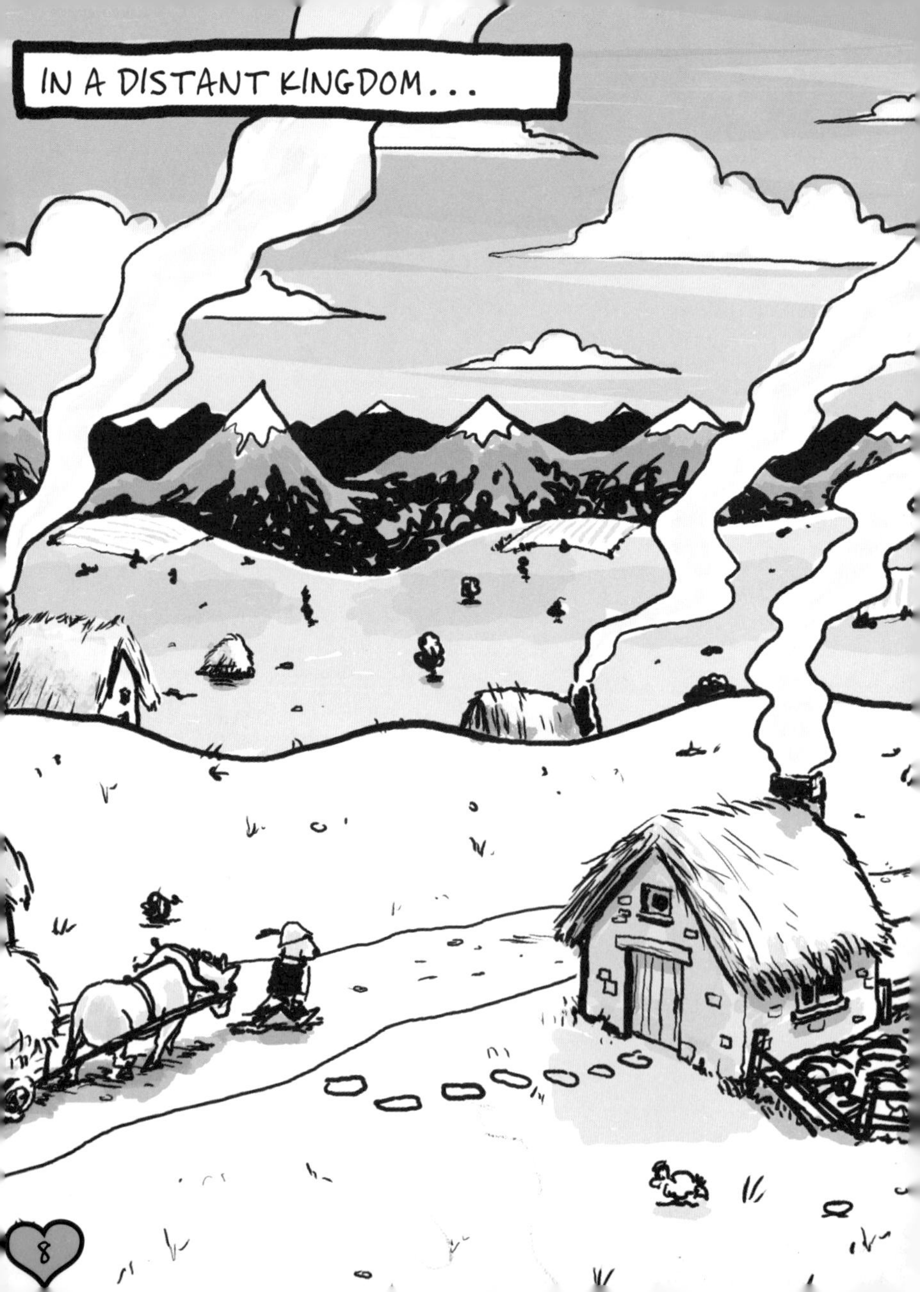
IN A DISTANT KINGDOM...

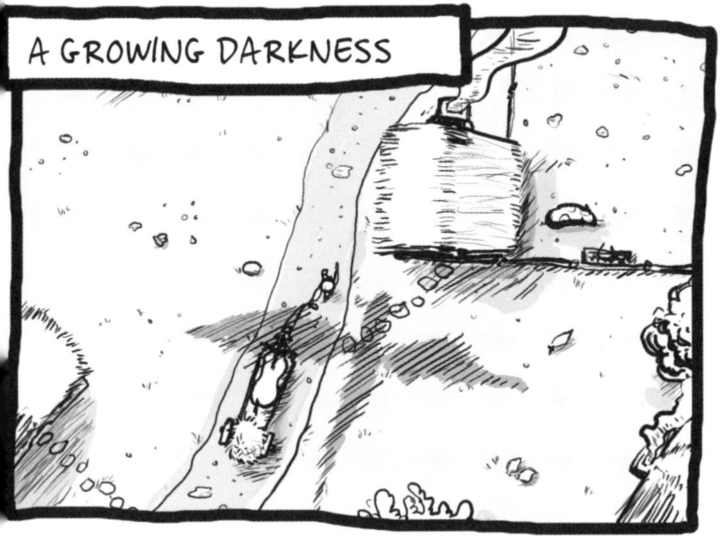
A GROWING DARKNESS

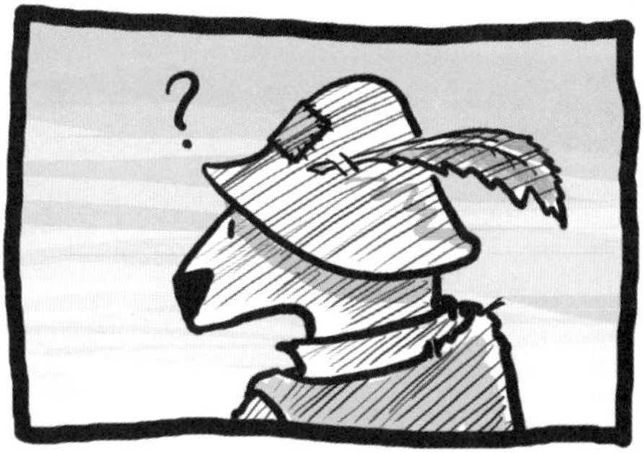
?

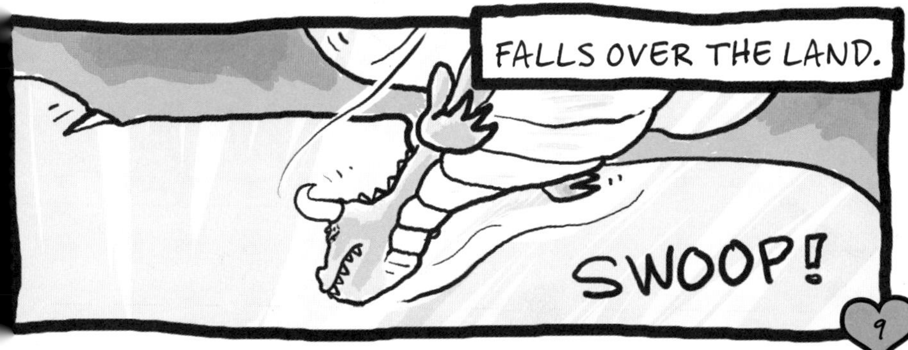
FALLS OVER THE LAND.
SWOOP!!

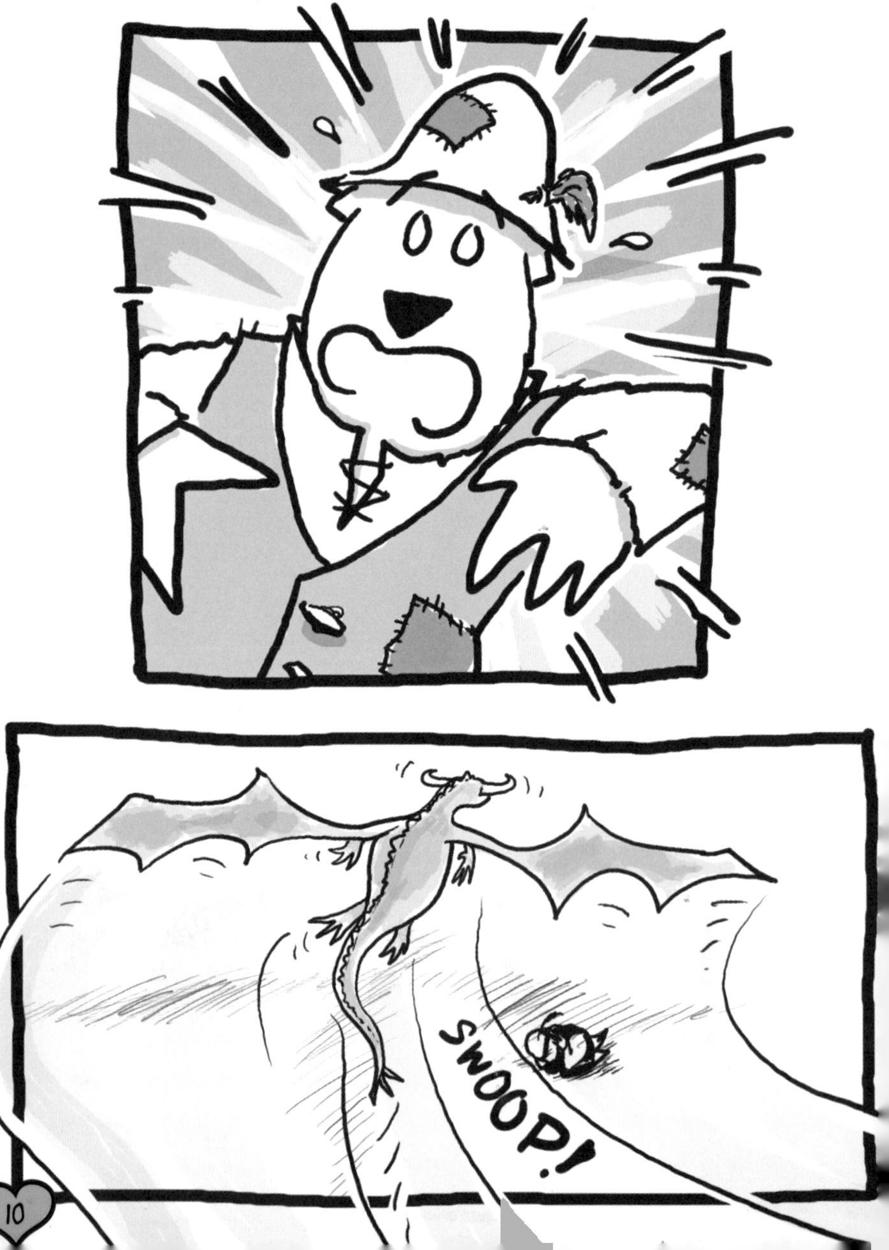
SWOOP!

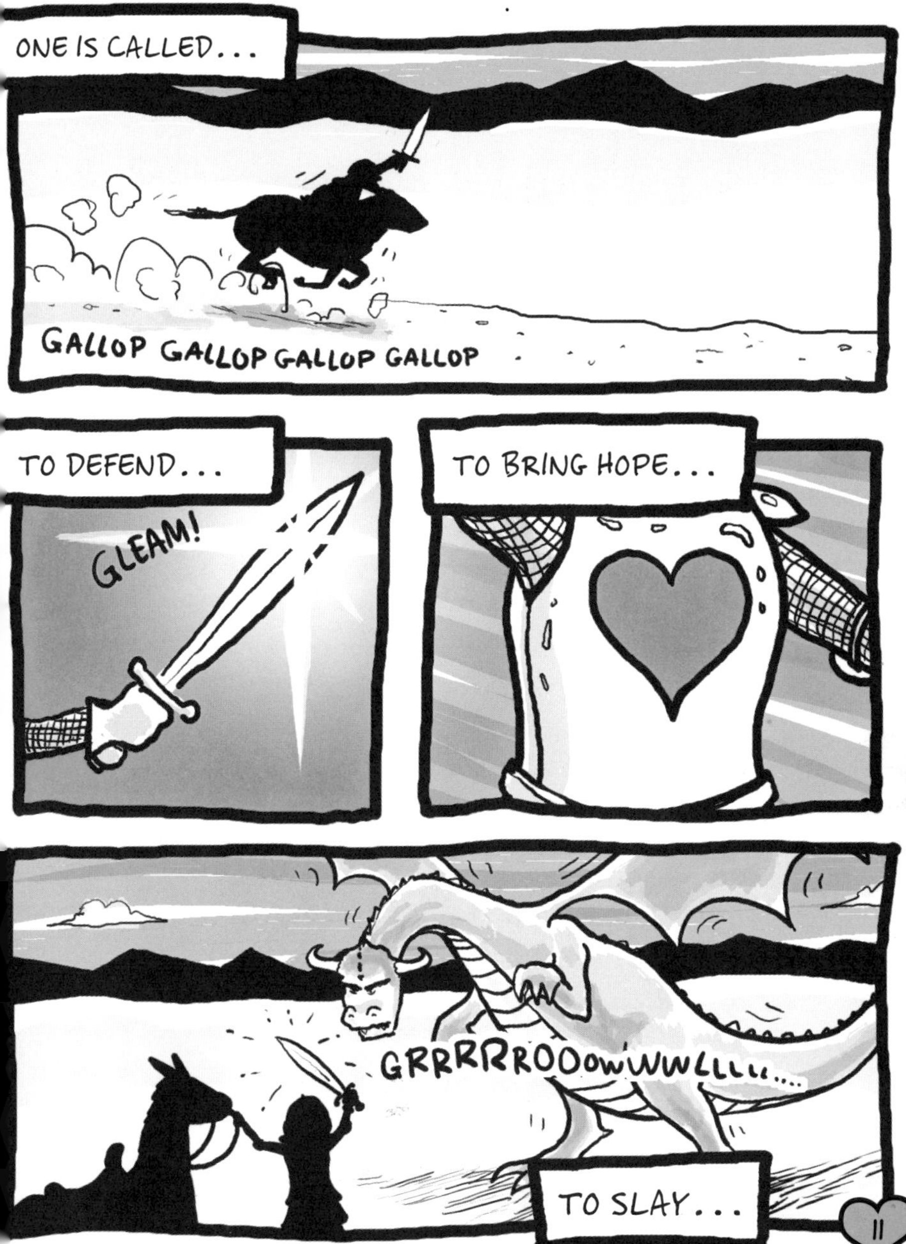
ONE IS CALLED...
GALLOP GALLOP GALLOP GALLOP
TO DEFEND...
GLEAM!
TO BRING HOPE...
GRRRRROOOowWWLLLL....
TO SLAY...

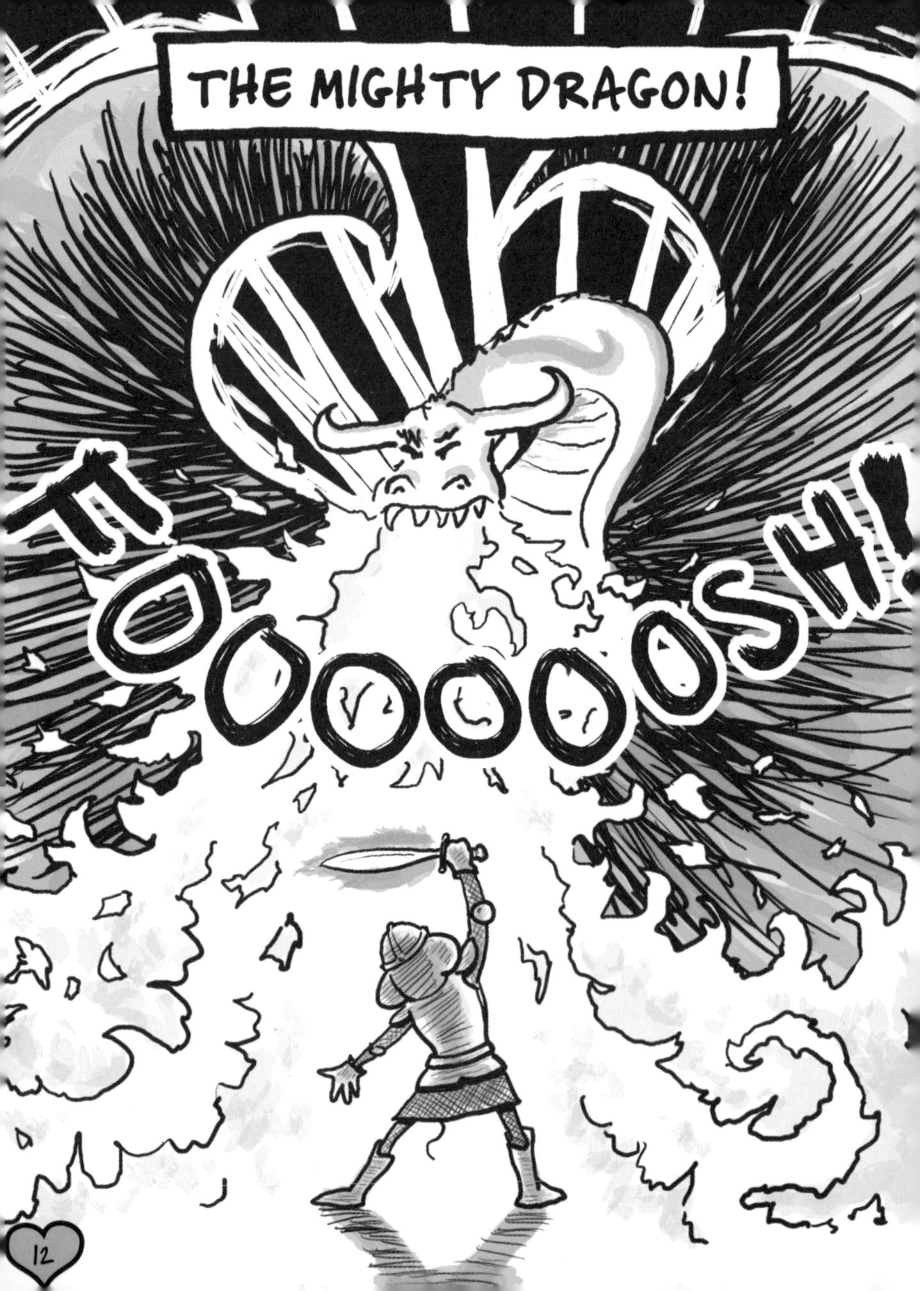
THE MIGHTY DRAGON!
FWOOOOOSH!

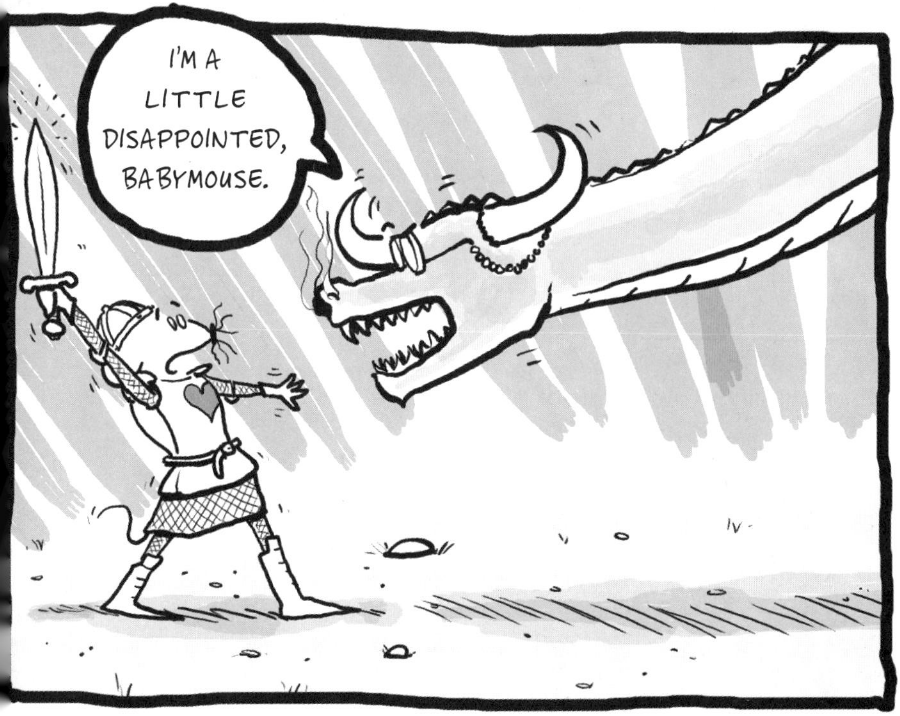
I'M A LITTLE DISAPPOINTED, BABYMOUSE.

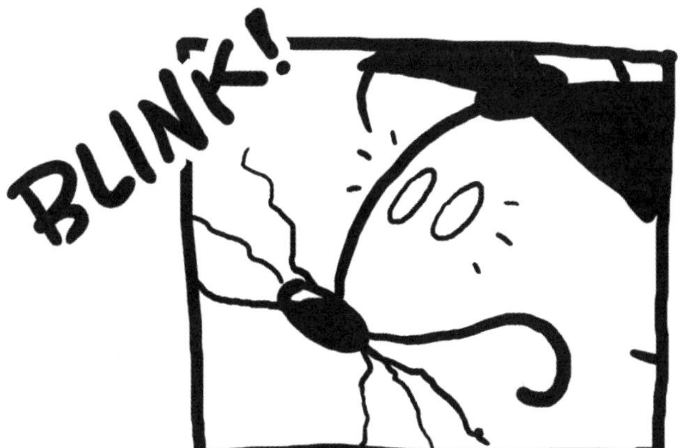
BLINK!

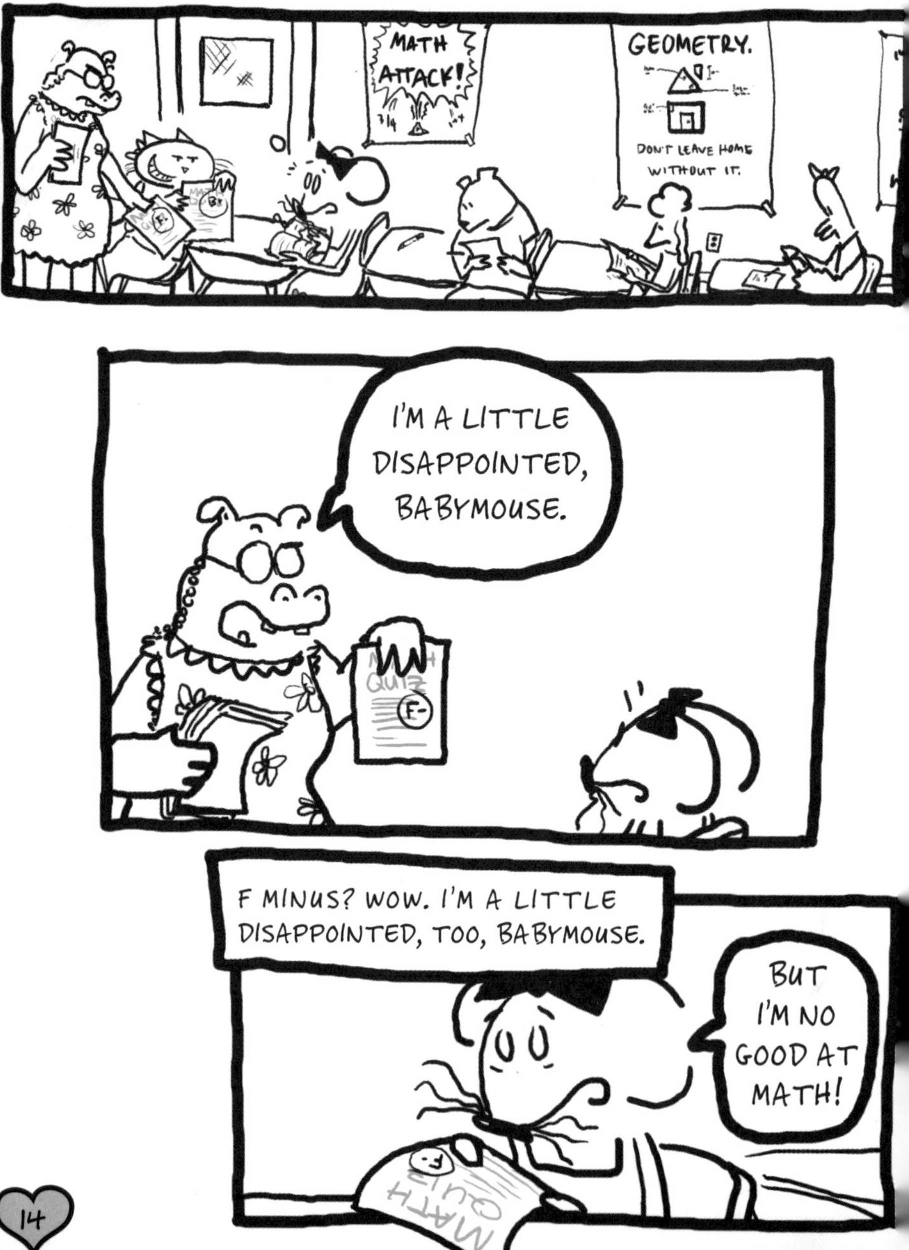
MATH ATTACK!
GEOMETRY.
DON'T LEAVE HOME WITHOUT IT.
I'M A LITTLE DISAPPOINTED, BABYMOUSE.
MATH QUIZ
F-
F MINUS? WOW. I'M A LITTLE DISAPPOINTED, TOO, BABYMOUSE.
BUT I'M NO GOOD AT MATH!
MATH QUIZ

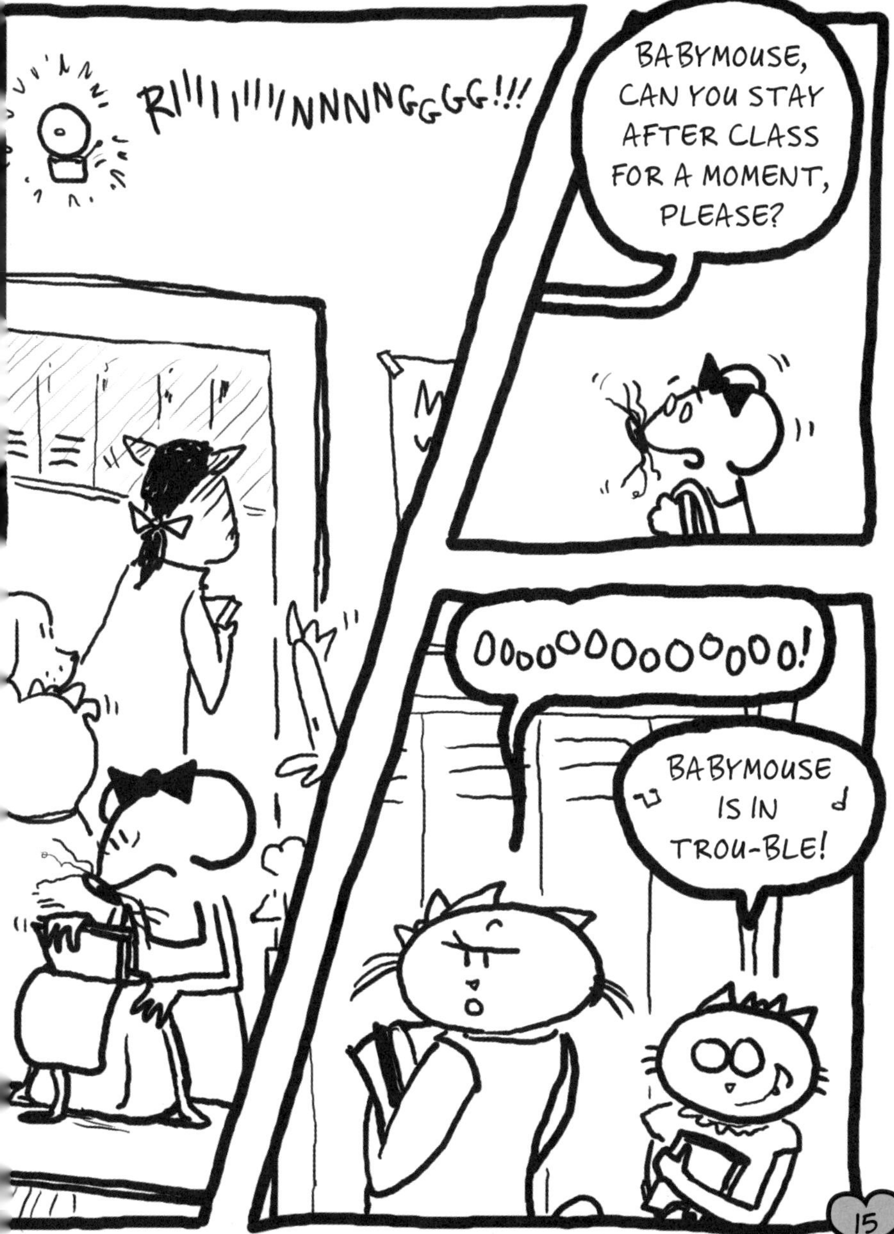
RI'''I I'''INNNNGGGG!!!
BABYMOUSE, CAN YOU STAY AFTER CLASS FOR A MOMENT, PLEASE?
OoooOOOOOOOOOOO!
BABYMOUSE IS IN TROU-BLE!

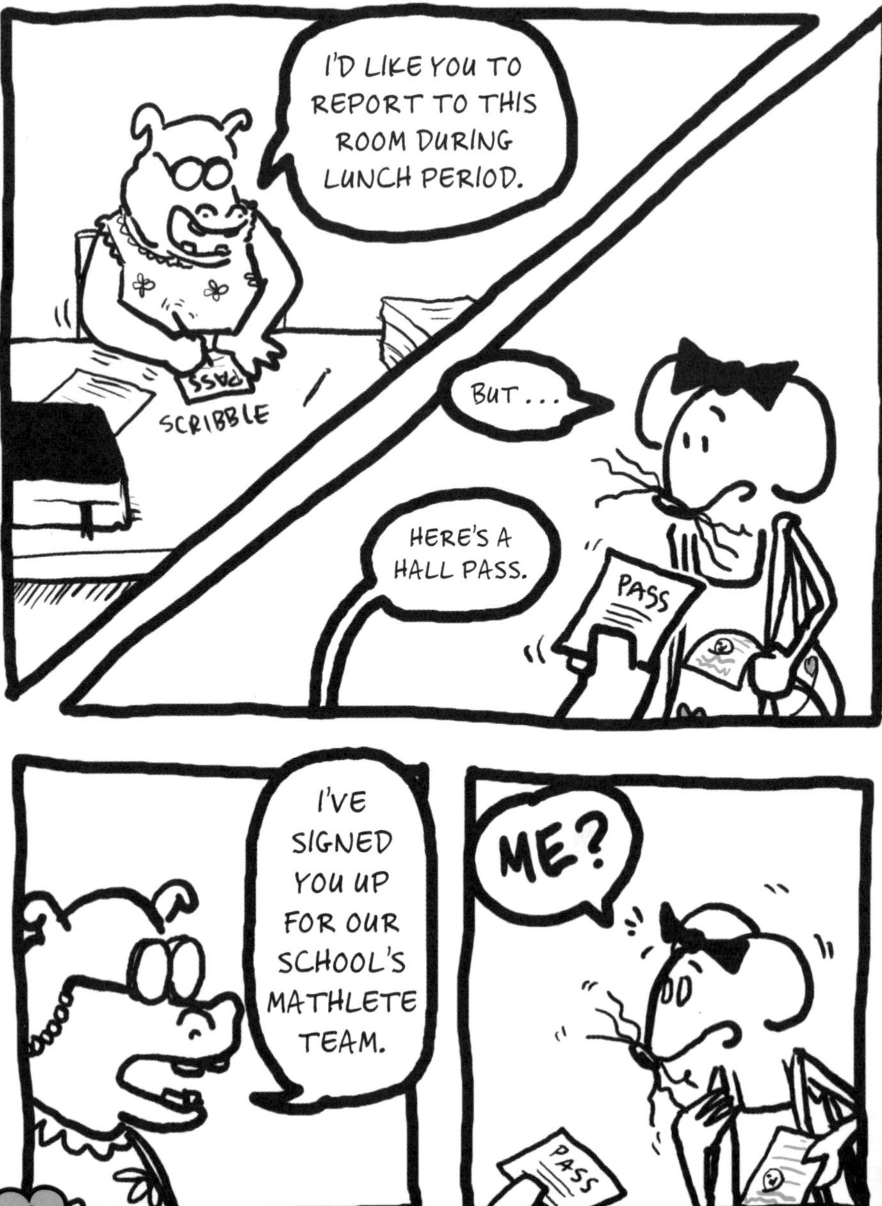

I'D LIKE YOU TO REPORT TO THIS ROOM DURING LUNCH PERIOD.
PASS
SCRIBBLE
BUT . . .
HERE'S A HALL PASS.
PASS
I'VE SIGNED YOU UP FOR OUR SCHOOL'S MATHLETE TEAM.
ME?
PASS

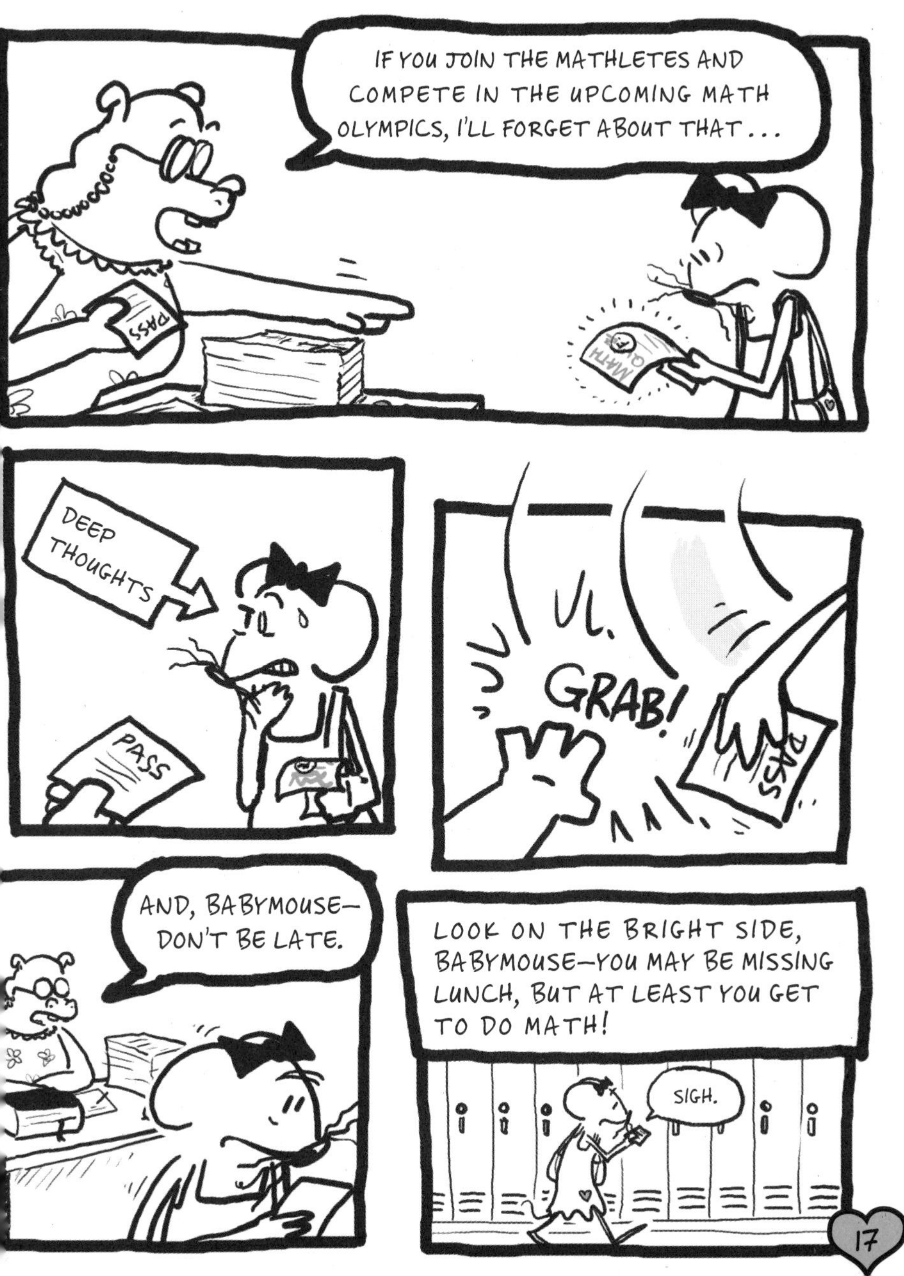
IF YOU JOIN THE MATHLETES AND COMPETE IN THE UPCOMING MATH OLYMPICS, I'LL FORGET ABOUT THAT . . .
PASS
MATH QUIZ
DEEP THOUGHTS
PASS
GRAB!
PASS
AND, BABYMOUSE— DON'T BE LATE.
LOOK ON THE BRIGHT SIDE, BABYMOUSE—YOU MAY BE MISSING LUNCH, BUT AT LEAST YOU GET TO DO MATH!
SIGH.

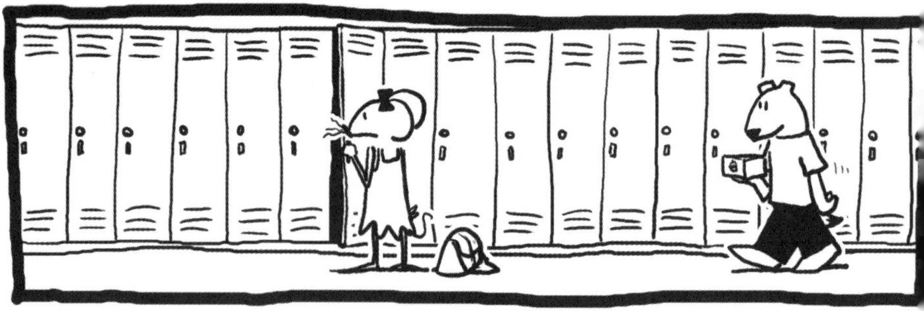

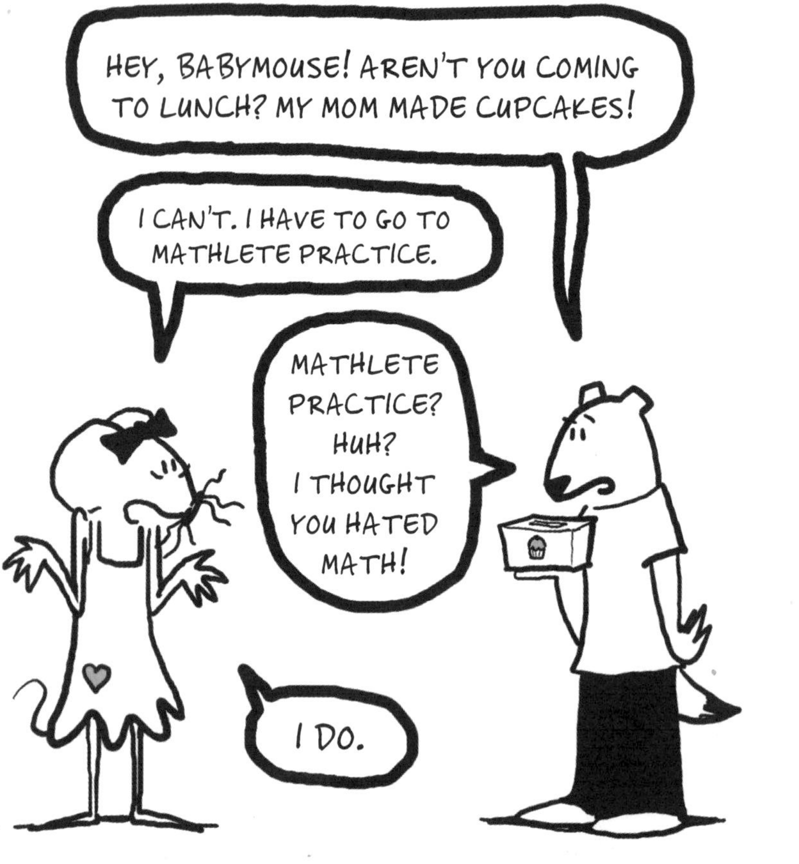
HEY, BABYMOUSE! AREN'T YOU COMING TO LUNCH? MY MOM MADE CUPCAKES!
I CAN'T. I HAVE TO GO TO MATHLETE PRACTICE.
MATHLETE PRACTICE? HUH? I THOUGHT YOU HATED MATH!
I DO.

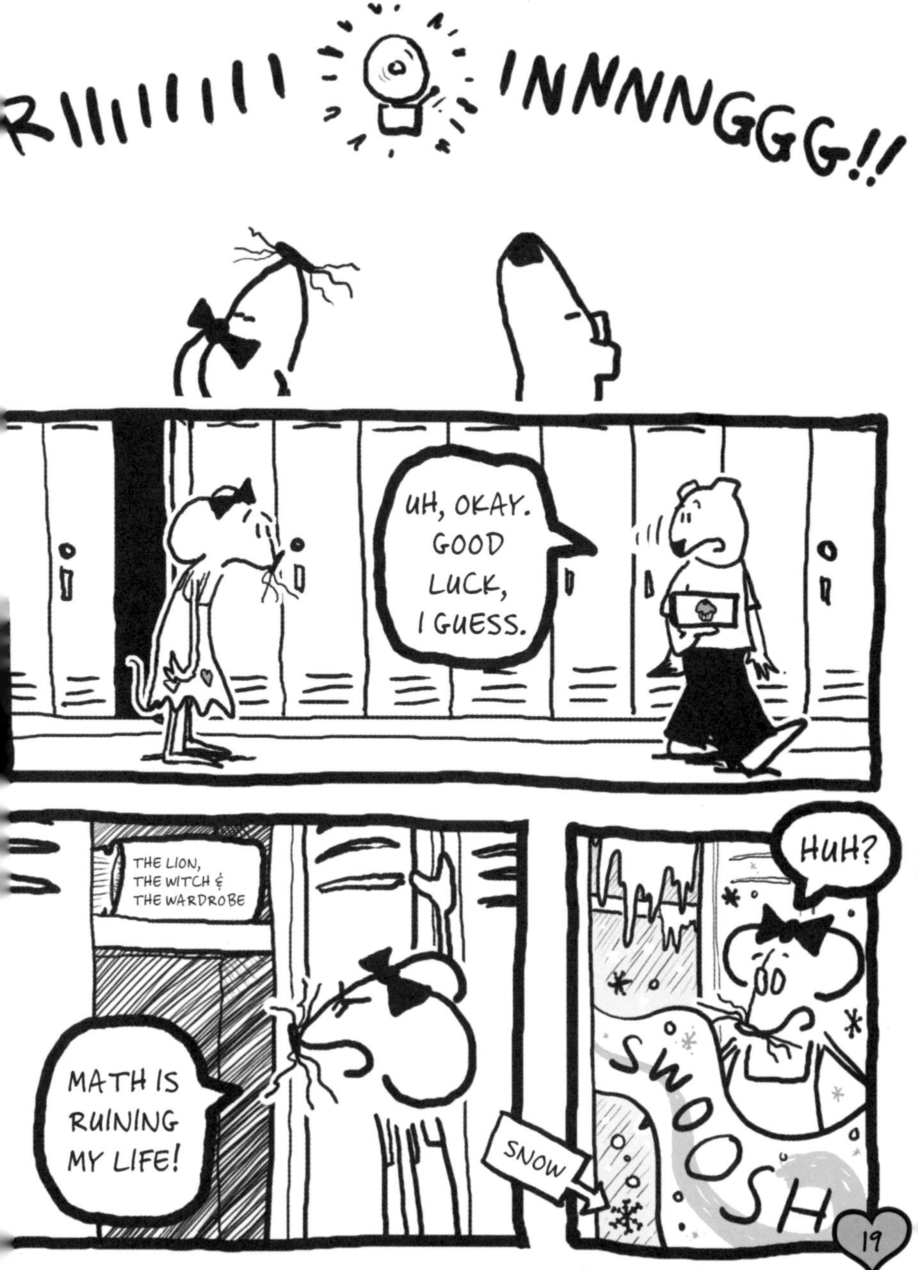
RIIIIIIII INNNNGGG!!
UH, OKAY. GOOD LUCK, I GUESS.
THE LION, THE WITCH & THE WARDROBE
MATH IS RUINING MY LIFE!
HUH?
SWOOSH
SNOW

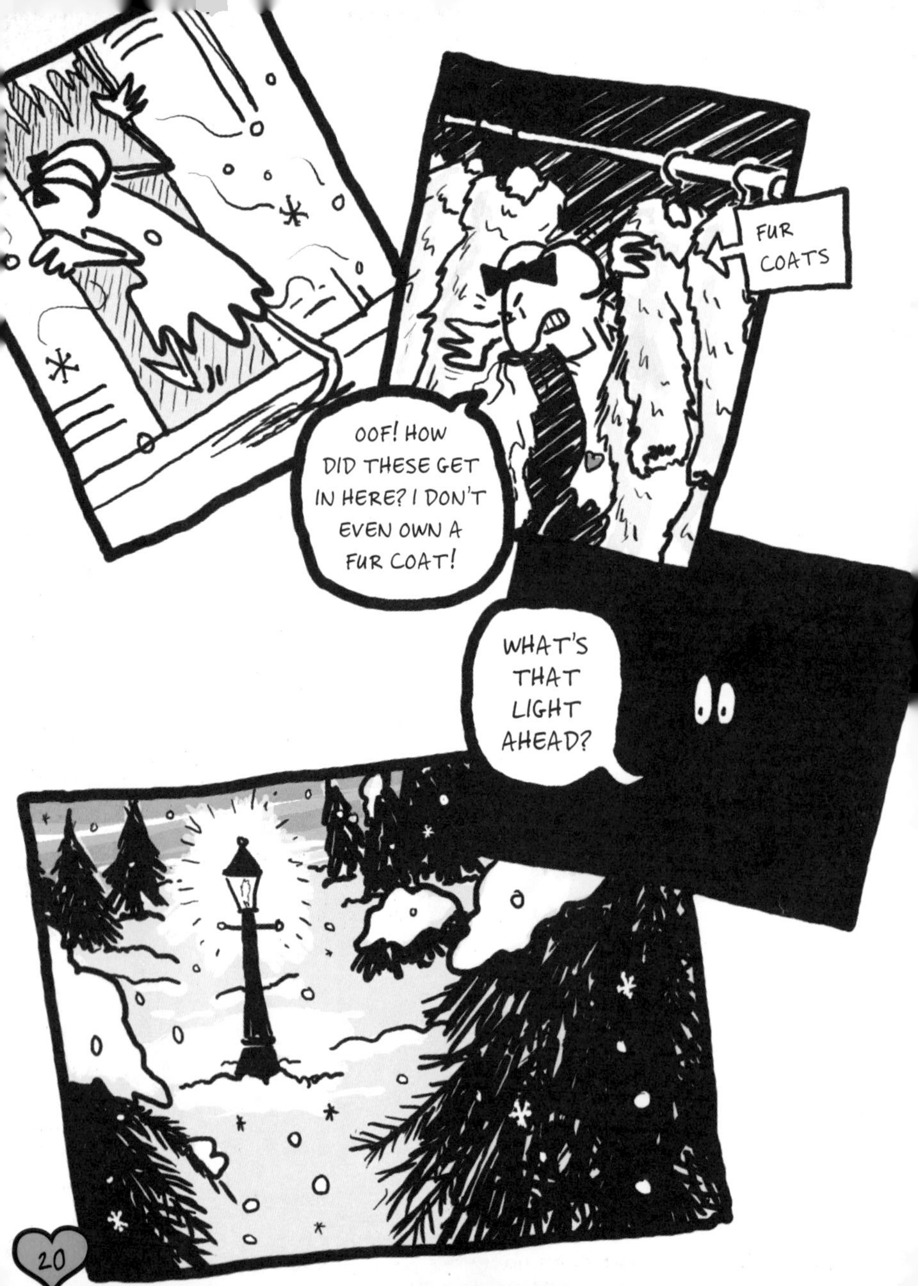
FUR COATS
OOF! HOW DID THESE GET IN HERE? I DON'T EVEN OWN A FUR COAT!
WHAT'S THAT LIGHT AHEAD?

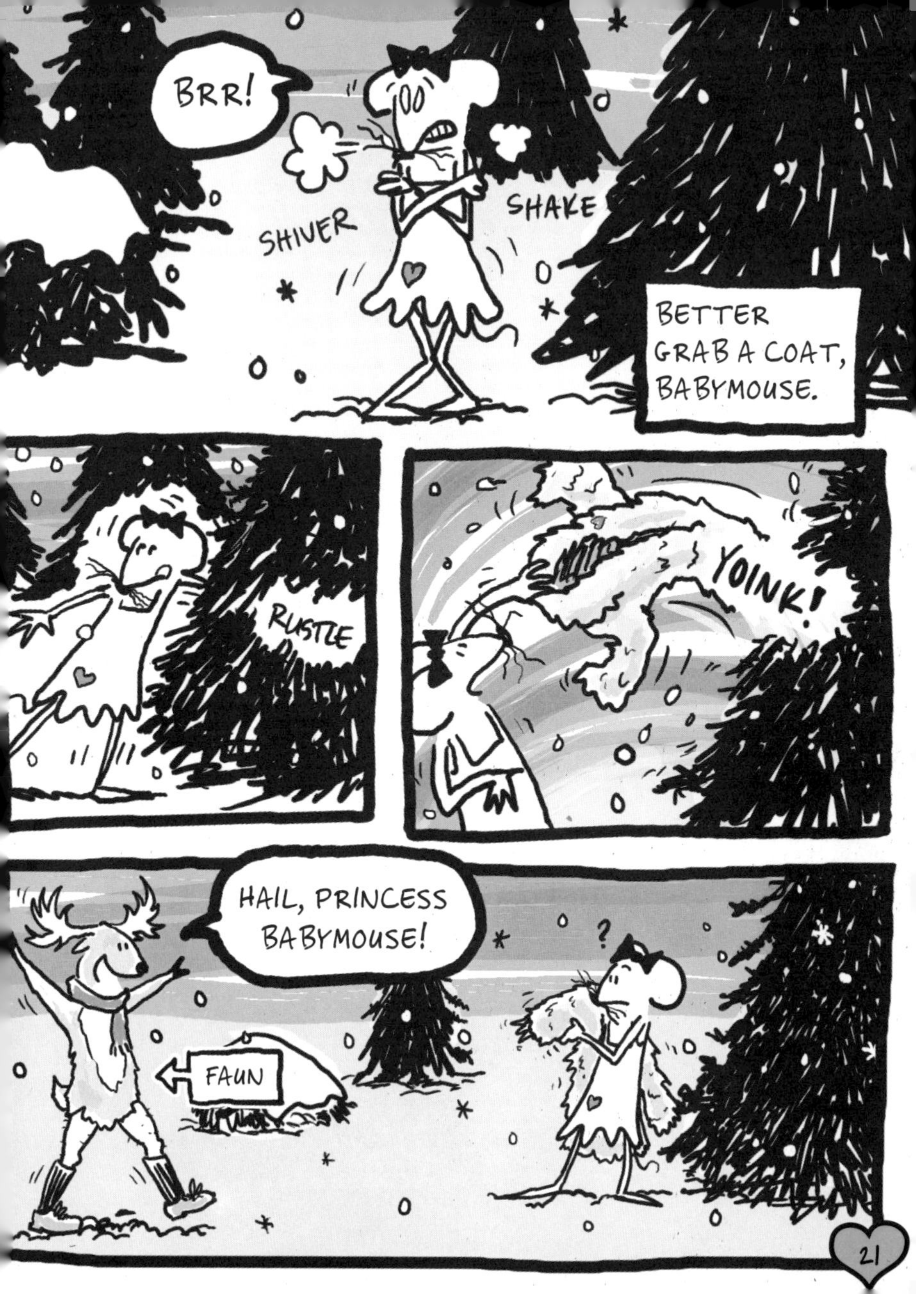

BRR!
SHIVER
SHAKE
BETTER GRAB A COAT, BABYMOUSE.
RUSTLE
YOINK!
HAIL, PRINCESS BABYMOUSE!
FAUN
?

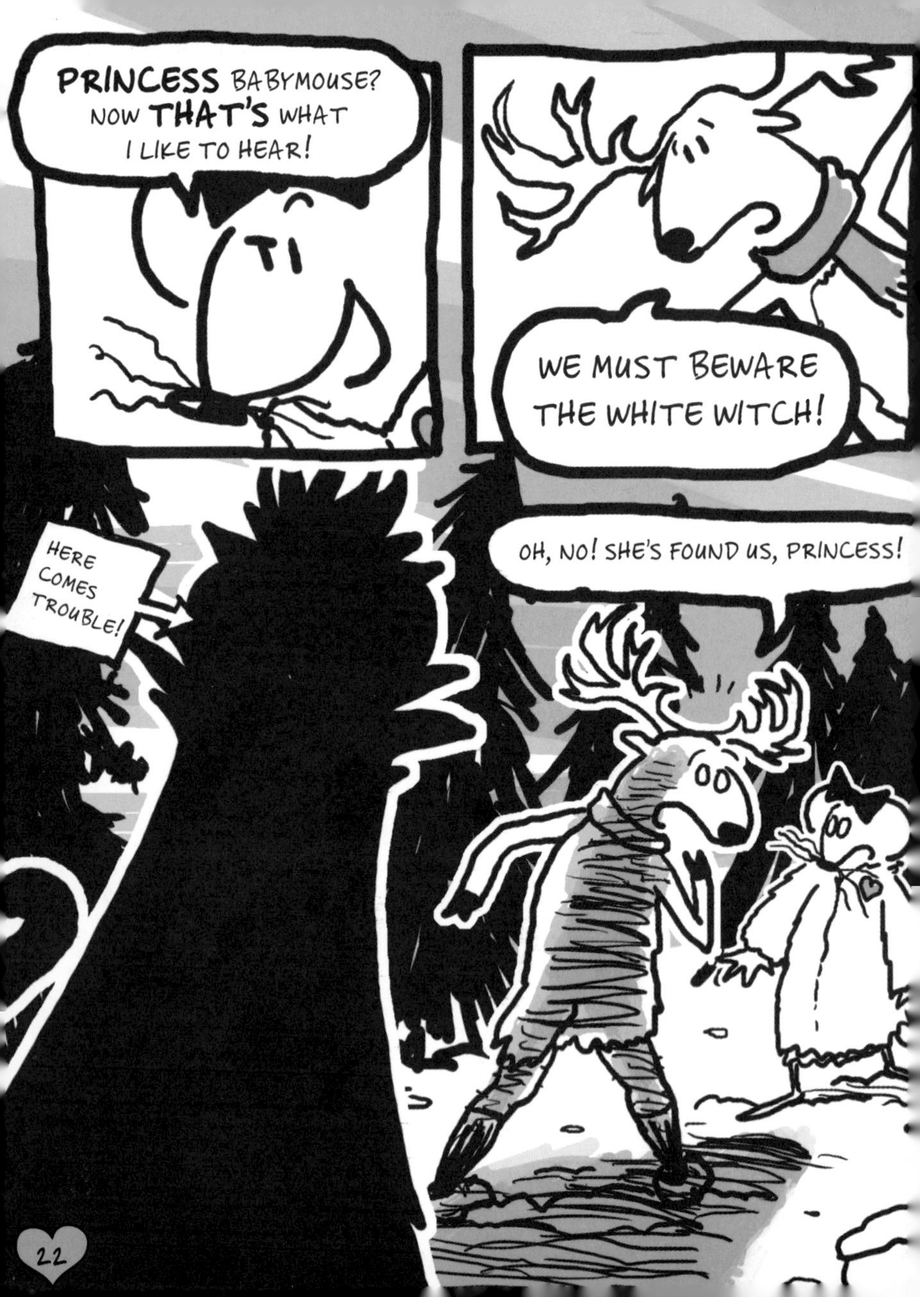
PRINCESS BABYMOUSE? NOW THAT'S WHAT I LIKE TO HEAR!
WE MUST BEWARE THE WHITE WITCH!
OH, NO! SHE'S FOUND US, PRINCESS!
HERE COMES TROUBLE!

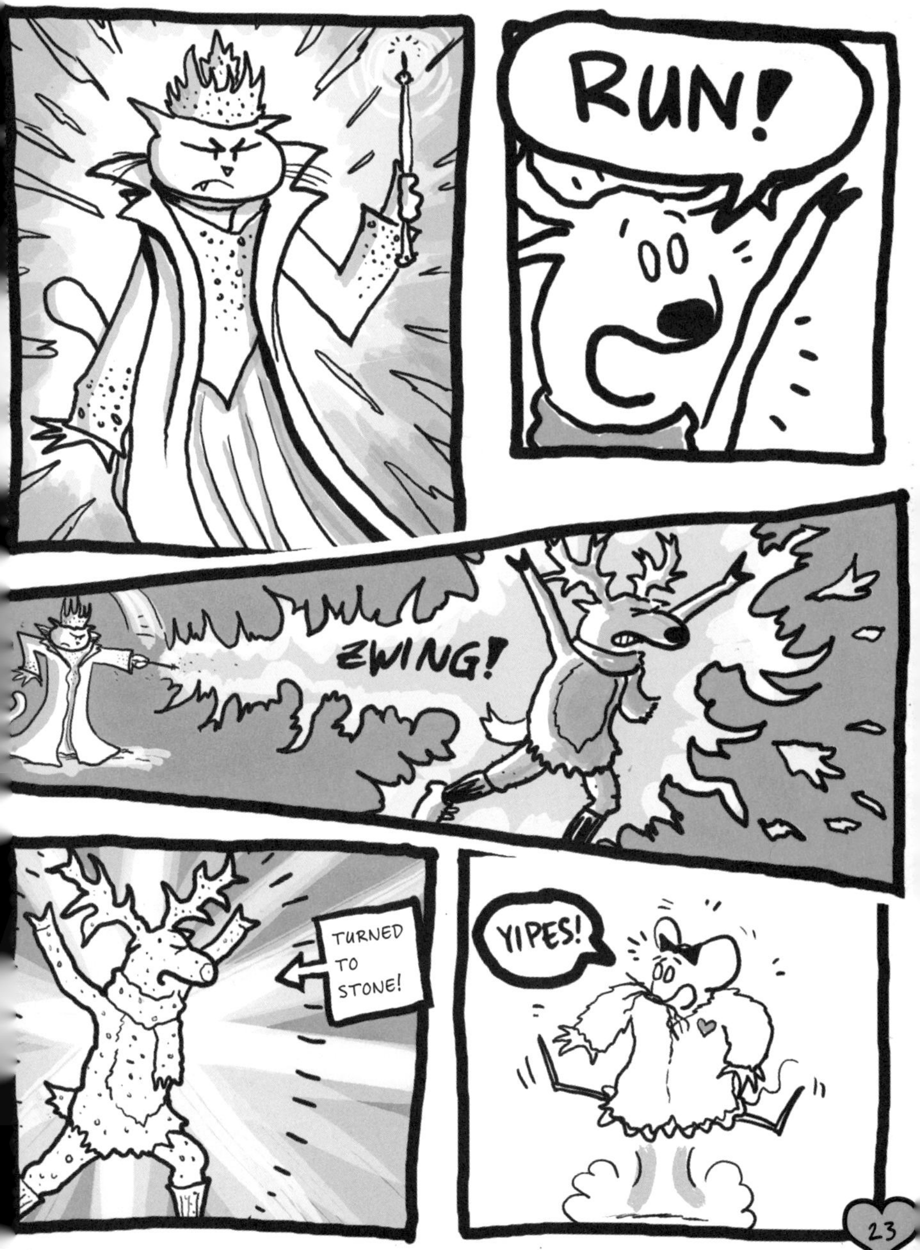
RUN!
ZWING!
TURNED TO STONE!
YIPES!

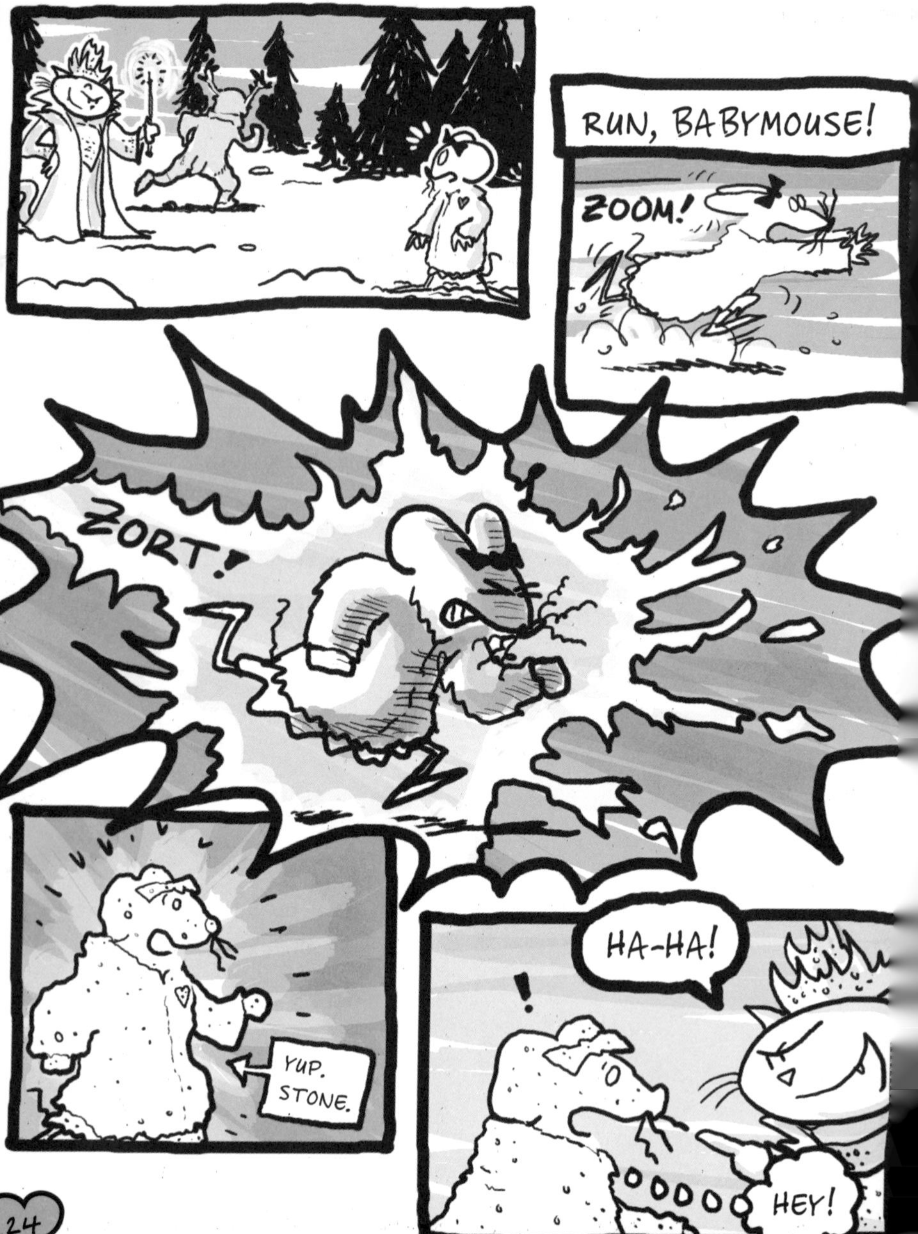
RUN, BABYMOUSE!
ZOOM!
ZORT!
YUP. STONE.
HA-HA!
!
OOOOO
HEY!

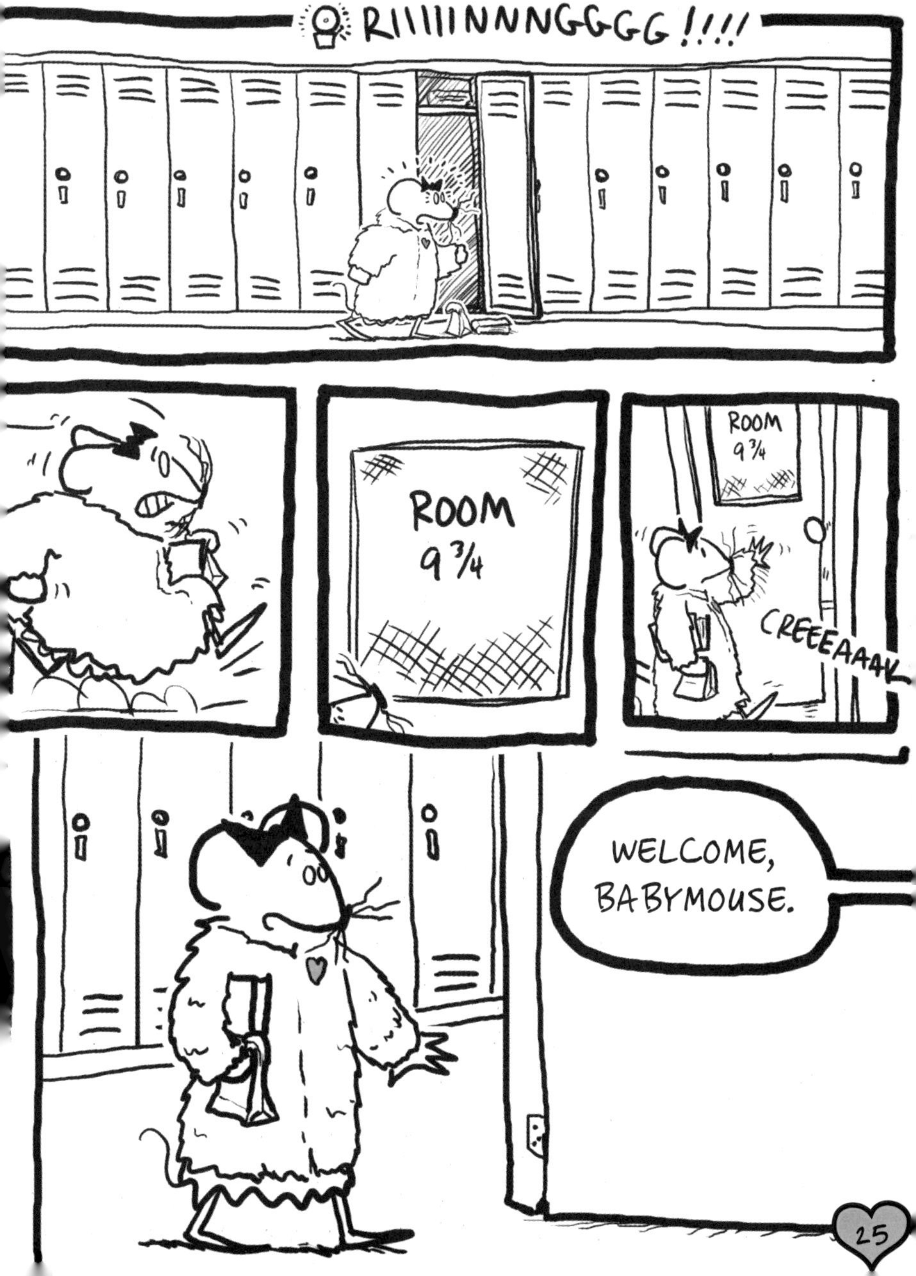
RIIIIINNNGGGG!!!!
ROOM 9 3/4
ROOM 9 3/4
CREEEAAAK
WELCOME, BABYMOUSE.

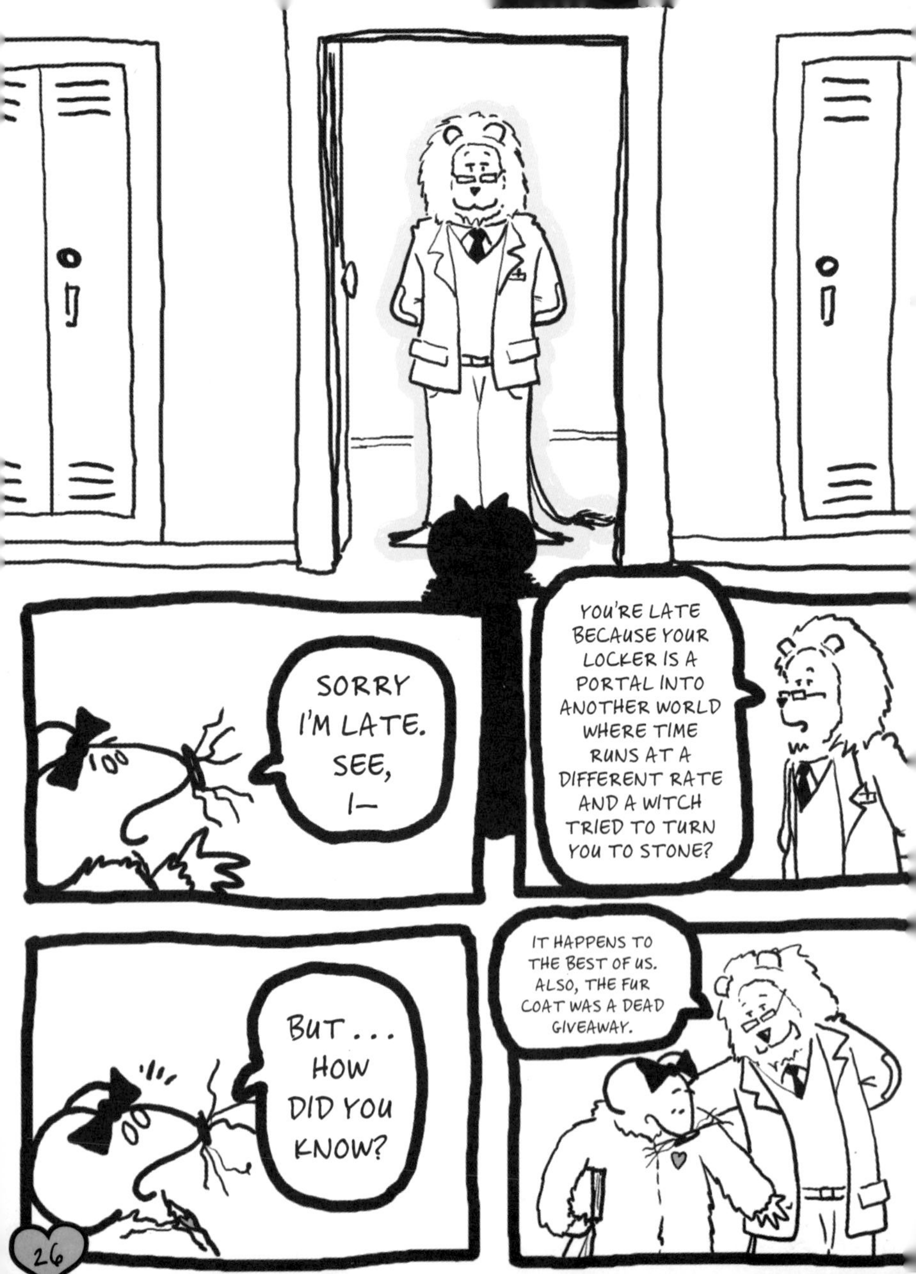
SORRY I'M LATE. SEE, I—
YOU'RE LATE BECAUSE YOUR LOCKER IS A PORTAL INTO ANOTHER WORLD WHERE TIME RUNS AT A DIFFERENT RATE AND A WITCH TRIED TO TURN YOU TO STONE?
BUT . . . HOW DID YOU KNOW?
IT HAPPENS TO THE BEST OF US. ALSO, THE FUR COAT WAS A DEAD GIVEAWAY.

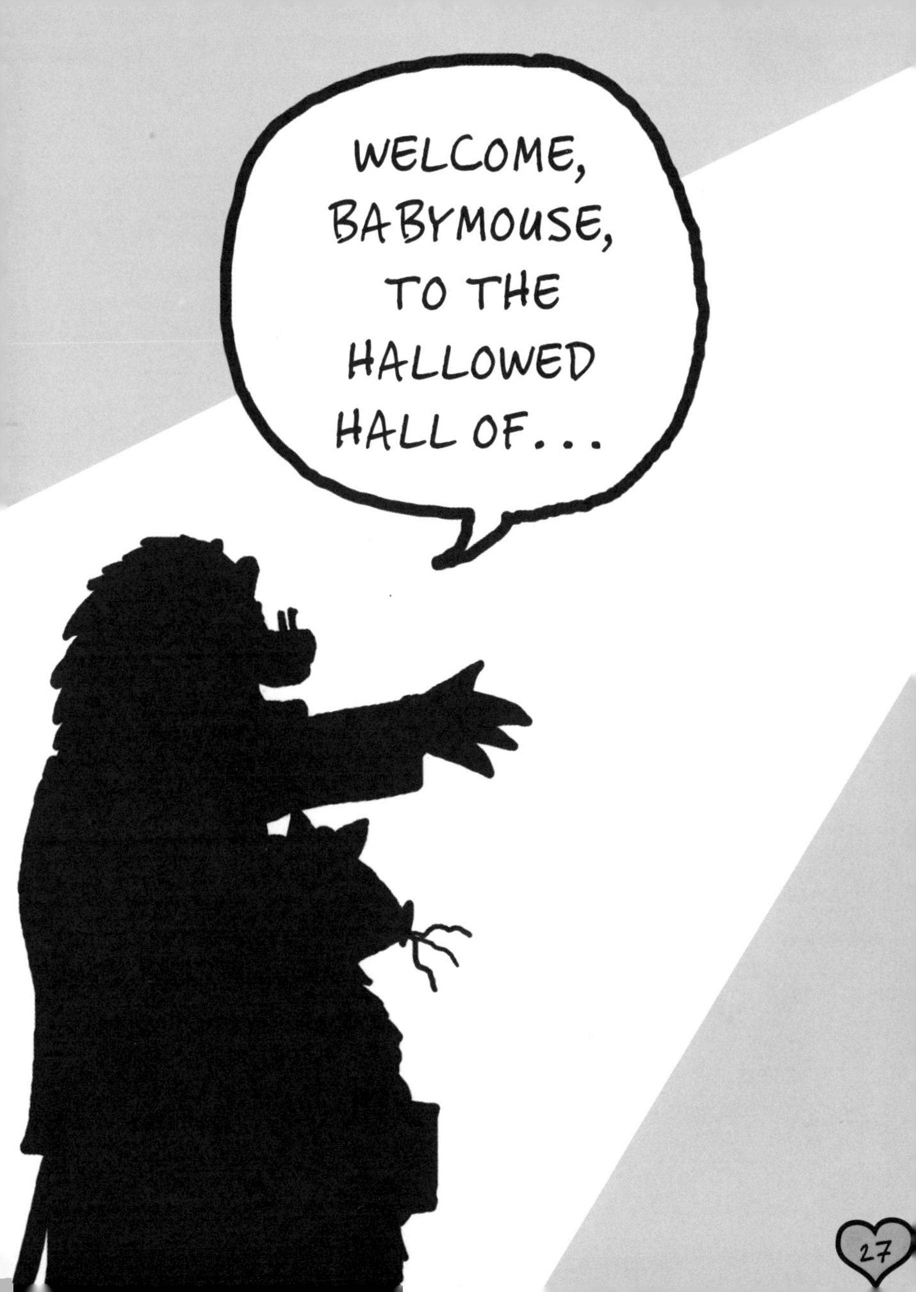
WELCOME, BABYMOUSE, TO THE HALLOWED HALL OF...

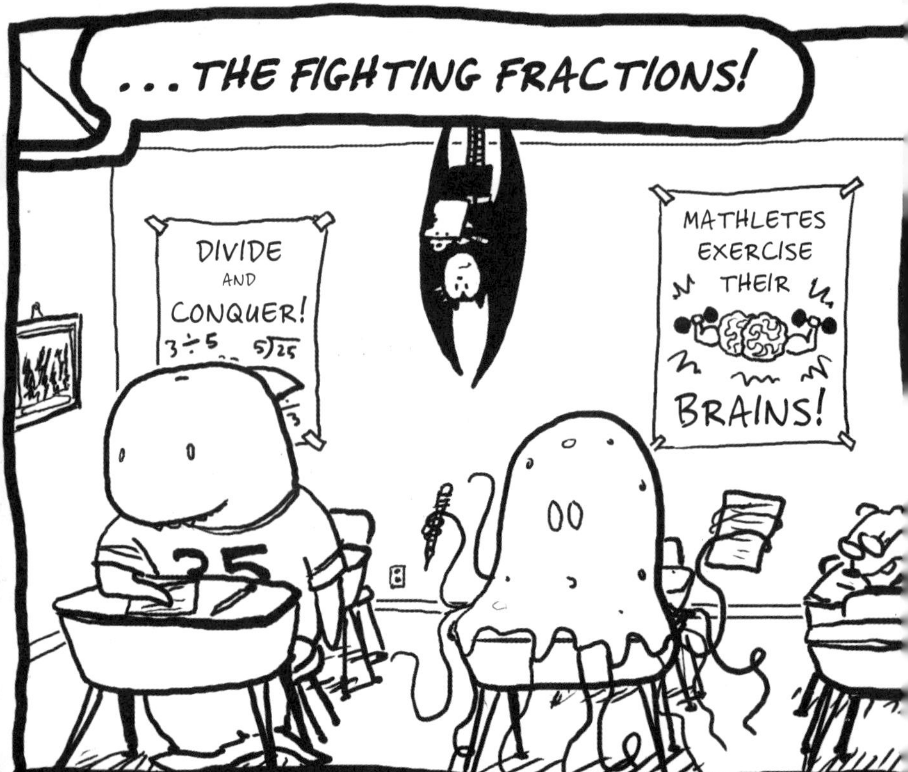
...THE FIGHTING FRACTIONS!
DIVIDE AND CONQUER!
MATHLETES EXERCISE THEIR BRAINS!
25

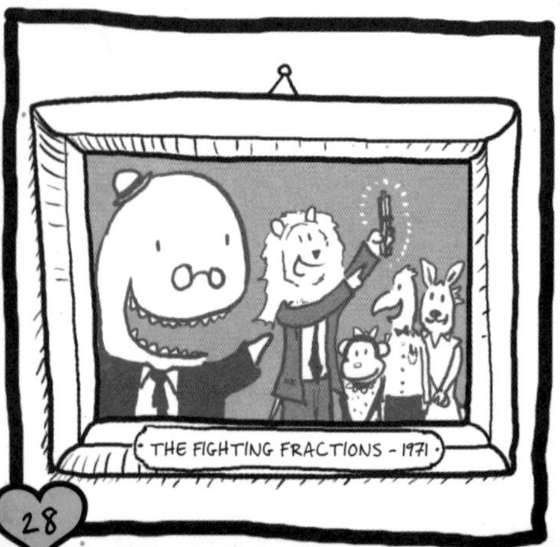
THE FIGHTING FRACTIONS - 1971

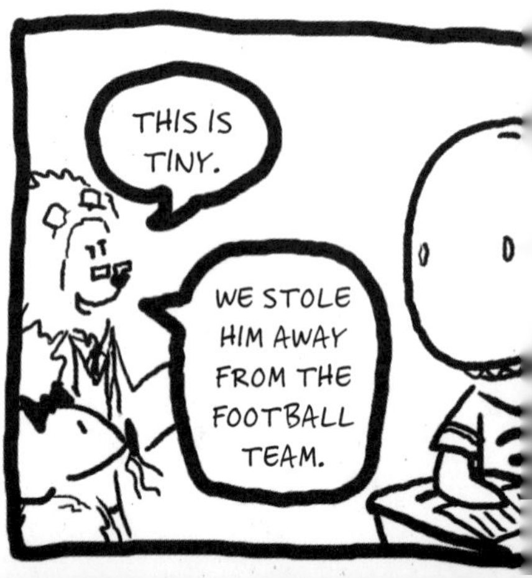
THIS IS TINY.
WE STOLE HIM AWAY FROM THE FOOTBALL TEAM.

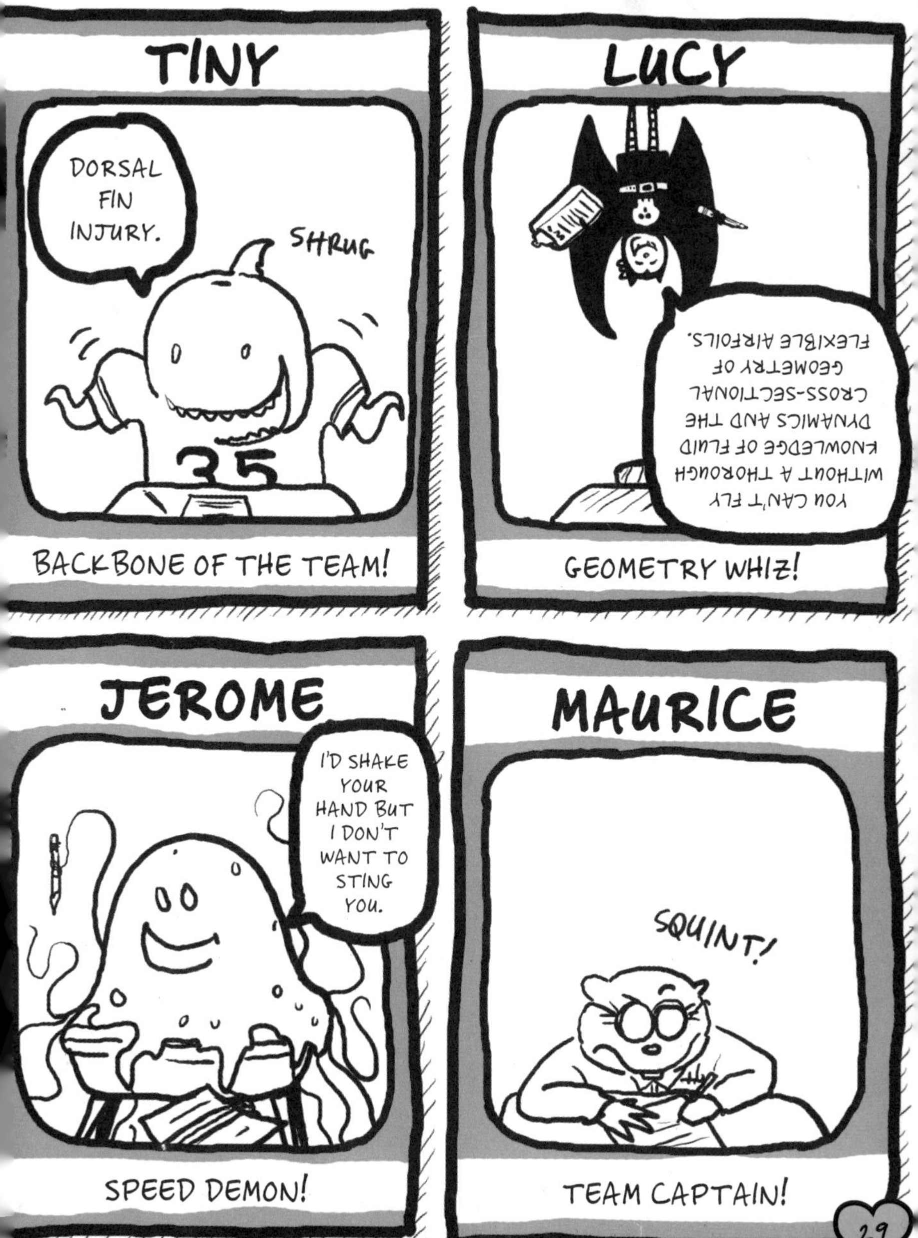
TINY
DORSAL FIN INJURY.
SHRUG
35
BACKBONE OF THE TEAM!
LUCY
YOU CAN'T FLY WITHOUT A THOROUGH KNOWLEDGE OF FLUID DYNAMICS AND THE CROSS-SECTIONAL GEOMETRY OF FLEXIBLE AIRFOILS.
GEOMETRY WHIZ!
JEROME
I'D SHAKE YOUR HAND BUT I DON'T WANT TO STING YOU.
SPEED DEMON!
MAURICE
SQUINT!
TEAM CAPTAIN!

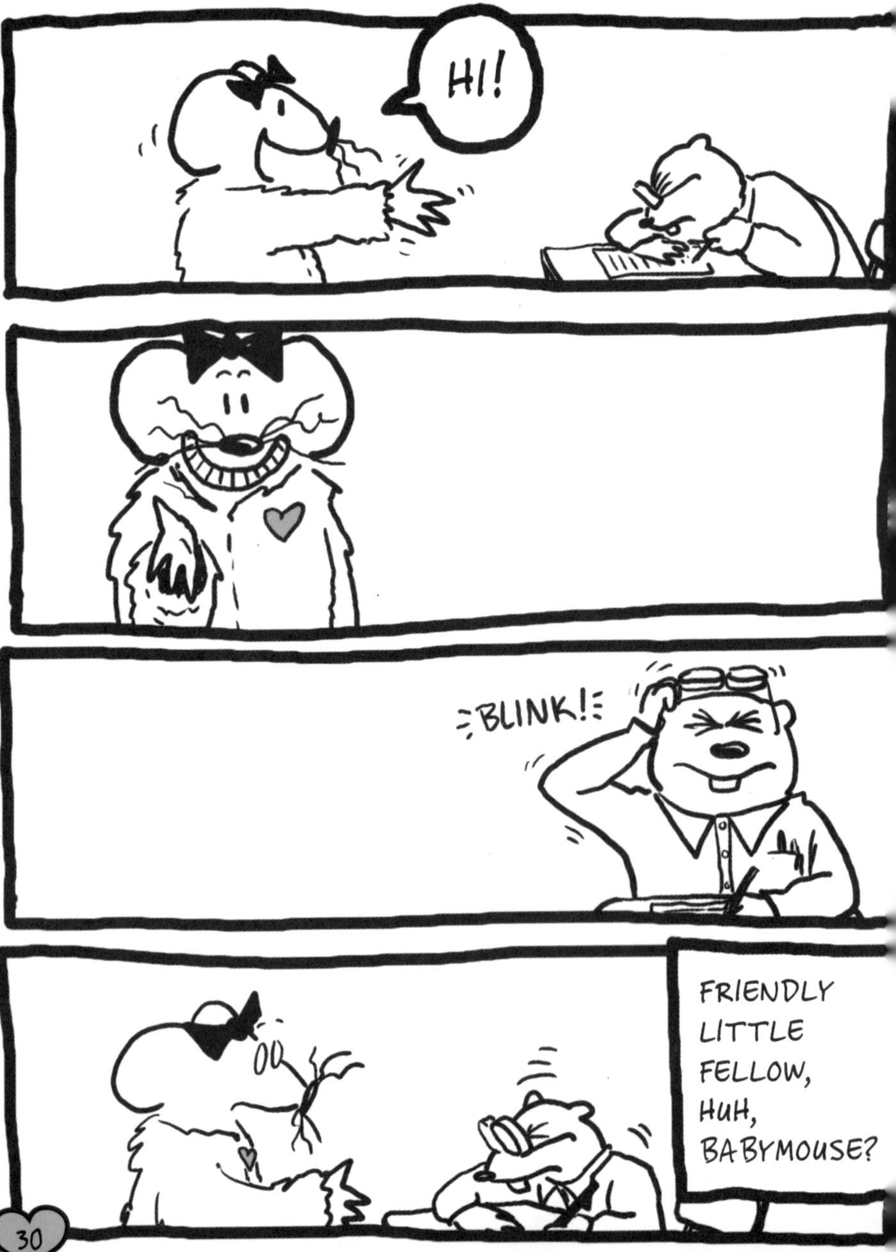
HI!
BLINK!
FRIENDLY LITTLE FELLOW, HUH, BABYMOUSE?

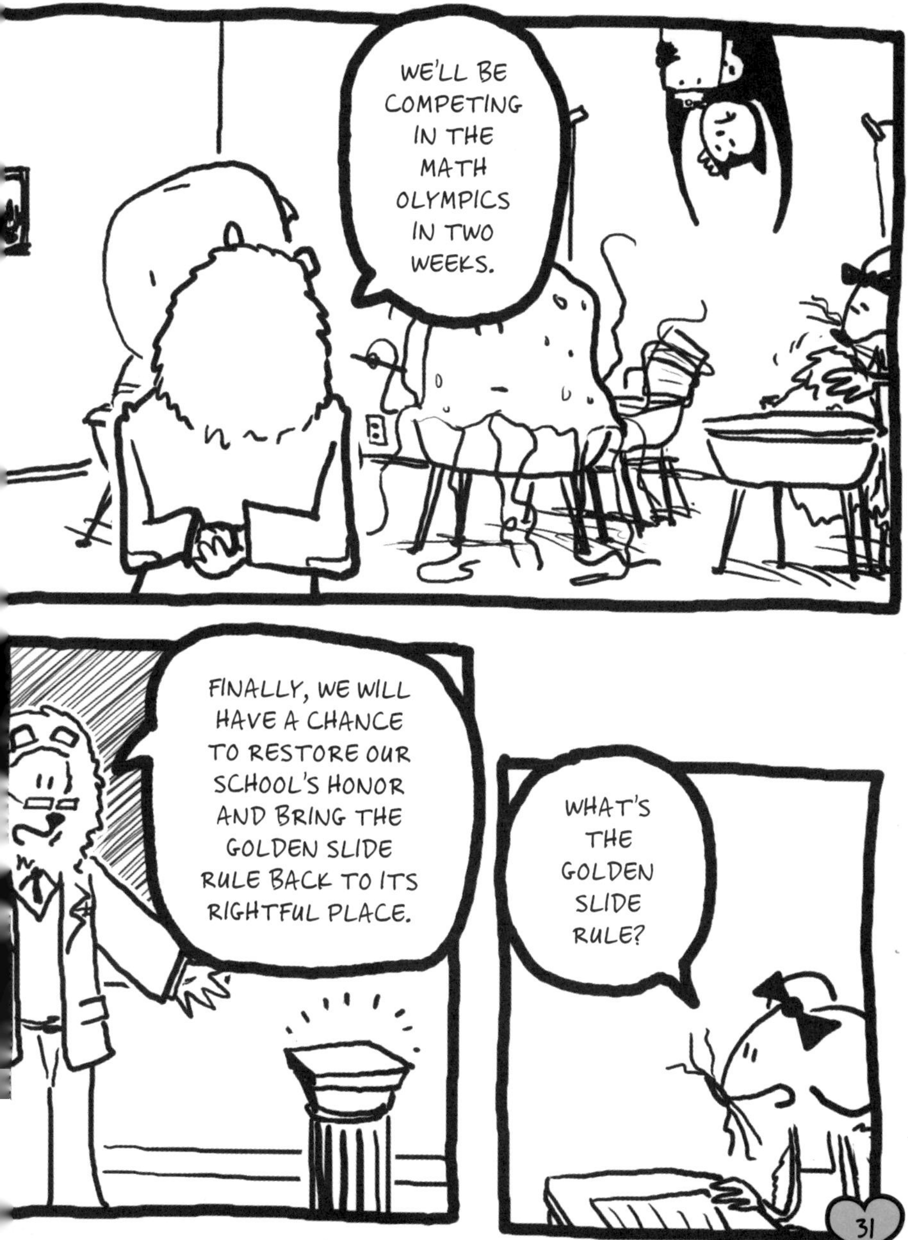
WE'LL BE COMPETING IN THE MATH OLYMPICS IN TWO WEEKS.
FINALLY, WE WILL HAVE A CHANCE TO RESTORE OUR SCHOOL'S HONOR AND BRING THE GOLDEN SLIDE RULE BACK TO ITS RIGHTFUL PLACE.
WHAT'S THE GOLDEN SLIDE RULE?

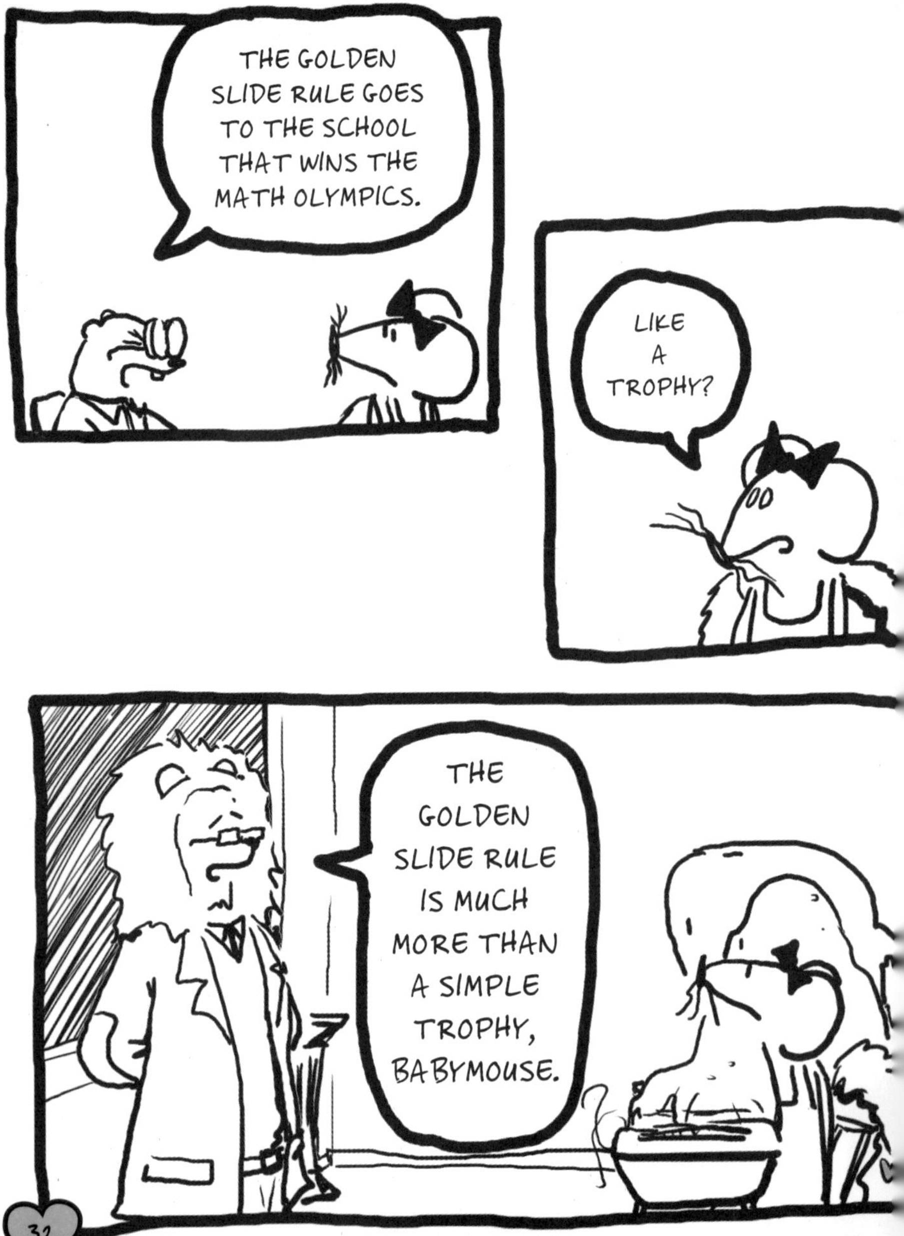

THE GOLDEN SLIDE RULE GOES TO THE SCHOOL THAT WINS THE MATH OLYMPICS.
LIKE A TROPHY?
THE GOLDEN SLIDE RULE IS MUCH MORE THAN A SIMPLE TROPHY, BABYMOUSE.

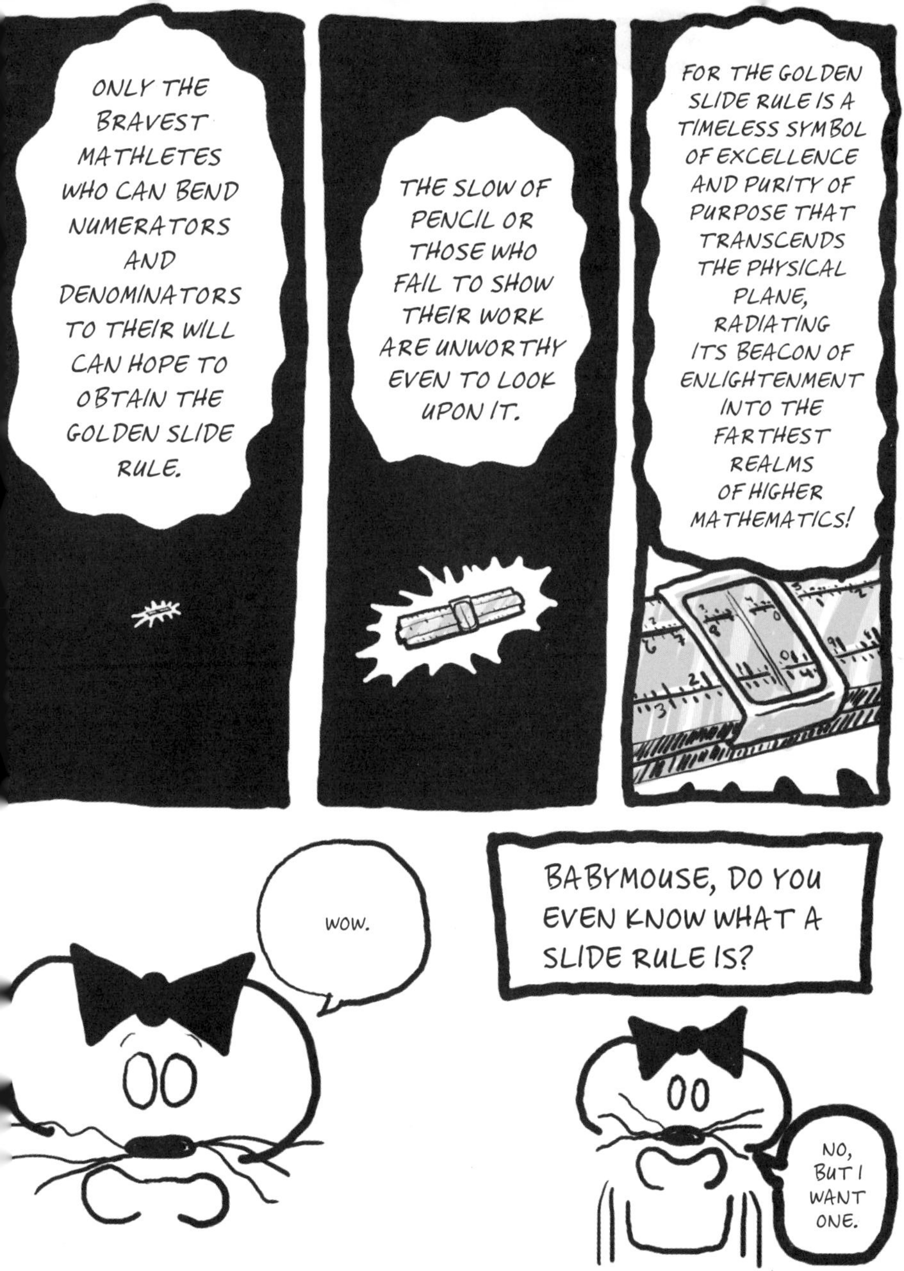
ONLY THE BRAVEST MATHLETES WHO CAN BEND NUMERATORS AND DENOMINATORS TO THEIR WILL CAN HOPE TO OBTAIN THE GOLDEN SLIDE RULE.
THE SLOW OF PENCIL OR THOSE WHO FAIL TO SHOW THEIR WORK ARE UNWORTHY EVEN TO LOOK UPON IT.
FOR THE GOLDEN SLIDE RULE IS A TIMELESS SYMBOL OF EXCELLENCE AND PURITY OF PURPOSE THAT TRANSCENDS THE PHYSICAL PLANE, RADIATING ITS BEACON OF ENLIGHTENMENT INTO THE FARTHEST REALMS OF HIGHER MATHEMATICS!
WOW.
BABYMOUSE, DO YOU EVEN KNOW WHAT A SLIDE RULE IS?
NO, BUT I WANT ONE.

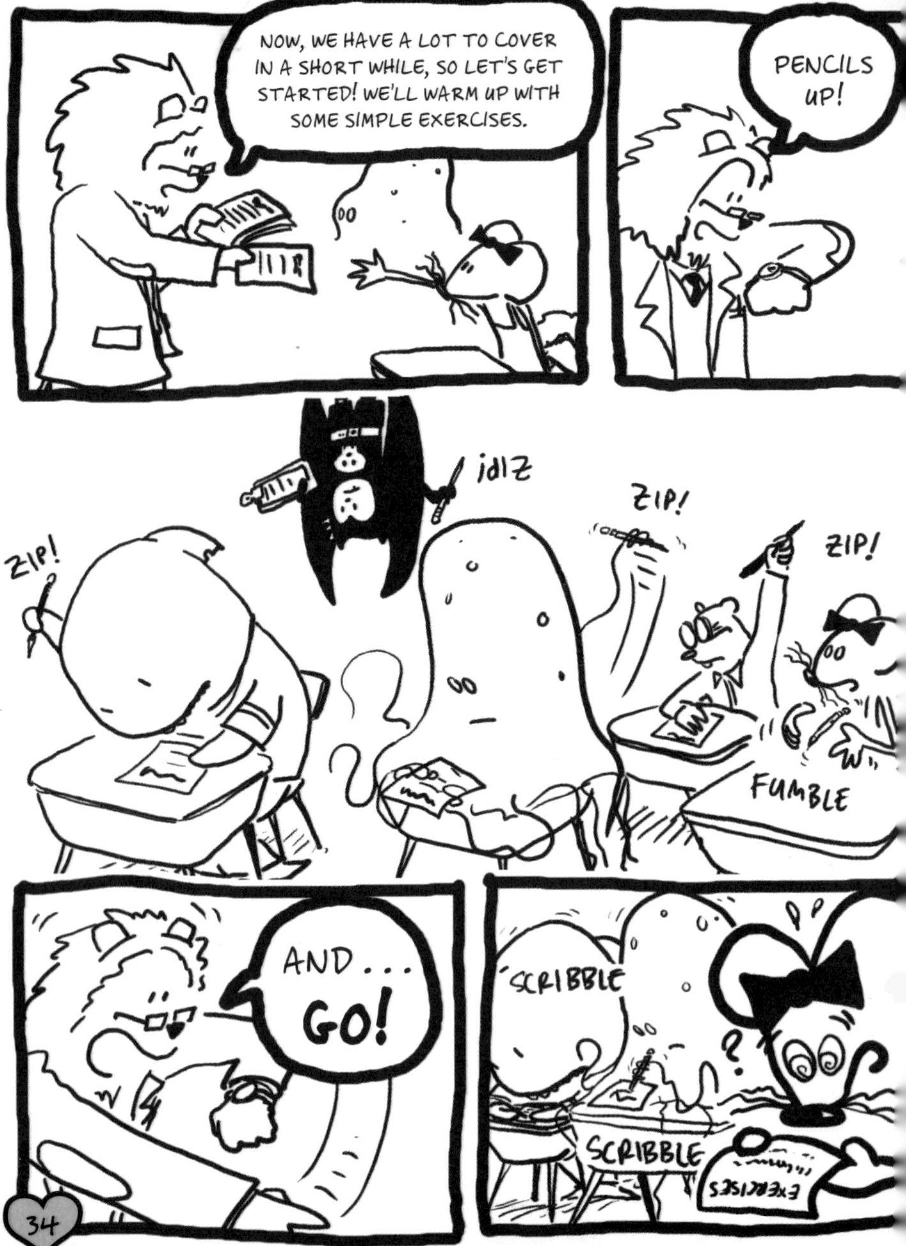

NOW, WE HAVE A LOT TO COVER IN A SHORT WHILE, SO LET'S GET STARTED! WE'LL WARM UP WITH SOME SIMPLE EXERCISES.
PENCILS UP!
ZIP!
ZIP!
ZIP!
ZIP!
FUMBLE
AND....
GO!
SCRIBBLE
SCRIBBLE
EXERCISES

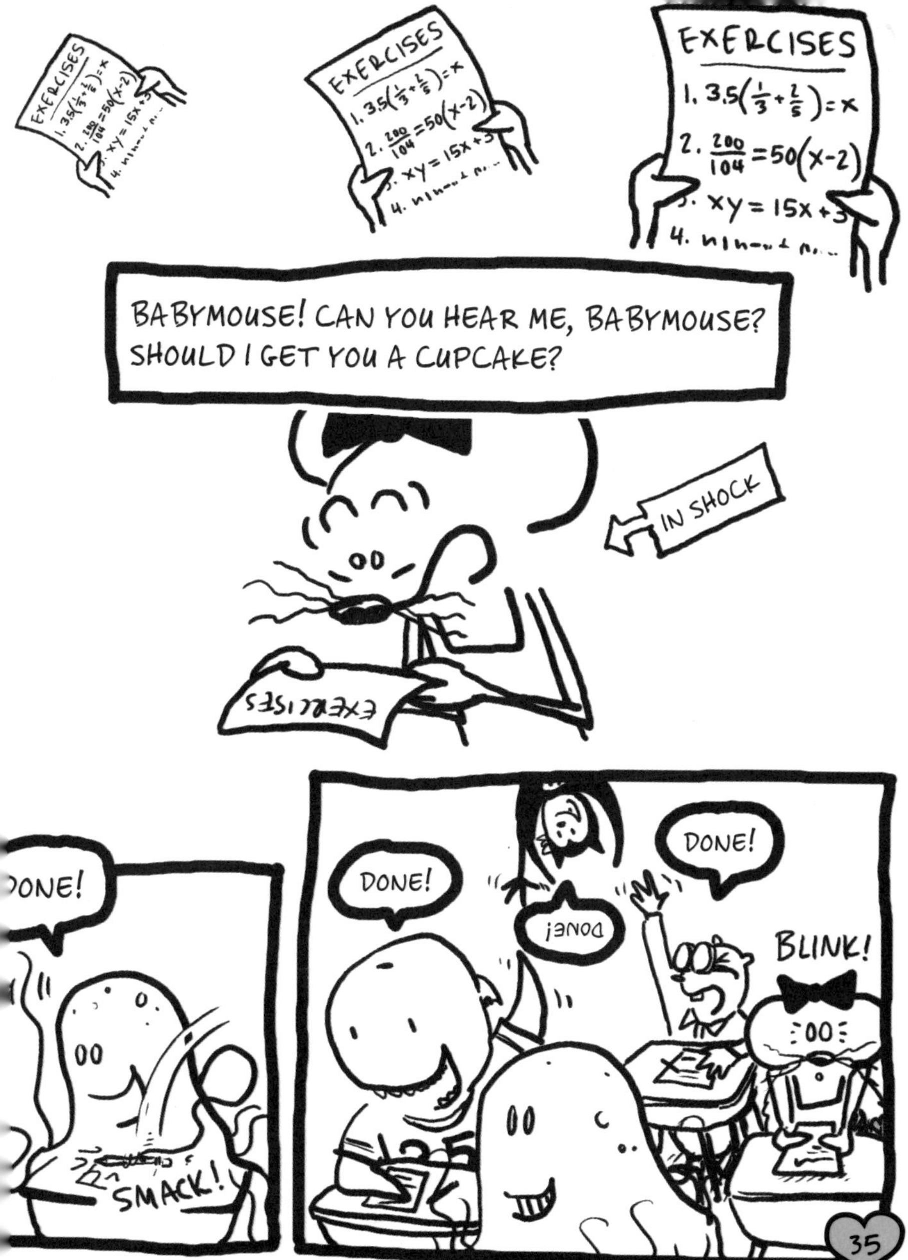
EXERCISES
1. 3.5(1/3 + 2/5) = x
2. 200/104 = 50(x-2)
3. xy = 15x + 3
BABYMOUSE! CAN YOU HEAR ME, BABYMOUSE? SHOULD I GET YOU A CUPCAKE?
IN SHOCK
EXERCISES
DONE!
SMACK!
DONE!
DONE!
DONE!
BLINK!

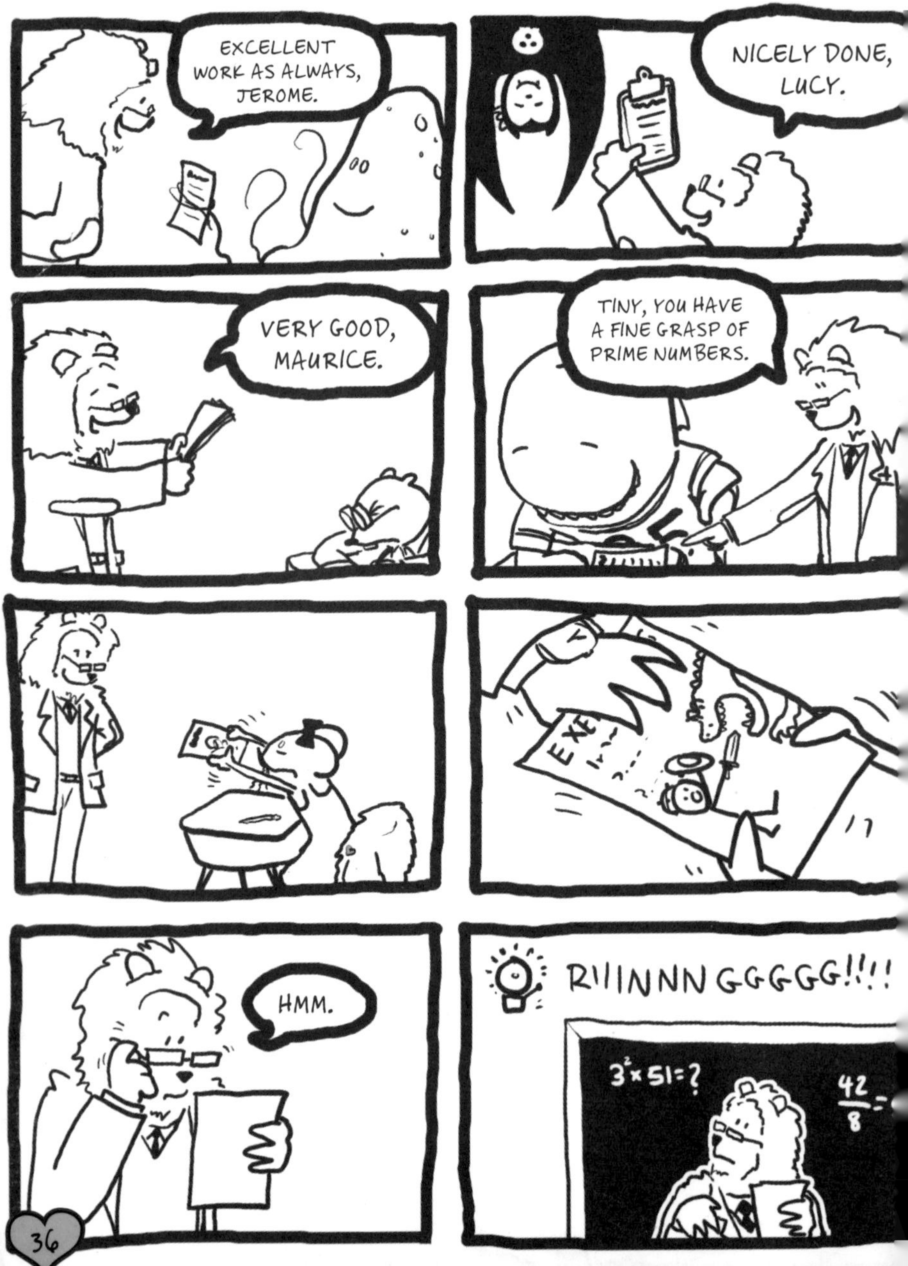
EXCELLENT WORK AS ALWAYS, JEROME.
NICELY DONE, LUCY.
VERY GOOD, MAURICE.
TINY, YOU HAVE A FINE GRASP OF PRIME NUMBERS.
EXE
HMM.
RIIINNNGGGGG!!!!
3² x 51 = ?
42/8 =

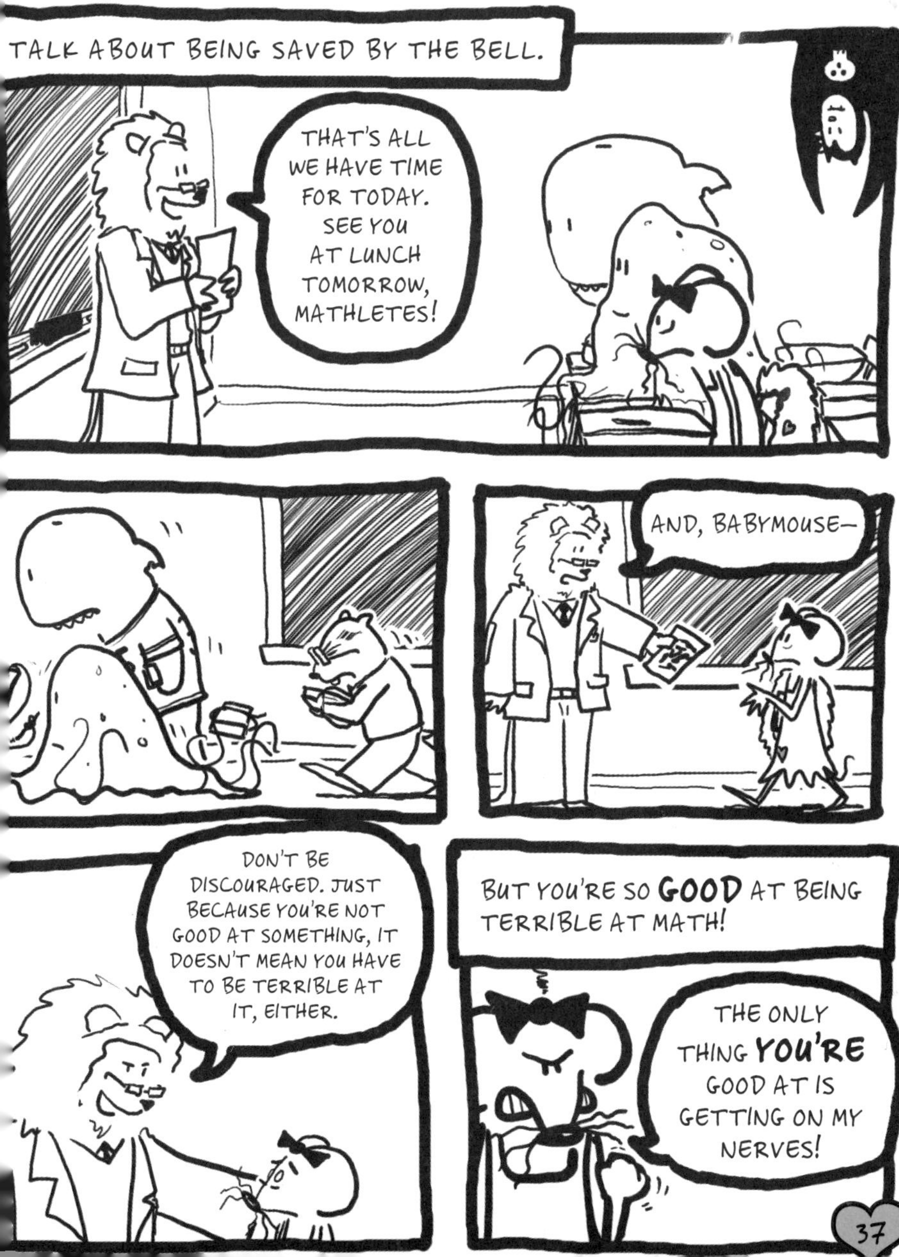

TALK ABOUT BEING SAVED BY THE BELL.
THAT'S ALL WE HAVE TIME FOR TODAY. SEE YOU AT LUNCH TOMORROW, MATHLETES!
AND, BABYMOUSE—
DON'T BE DISCOURAGED. JUST BECAUSE YOU'RE NOT GOOD AT SOMETHING, IT DOESN'T MEAN YOU HAVE TO BE TERRIBLE AT IT, EITHER.
BUT YOU'RE SO **GOOD** AT BEING TERRIBLE AT MATH!
THE ONLY THING **YOU'RE** GOOD AT IS GETTING ON MY NERVES!

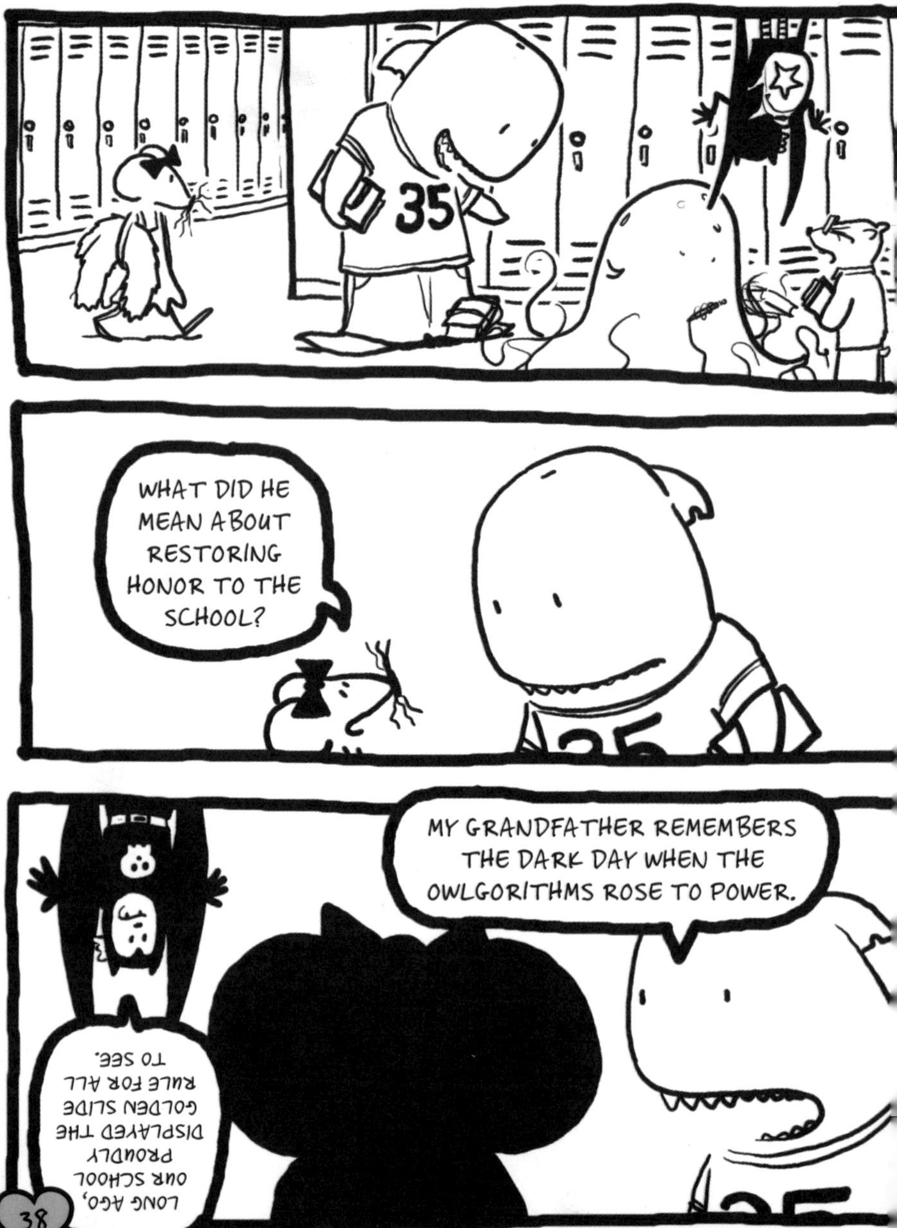
WHAT DID HE MEAN ABOUT RESTORING HONOR TO THE SCHOOL?
MY GRANDFATHER REMEMBERS THE DARK DAY WHEN THE OWLGORITHMS ROSE TO POWER.
LONG AGO, OUR SCHOOL PROUDLY DISPLAYED THE GOLDEN SLIDE RULE FOR ALL TO SEE.

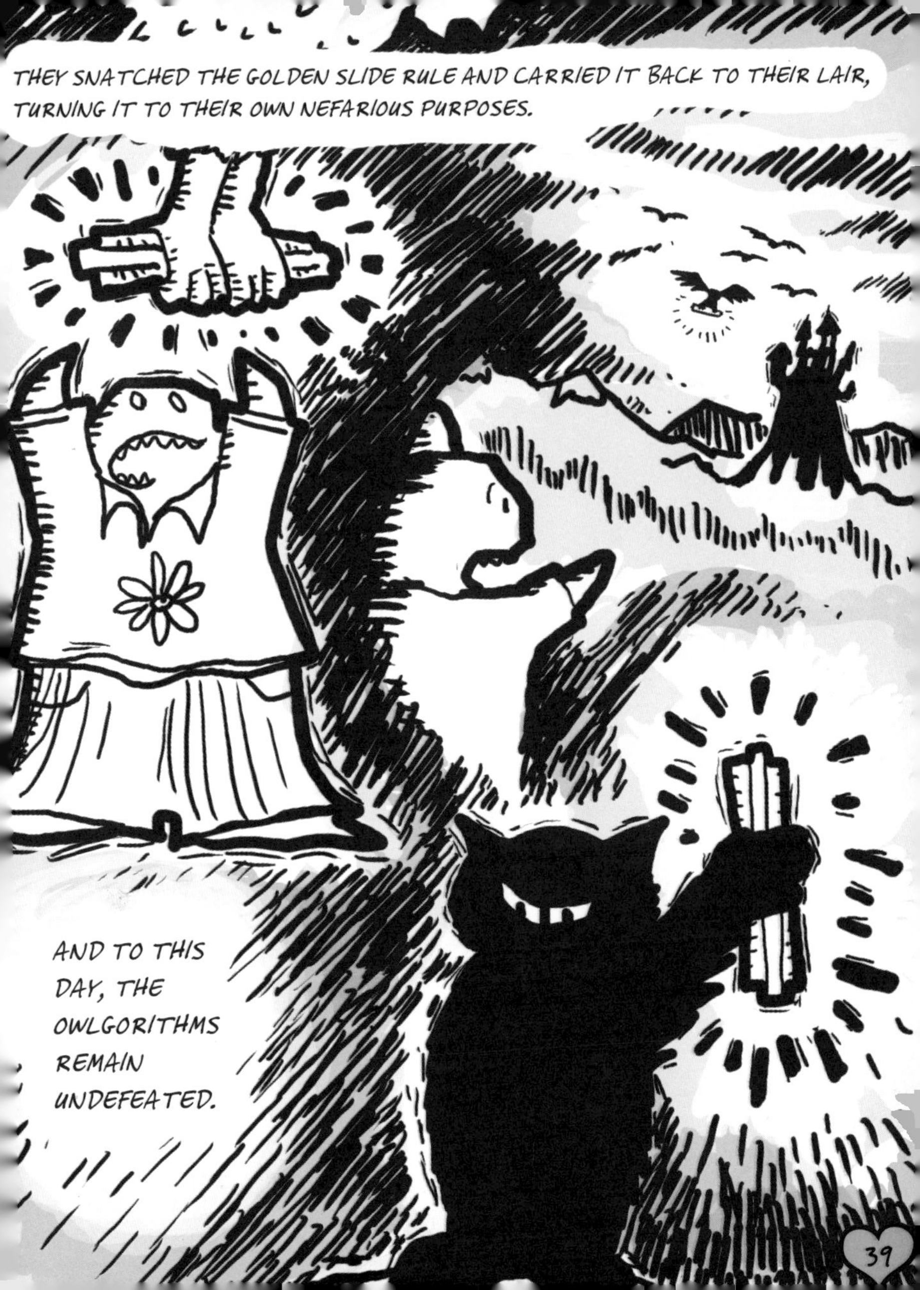
THEY SNATCHED THE GOLDEN SLIDE RULE AND CARRIED IT BACK TO THEIR LAIR, TURNING IT TO THEIR OWN NEFARIOUS PURPOSES.
AND TO THIS DAY, THE OWLGORITHMS REMAIN UNDEFEATED.

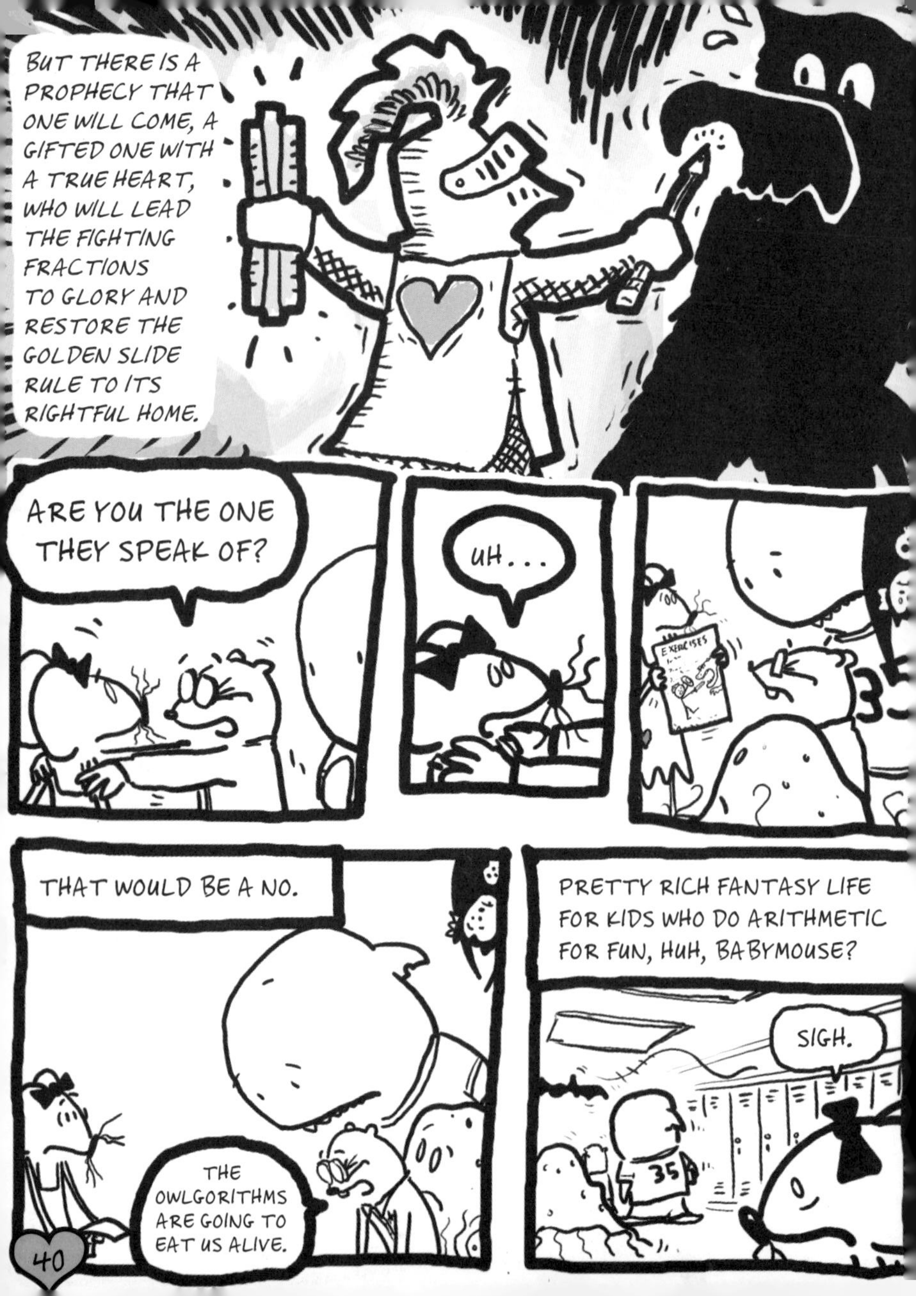
BUT THERE IS A PROPHECY THAT ONE WILL COME, A GIFTED ONE WITH A TRUE HEART, WHO WILL LEAD THE FIGHTING FRACTIONS TO GLORY AND RESTORE THE GOLDEN SLIDE RULE TO ITS RIGHTFUL HOME.
ARE YOU THE ONE THEY SPEAK OF?
UH...
EXERCISES
THAT WOULD BE A NO.
THE OWLGORITHMS ARE GOING TO EAT US ALIVE.
PRETTY RICH FANTASY LIFE FOR KIDS WHO DO ARITHMETIC FOR FUN, HUH, BABYMOUSE?
SIGH.
35

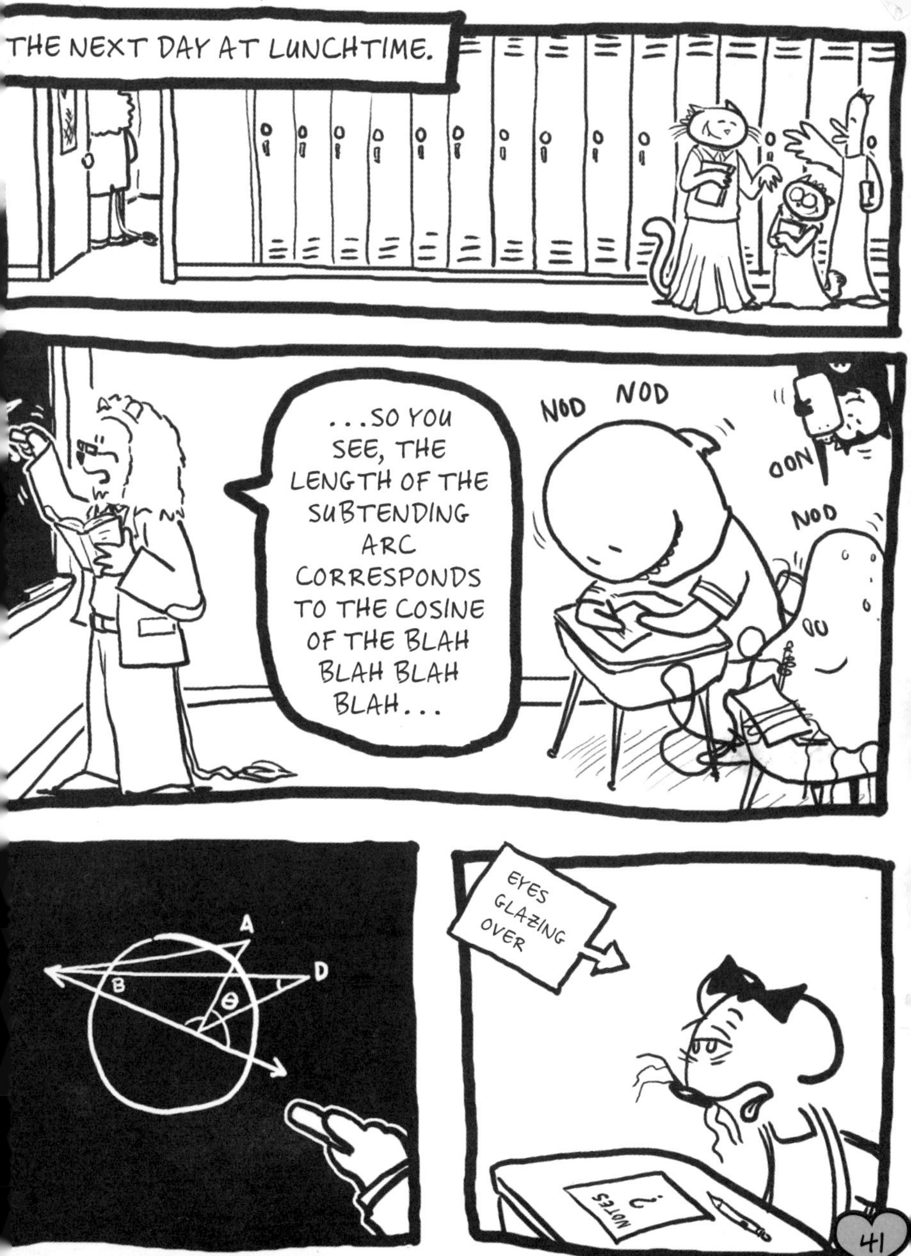
THE NEXT DAY AT LUNCHTIME.
...SO YOU SEE, THE LENGTH OF THE SUBTENDING ARC CORRESPONDS TO THE COSINE OF THE BLAH BLAH BLAH BLAH...
NOD NOD
NOD
NOD
A
D
B
θ
EYES GLAZING OVER
NOTES

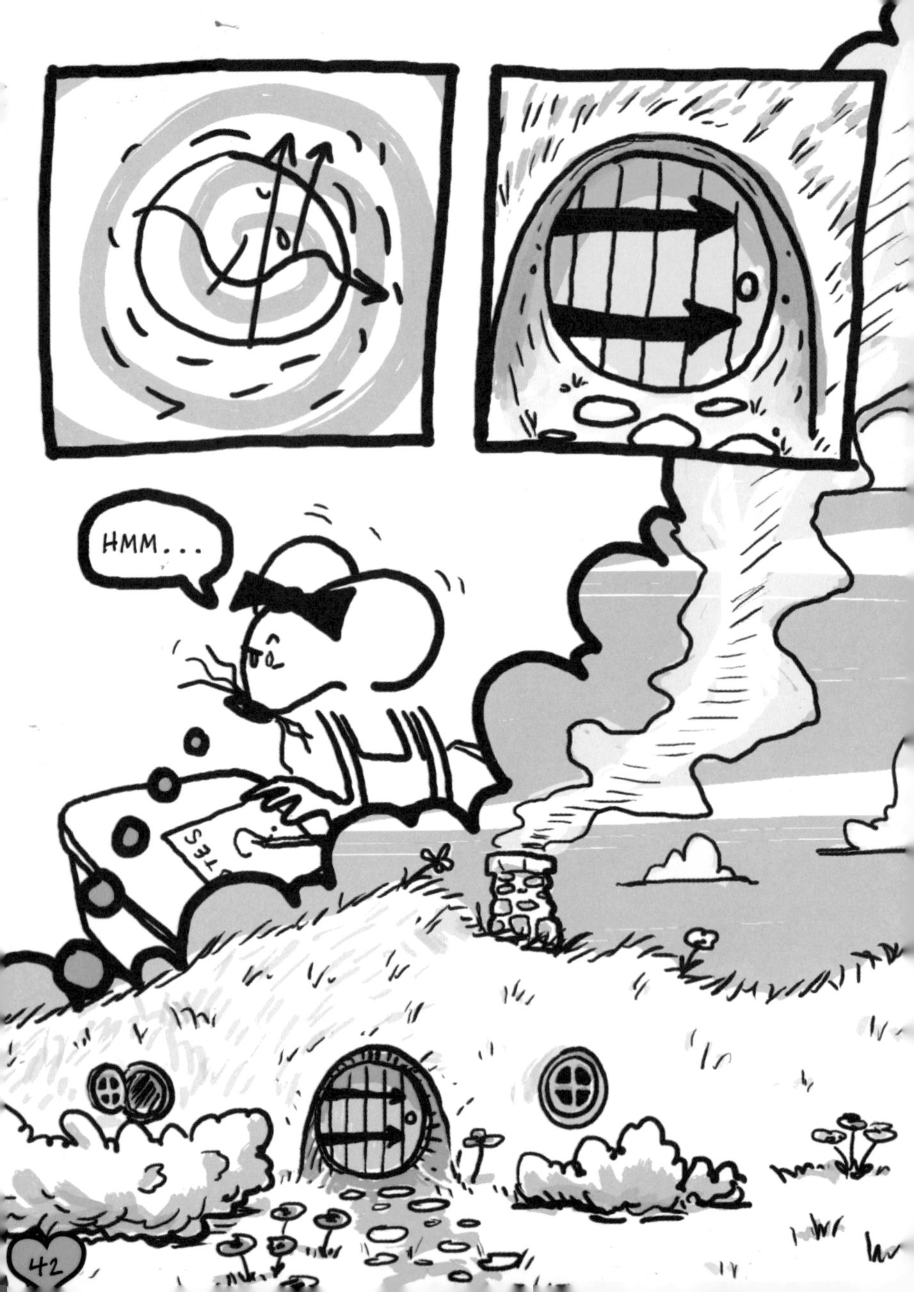
HMM...

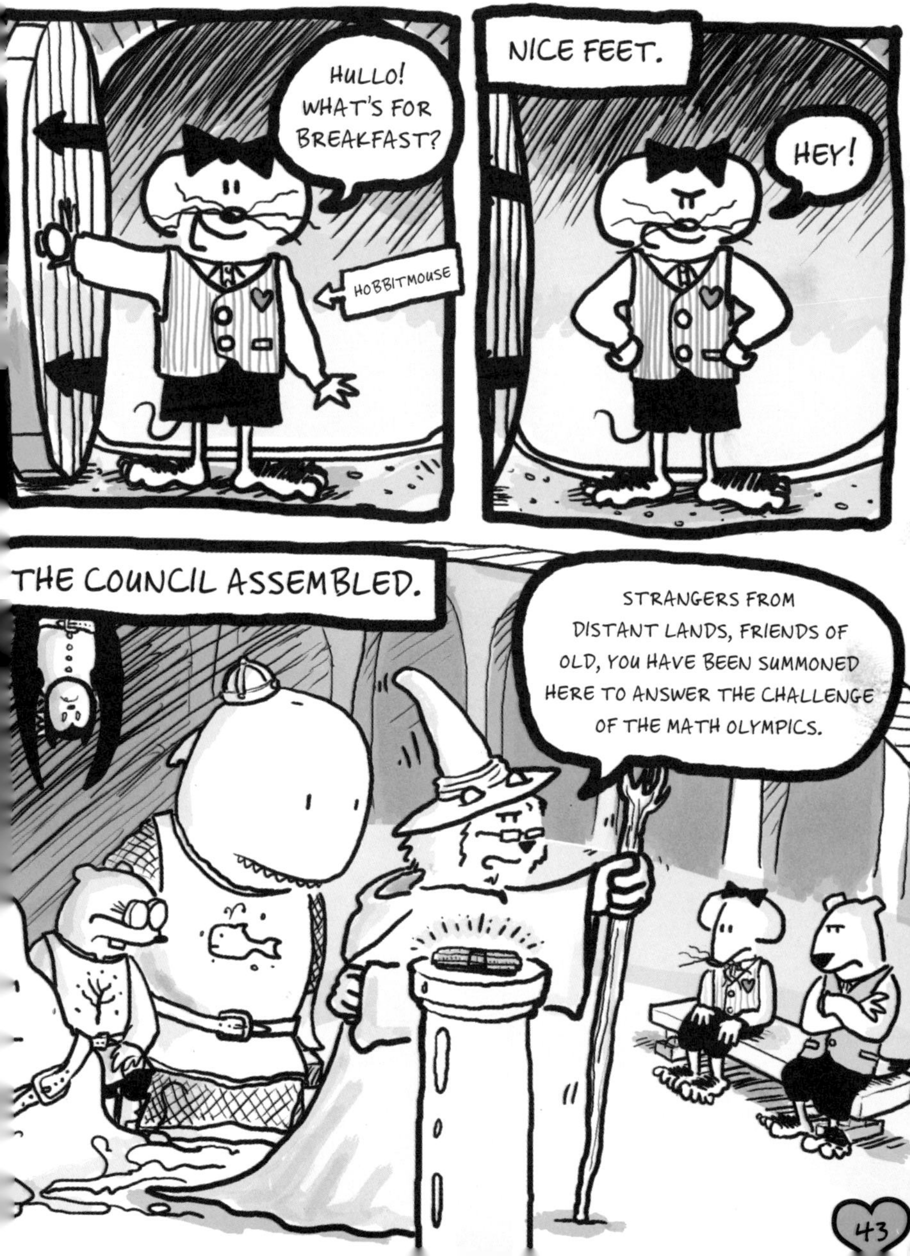

HULLO! WHAT'S FOR BREAKFAST?
HOBBITMOUSE
NICE FEET.
HEY!
THE COUNCIL ASSEMBLED.
STRANGERS FROM DISTANT LANDS, FRIENDS OF OLD, YOU HAVE BEEN SUMMONED HERE TO ANSWER THE CHALLENGE OF THE MATH OLYMPICS.

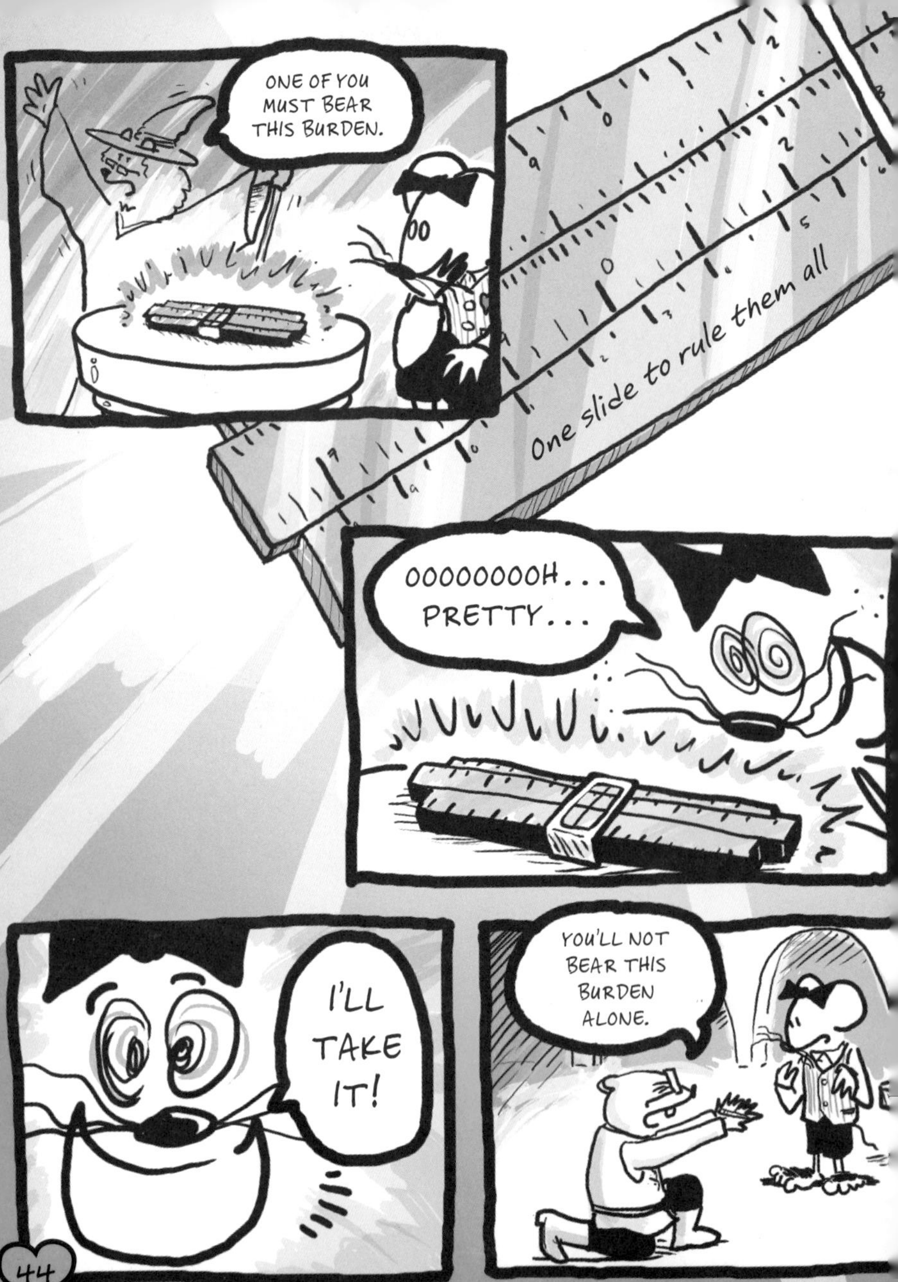
ONE OF YOU MUST BEAR THIS BURDEN.
One slide to rule them all
OOOOOOOOH... PRETTY...
I'LL TAKE IT!
YOU'LL NOT BEAR THIS BURDEN ALONE.

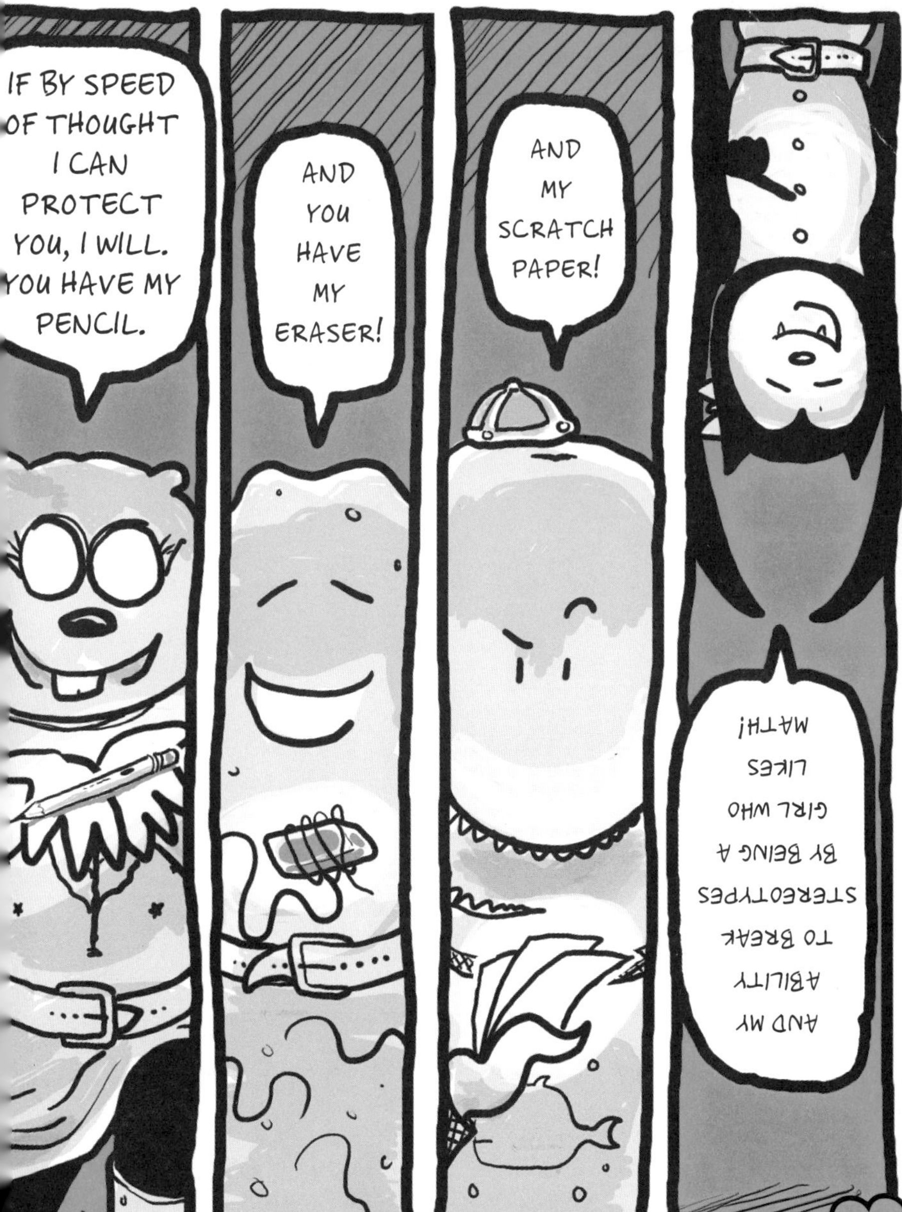
IF BY SPEED OF THOUGHT I CAN PROTECT YOU, I WILL. YOU HAVE MY PENCIL.
AND YOU HAVE MY ERASER!
AND MY SCRATCH PAPER!
AND MY ABILITY TO BREAK STEREOTYPES BY BEING A GIRL WHO LIKES MATH!

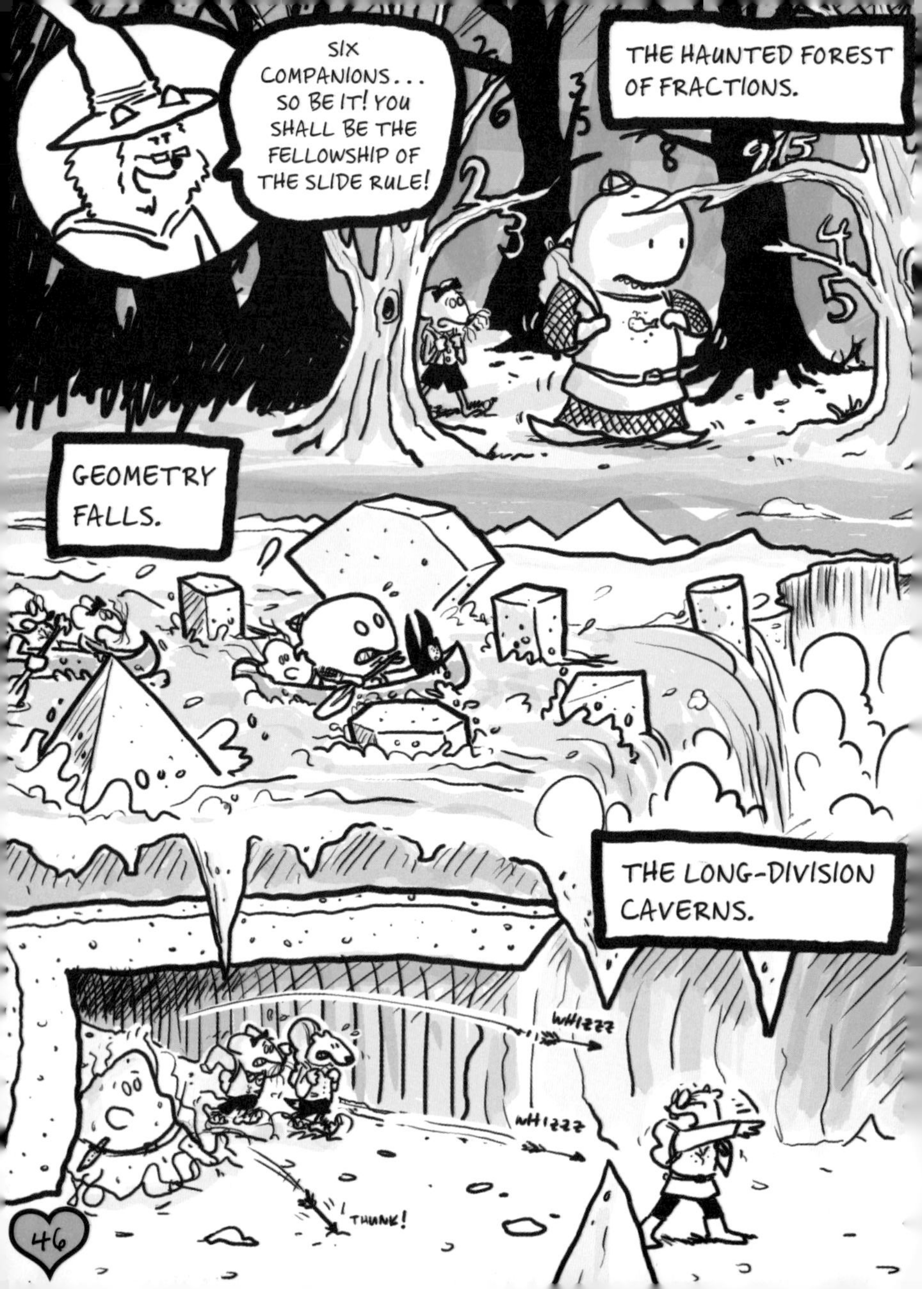
SIX COMPANIONS... SO BE IT! YOU SHALL BE THE FELLOWSHIP OF THE SLIDE RULE!
THE HAUNTED FOREST OF FRACTIONS.
GEOMETRY FALLS.
THE LONG-DIVISION CAVERNS.
WHIZZZ
WHIZZZ
THUNK!

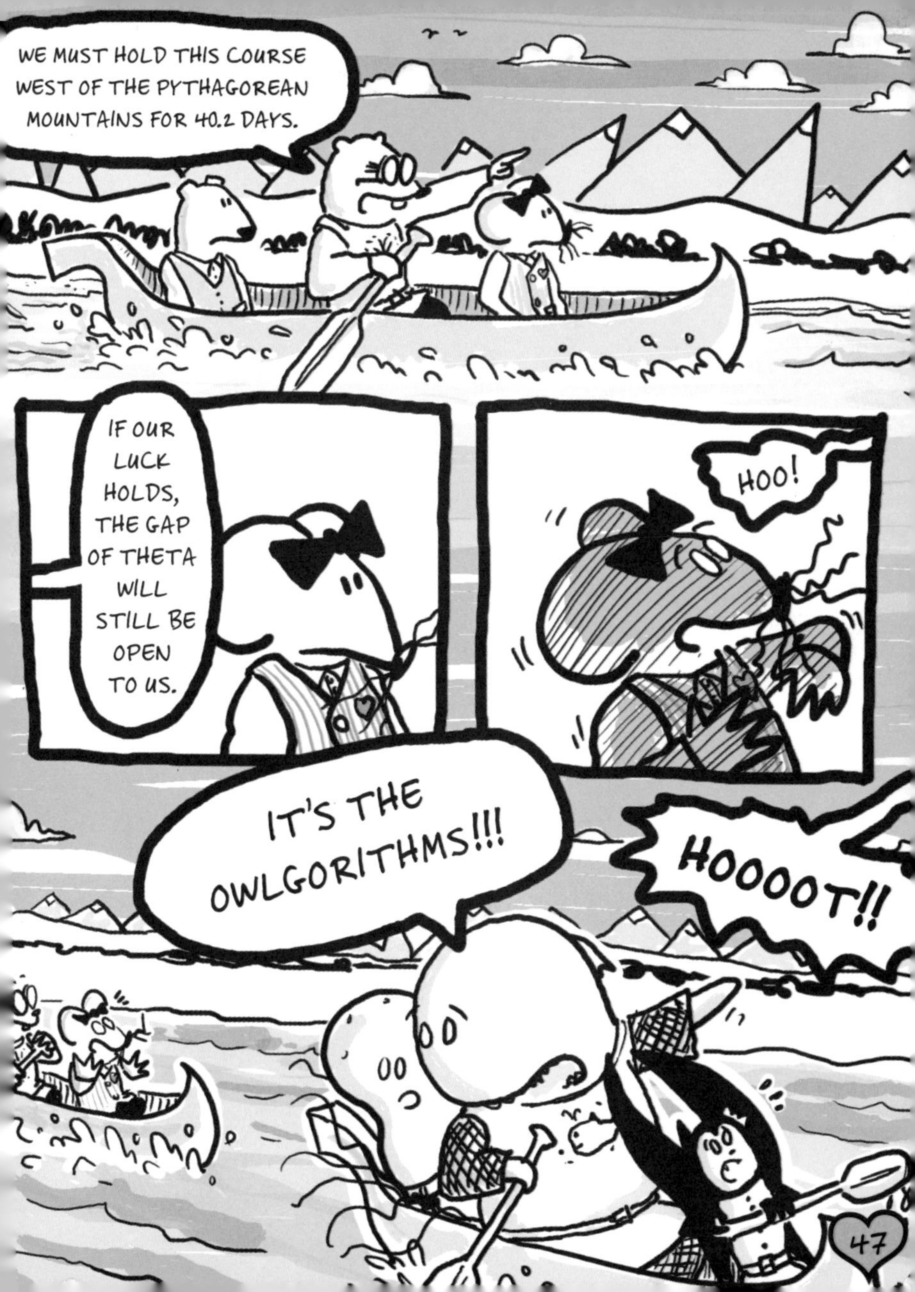
WE MUST HOLD THIS COURSE WEST OF THE PYTHAGOREAN MOUNTAINS FOR 40.2 DAYS.
IF OUR LUCK HOLDS, THE GAP OF THETA WILL STILL BE OPEN TO US.
HOO!
IT'S THE OWLGORITHMS!!!
HOOOOOT!!
47

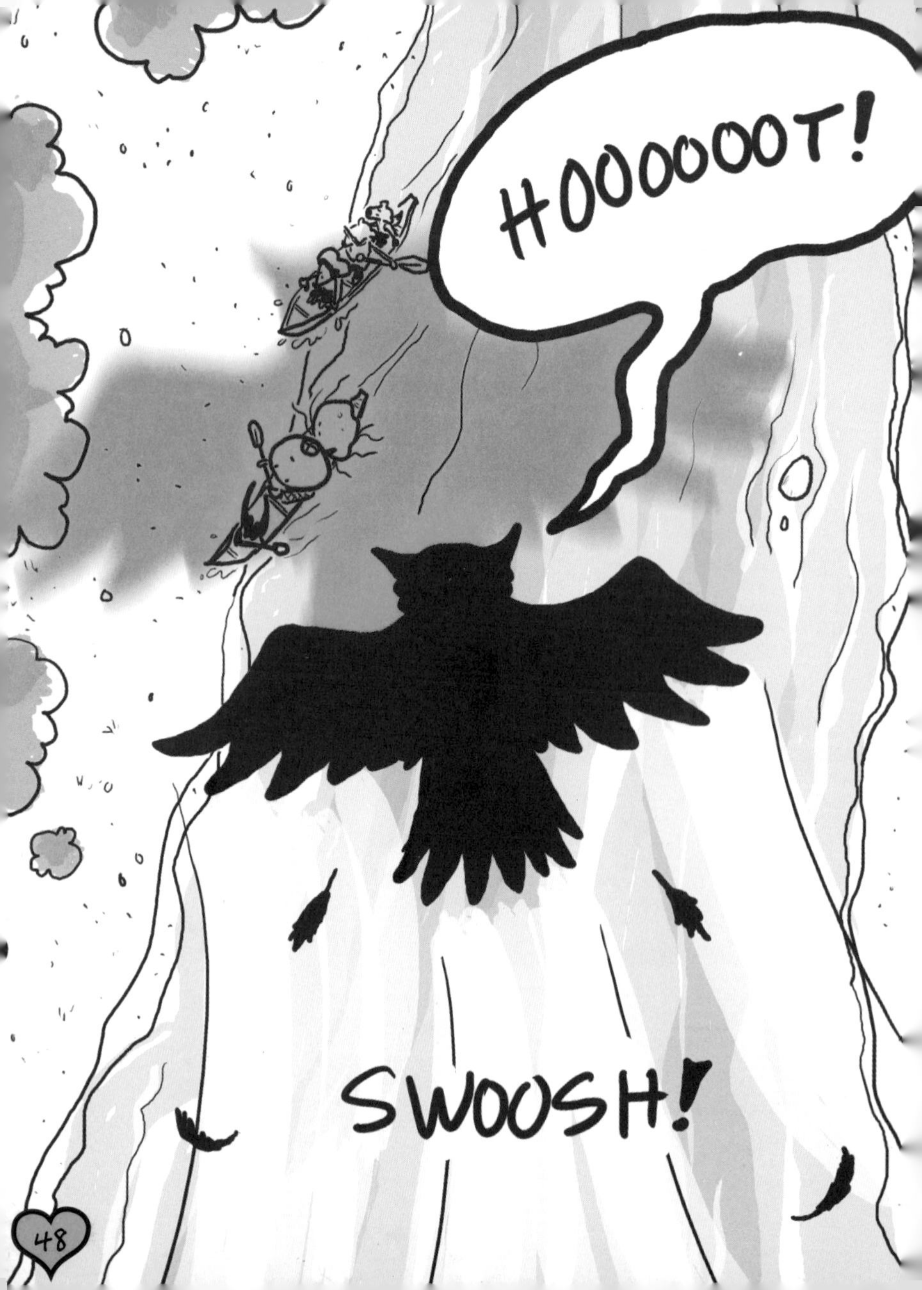
HOOOOOOT!
SWOOSH!

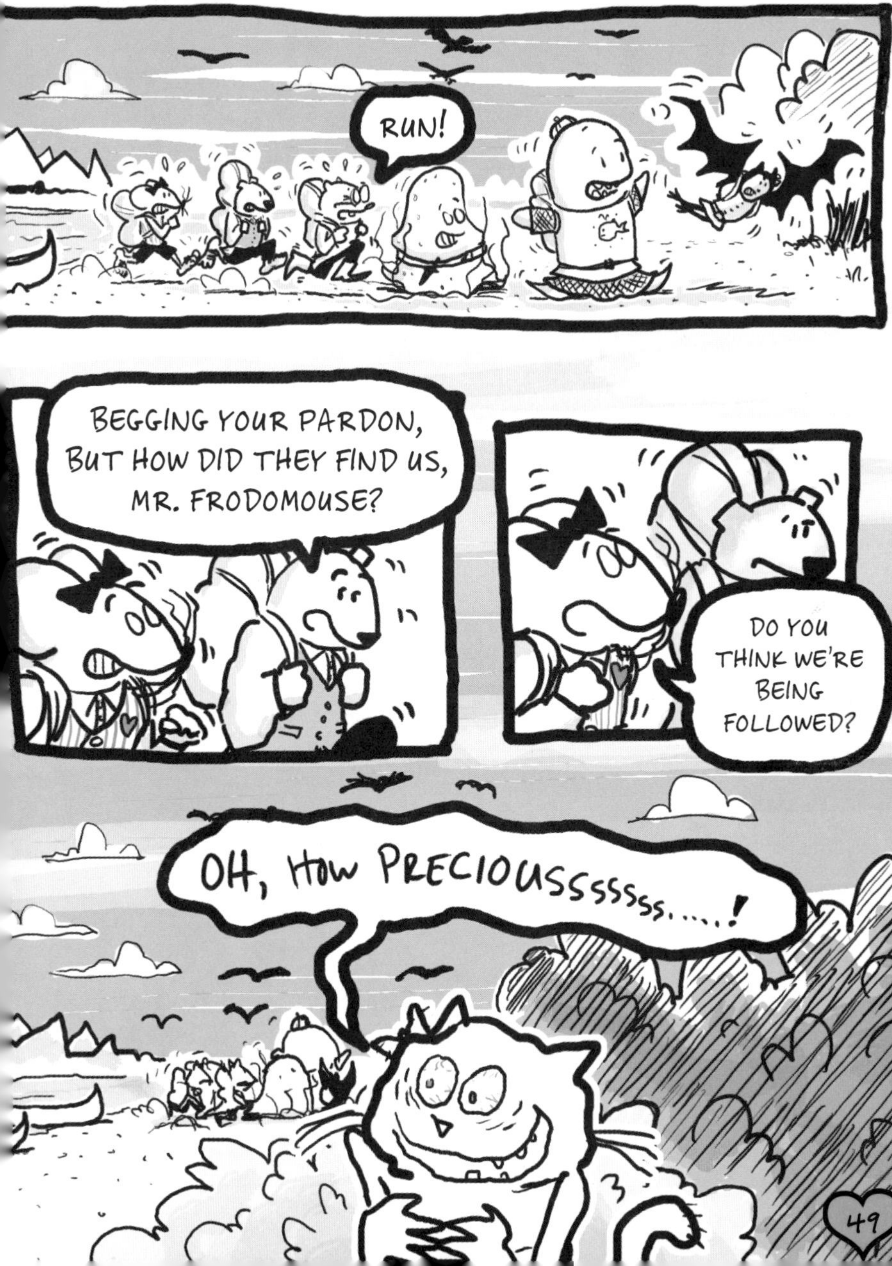

RUN!
BEGGING YOUR PARDON, BUT HOW DID THEY FIND US, MR. FRODOMOUSE?
DO YOU THINK WE'RE BEING FOLLOWED?
OH, HOW PRECIOUSSSSSSSS.....!

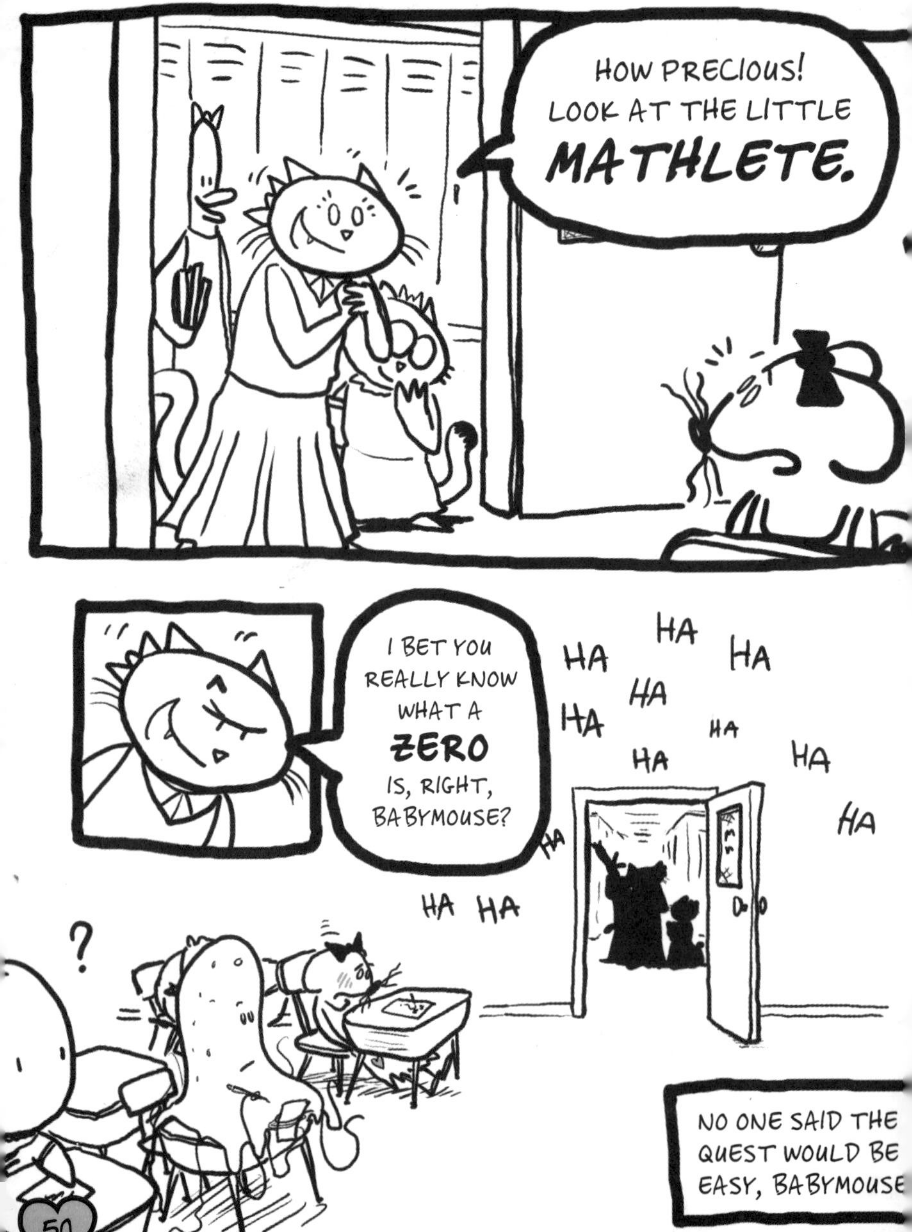
HOW PRECIOUS! LOOK AT THE LITTLE MATHLETE.
I BET YOU REALLY KNOW WHAT A ZERO IS, RIGHT, BABYMOUSE?
HA HA HA HA HA HA HA HA HA HA HA HA HA
?
NO ONE SAID THE QUEST WOULD BE EASY, BABYMOUSE

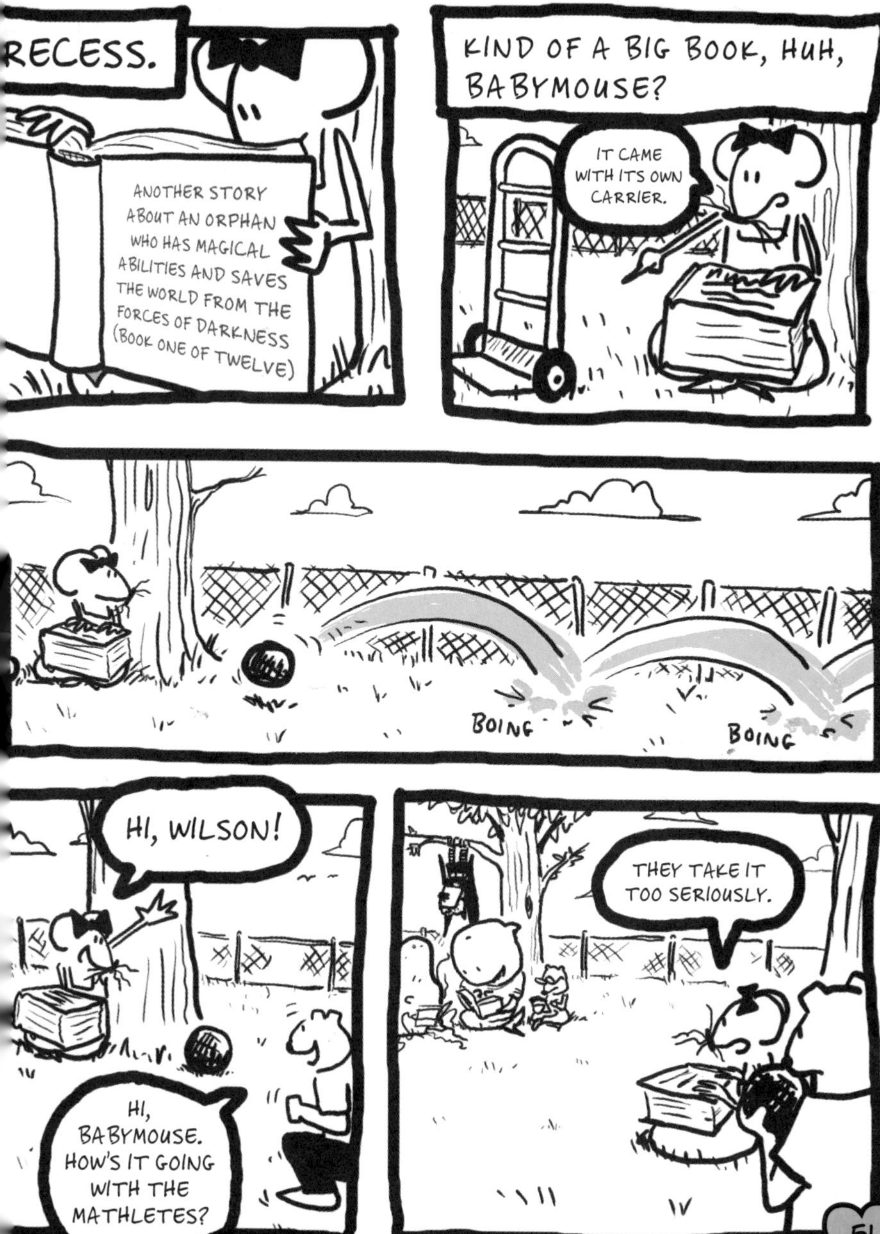

RECESS.
ANOTHER STORY ABOUT AN ORPHAN WHO HAS MAGICAL ABILITIES AND SAVES THE WORLD FROM THE FORCES OF DARKNESS (BOOK ONE OF TWELVE)
KIND OF A BIG BOOK, HUH, BABYMOUSE?
IT CAME WITH ITS OWN CARRIER.
BOING
BOING
HI, WILSON!
HI, BABYMOUSE. HOW'S IT GOING WITH THE MATHLETES?
THEY TAKE IT TOO SERIOUSLY.

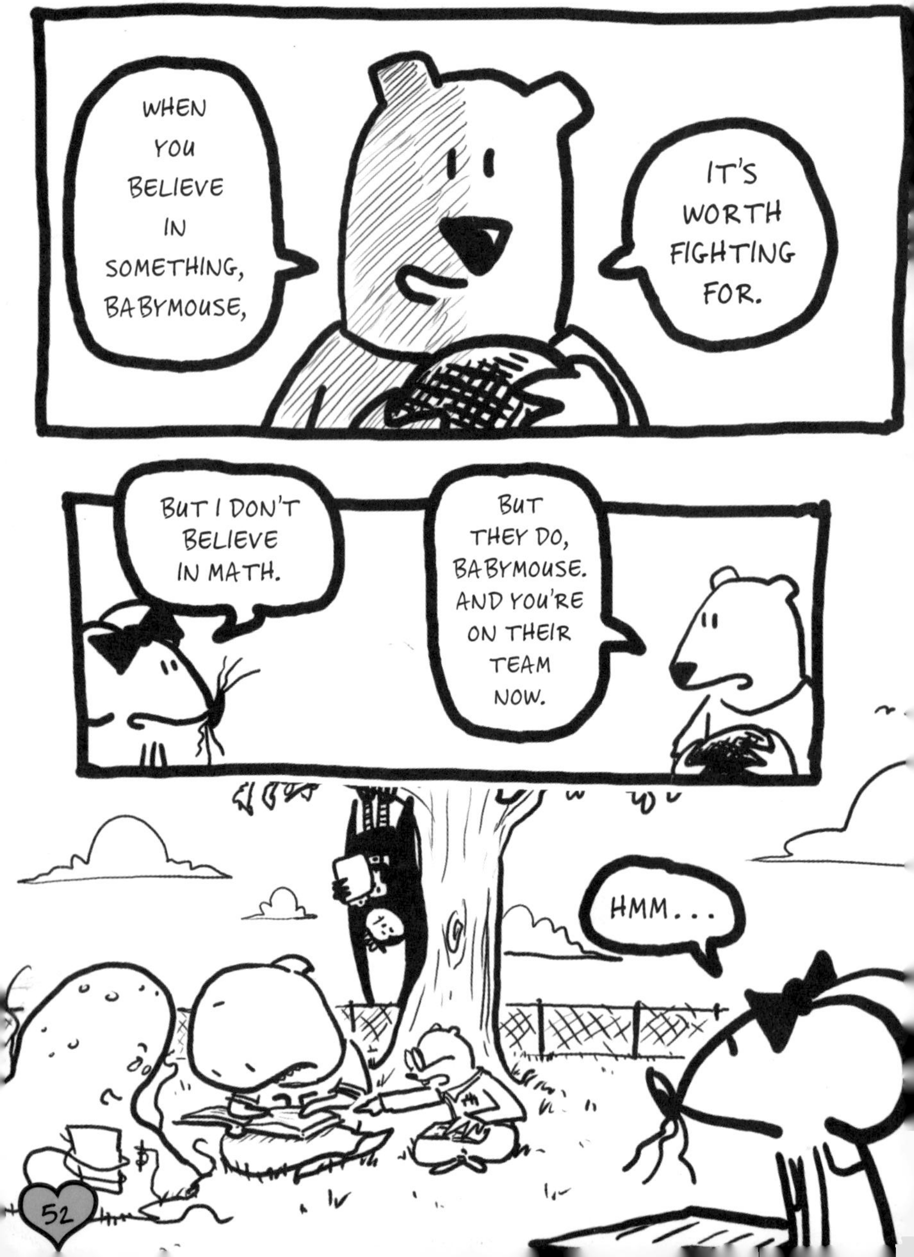
WHEN YOU BELIEVE IN SOMETHING, BABYMOUSE,
IT'S WORTH FIGHTING FOR.
BUT I DON'T BELIEVE IN MATH.
BUT THEY DO, BABYMOUSE. AND YOU'RE ON THEIR TEAM NOW.
HMM...

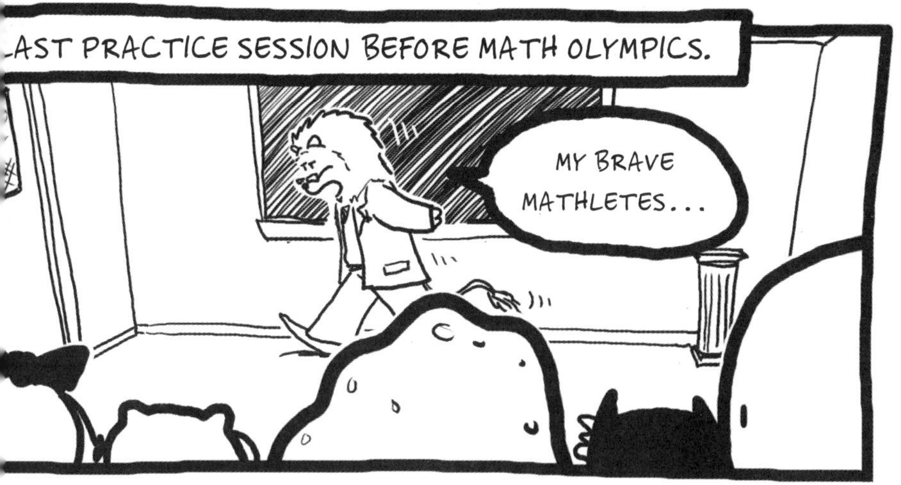
LAST PRACTICE SESSION BEFORE MATH OLYMPICS.
MY BRAVE MATHLETES...

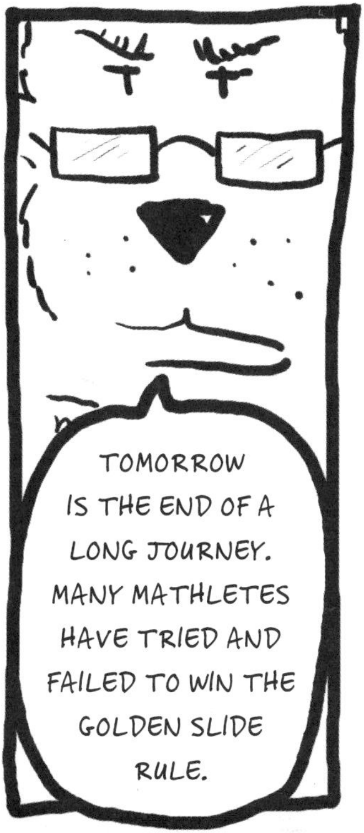
TOMORROW IS THE END OF A LONG JOURNEY. MANY MATHLETES HAVE TRIED AND FAILED TO WIN THE GOLDEN SLIDE RULE.

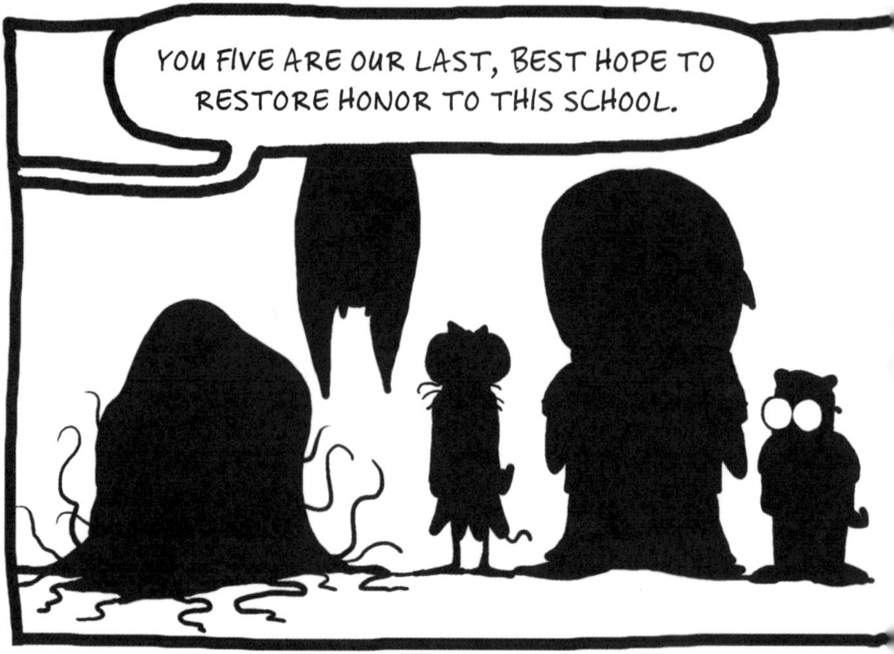
YOU FIVE ARE OUR LAST, BEST HOPE TO RESTORE HONOR TO THIS SCHOOL.

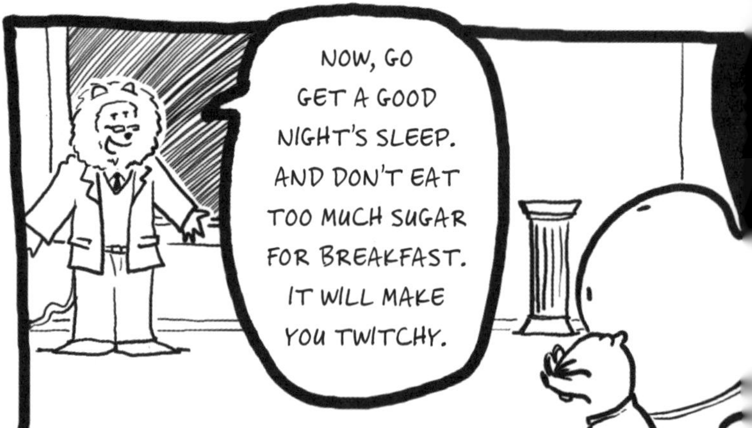
NOW, GO GET A GOOD NIGHT'S SLEEP. AND DON'T EAT TOO MUCH SUGAR FOR BREAKFAST. IT WILL MAKE YOU TWITCHY.

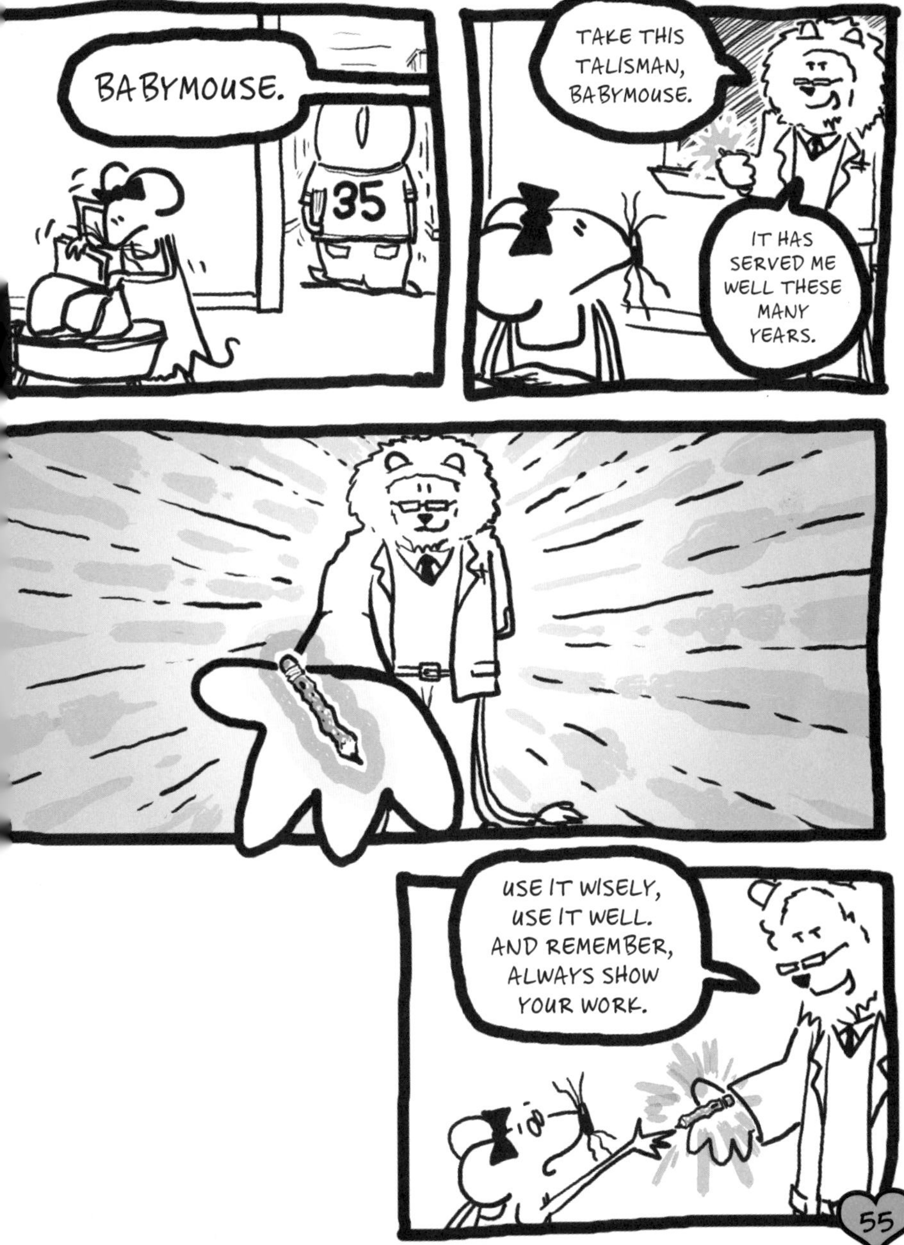
BABYMOUSE.
35
TAKE THIS TALISMAN, BABYMOUSE.
IT HAS SERVED ME WELL THESE MANY YEARS.
USE IT WISELY, USE IT WELL. AND REMEMBER, ALWAYS SHOW YOUR WORK.

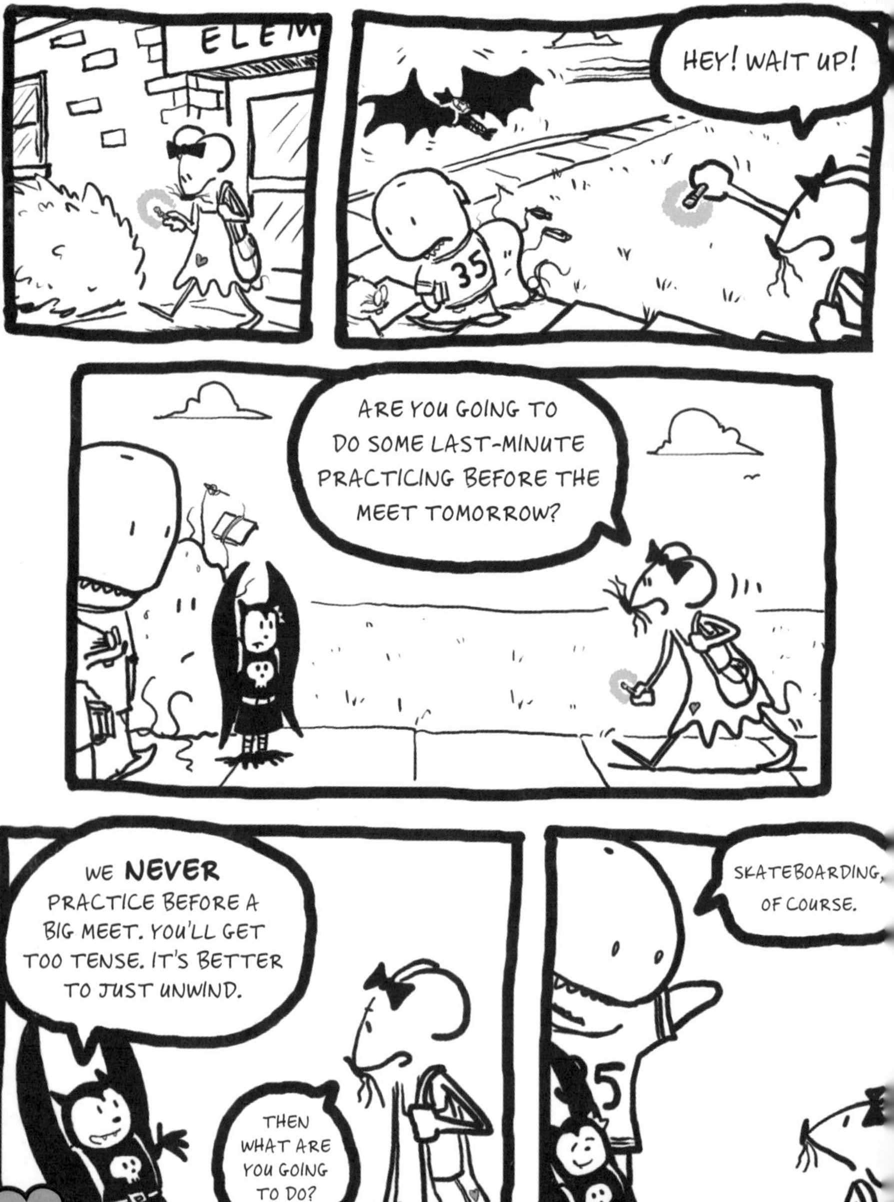

ELEM
HEY! WAIT UP!
ARE YOU GOING TO DO SOME LAST-MINUTE PRACTICING BEFORE THE MEET TOMORROW?
WE **NEVER** PRACTICE BEFORE A BIG MEET. YOU'LL GET TOO TENSE. IT'S BETTER TO JUST UNWIND.
THEN WHAT ARE YOU GOING TO DO?
SKATEBOARDING, OF COURSE.

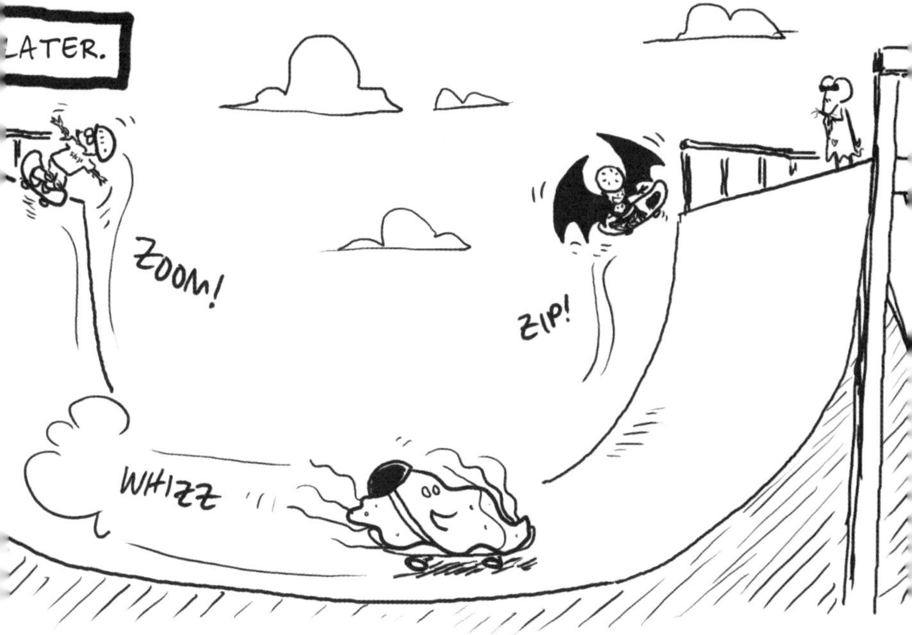
LATER.
ZOOM!
ZIP!
WHIZZ

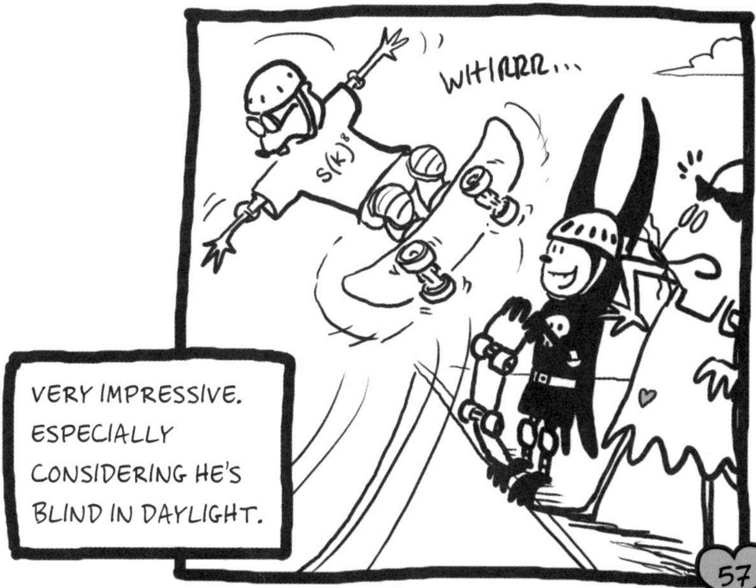
WHIRRR...
S(K)8
VERY IMPRESSIVE. ESPECIALLY CONSIDERING HE'S BLIND IN DAYLIGHT.

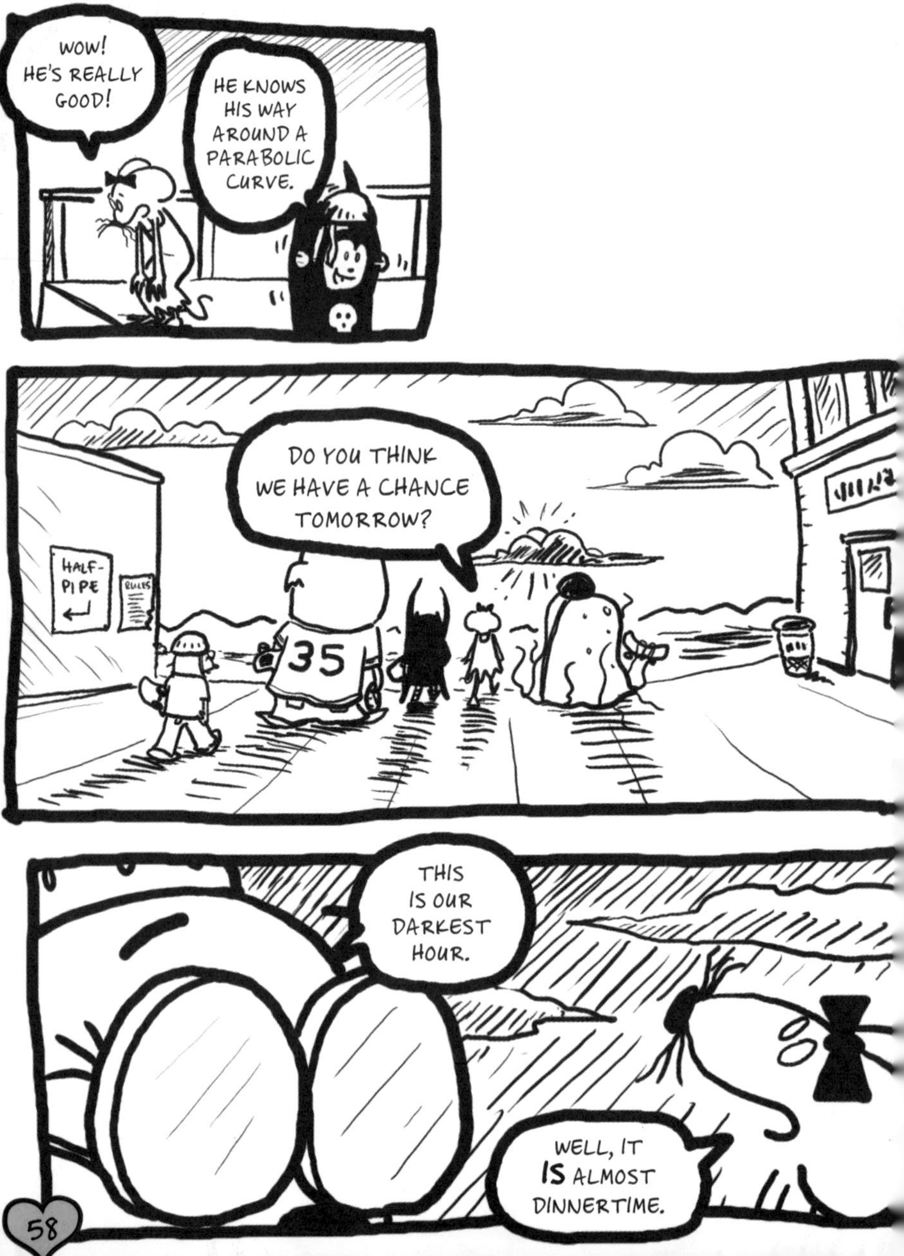
WOW! HE'S REALLY GOOD!
HE KNOWS HIS WAY AROUND A PARABOLIC CURVE.
HALF-PIPE
RULES
35
DO YOU THINK WE HAVE A CHANCE TOMORROW?
THIS IS OUR DARKEST HOUR.
WELL, IT **IS** ALMOST DINNERTIME.

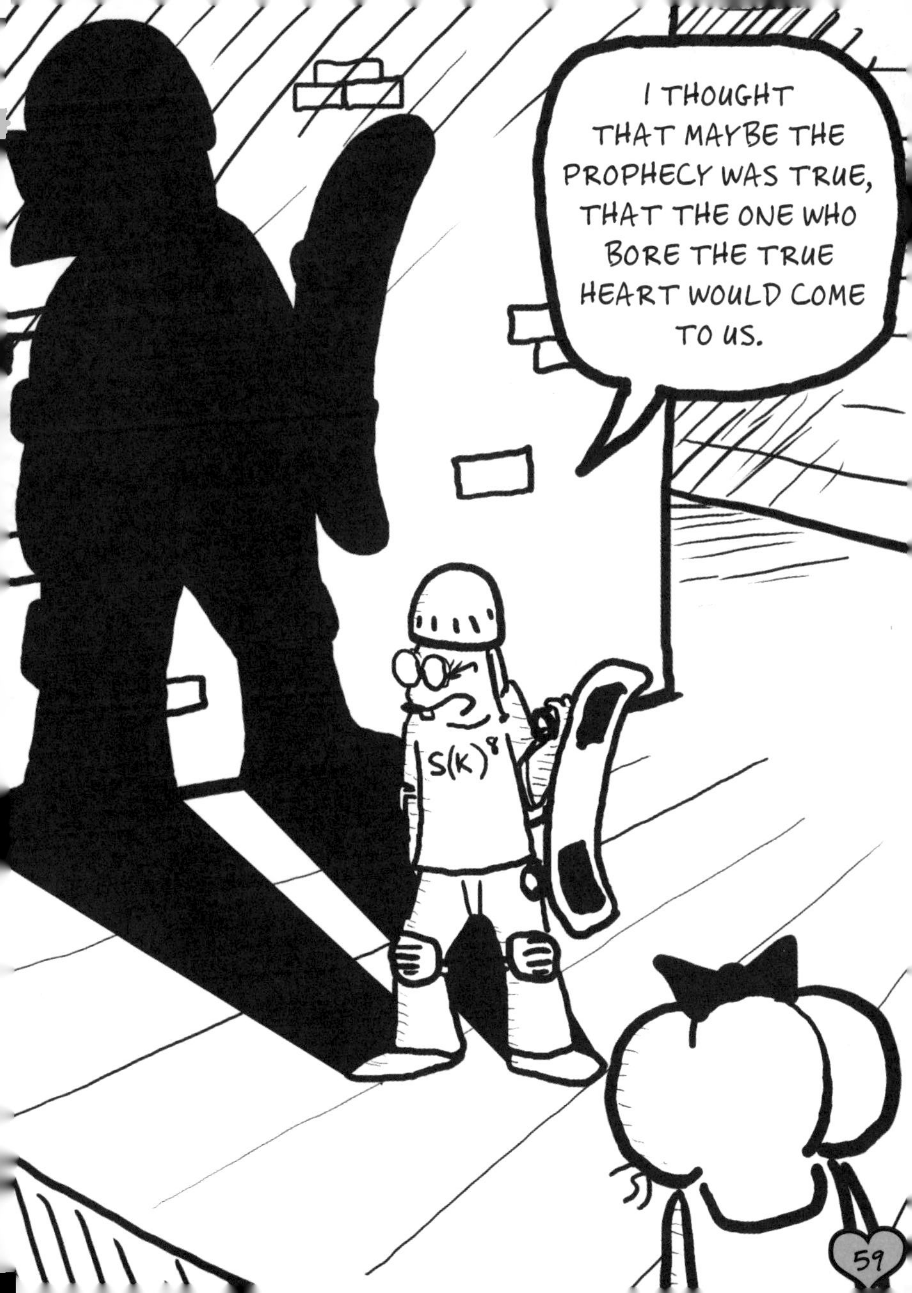
I THOUGHT THAT MAYBE THE PROPHECY WAS TRUE, THAT THE ONE WHO BORE THE TRUE HEART WOULD COME TO US.
S(K)8

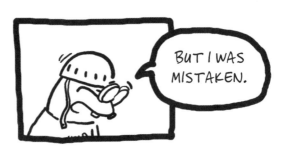

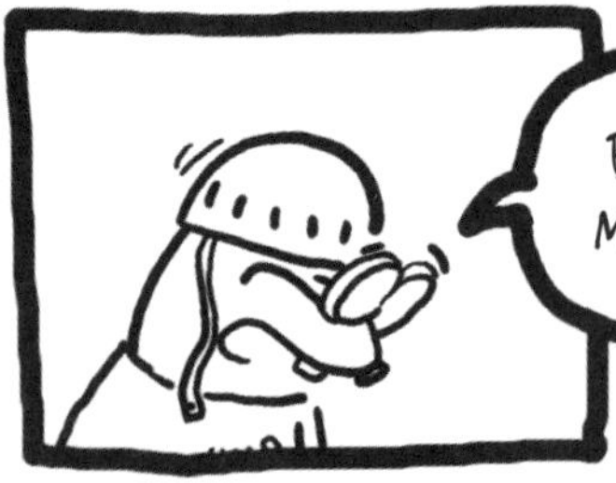
BUT I WAS MISTAKEN.

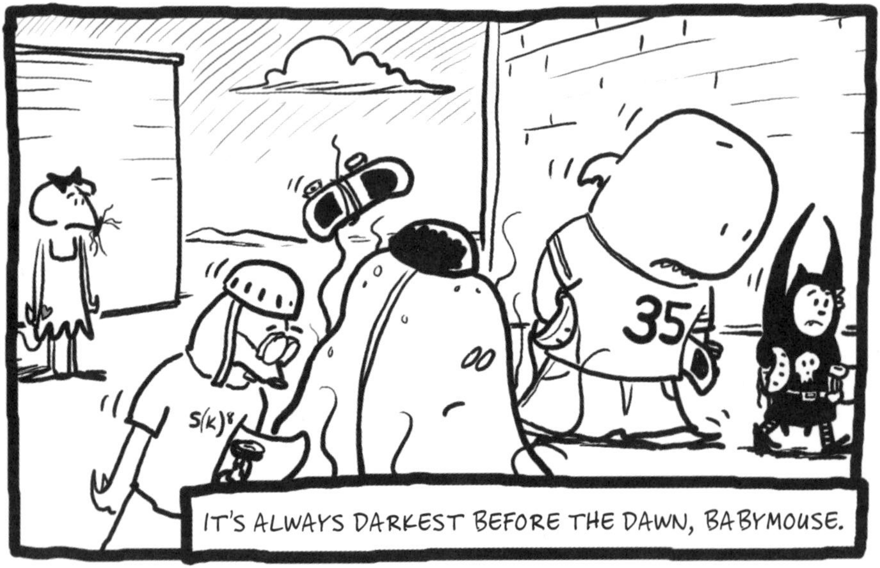
35
S(K)8
IT'S ALWAYS DARKEST BEFORE THE DAWN, BABYMOUSE.

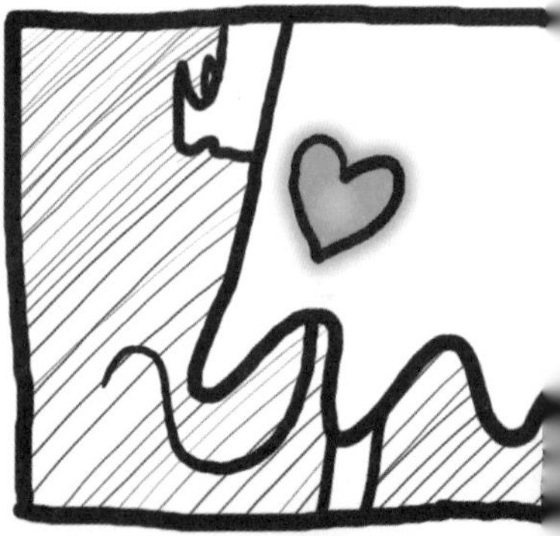

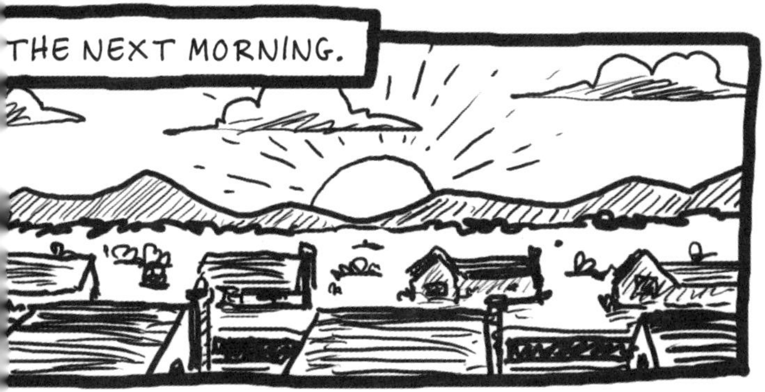
THE NEXT MORNING.

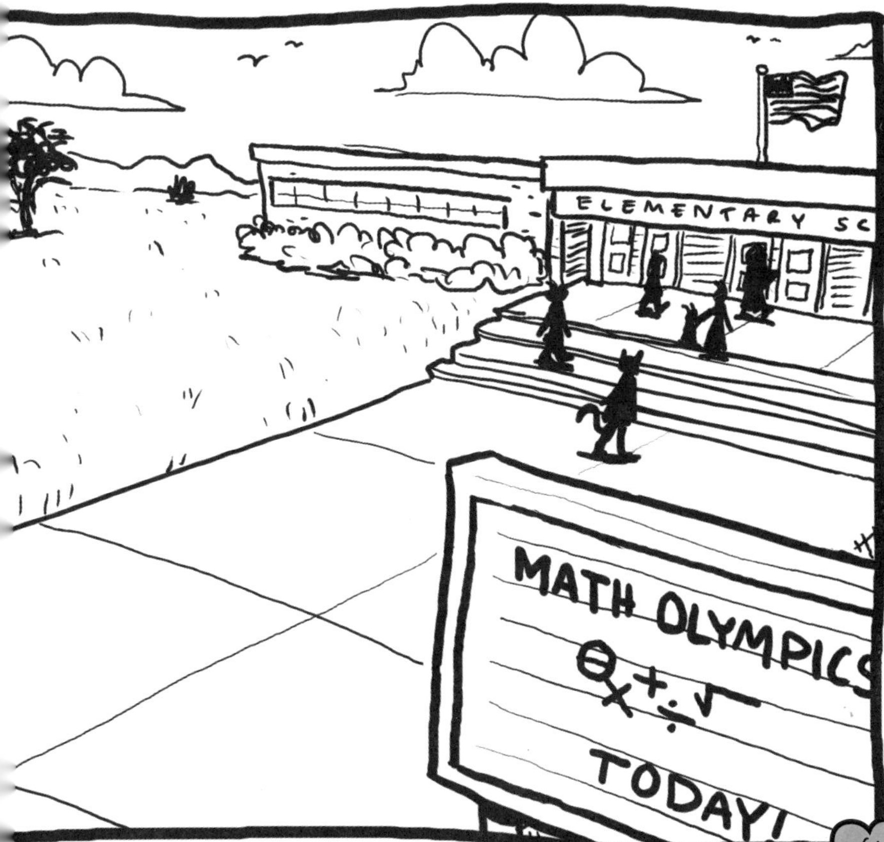
ELEMENTARY SC
MATH OLYMPICS
TODAY!

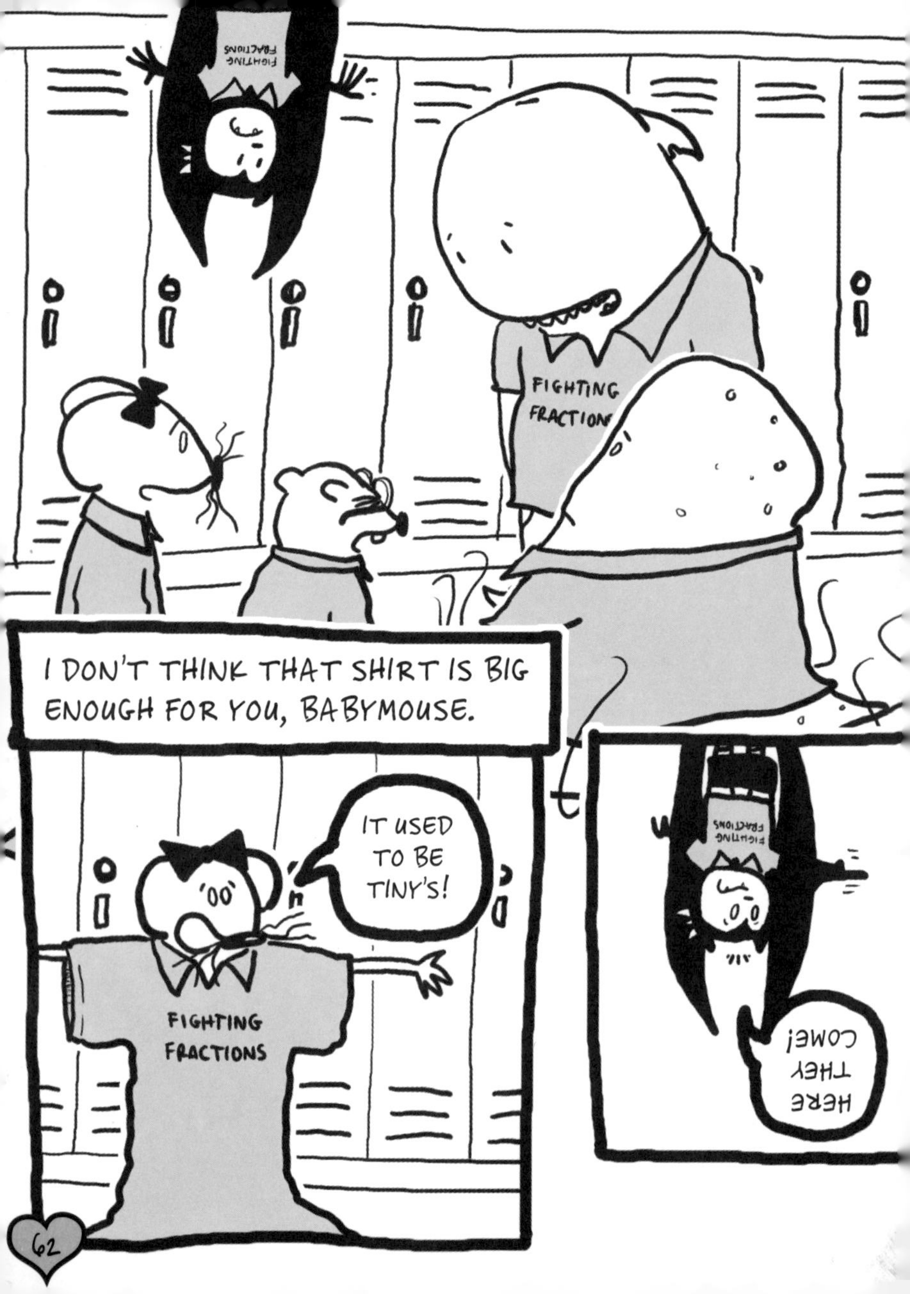
FIGHTING FRACTIONS
FIGHTING FRACTIONS
I DON'T THINK THAT SHIRT IS BIG ENOUGH FOR YOU, BABYMOUSE.
IT USED TO BE TINY'S!
FIGHTING FRACTIONS
FIGHTING FRACTIONS
HERE THEY COME!

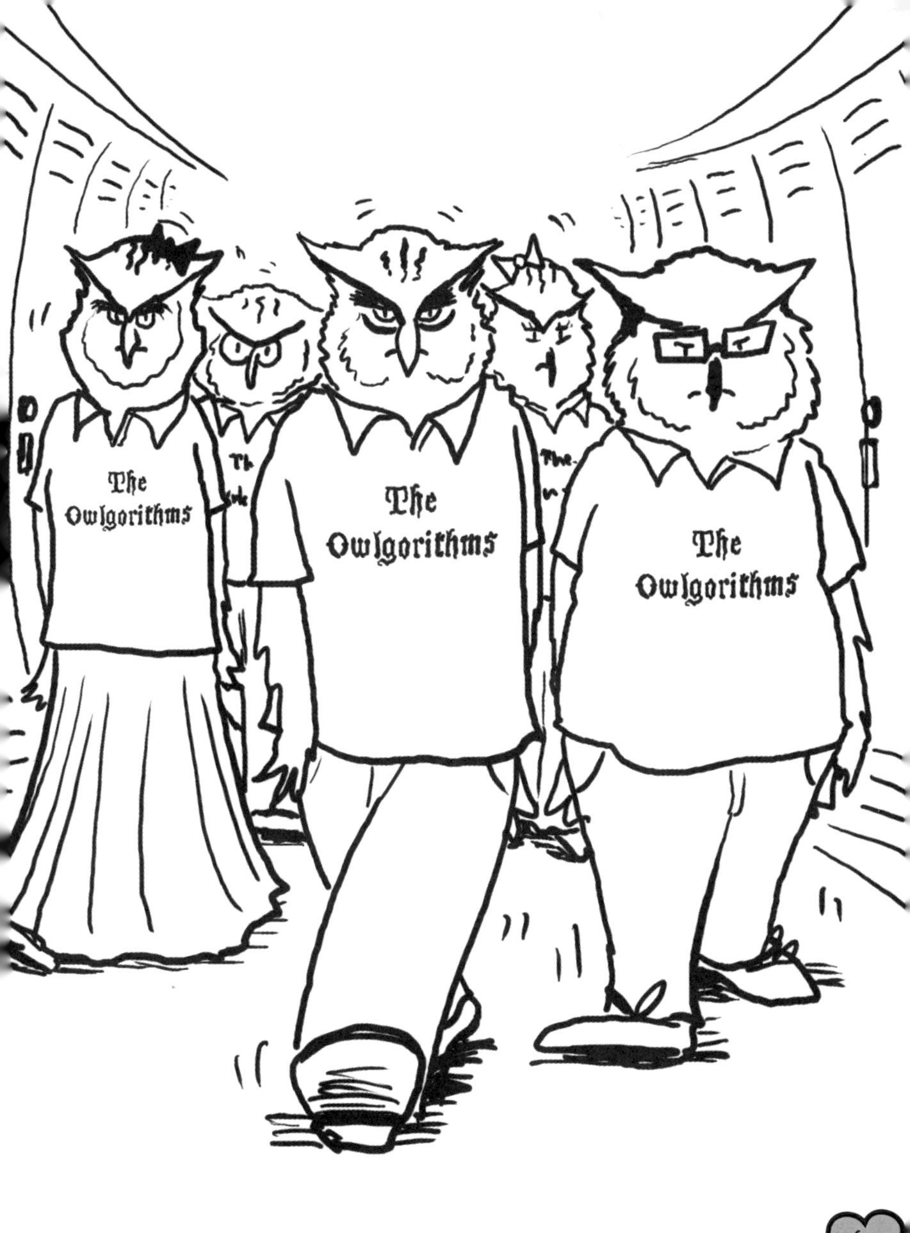
The Owlgorithms
The Owlgorithms
The Owlgorithms

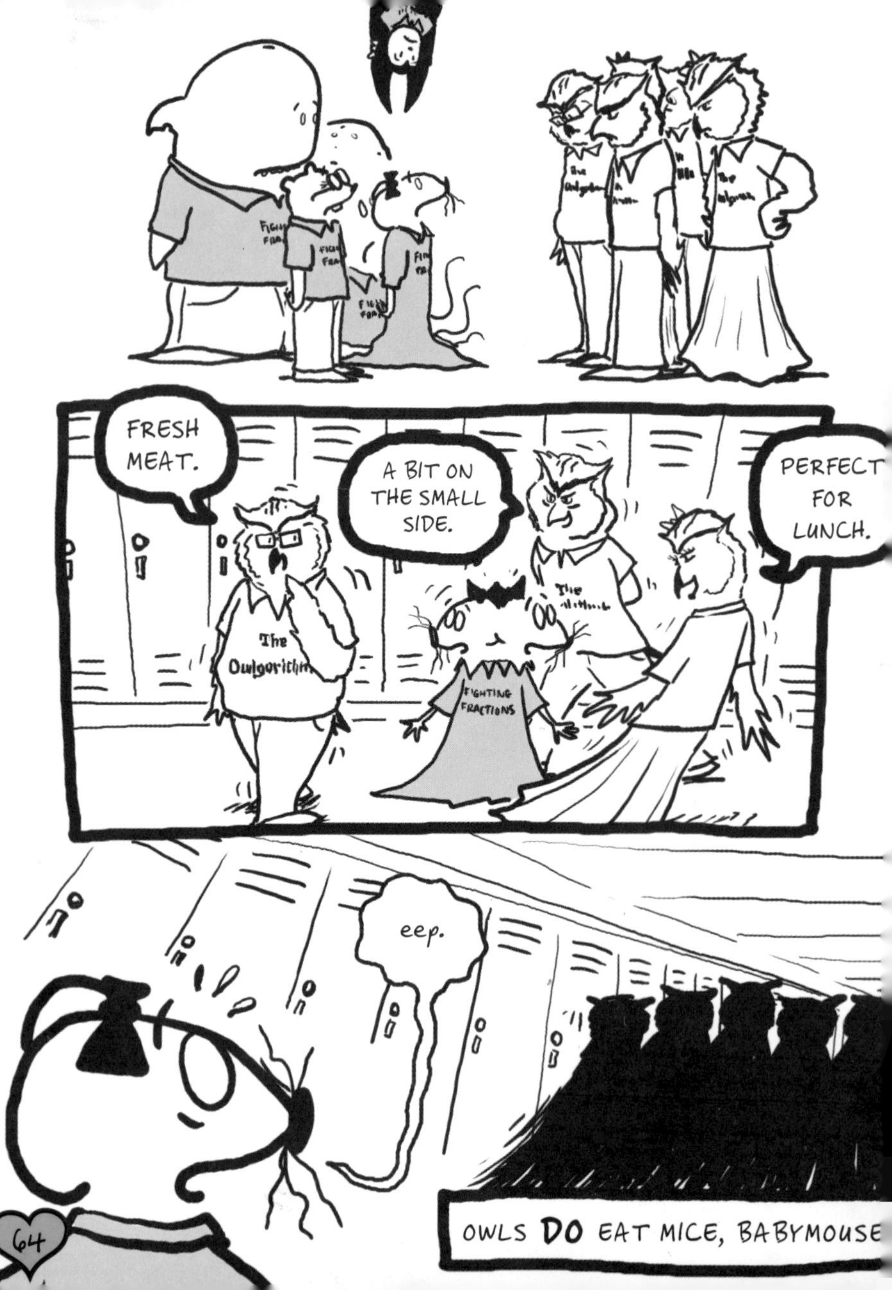
FRESH MEAT.
A BIT ON THE SMALL SIDE.
PERFECT FOR LUNCH.
The Owlgorithm
FIGHTING FRACTIONS
eep.
OWLS DO EAT MICE, BABYMOUSE

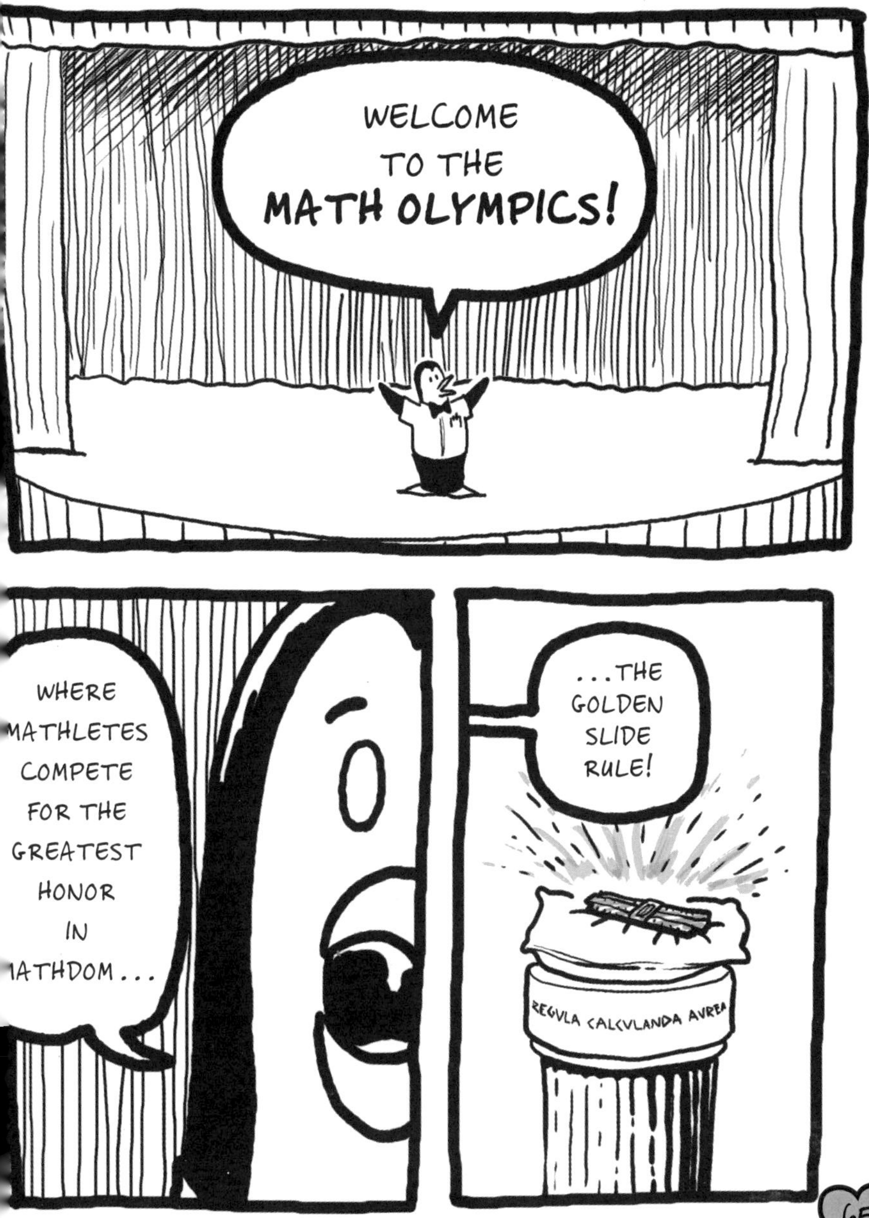
WELCOME TO THE MATH OLYMPICS!
WHERE MATHLETES COMPETE FOR THE GREATEST HONOR IN MATHDOM...
...THE GOLDEN SLIDE RULE!
REGVLA CALCVLANDA AVREA

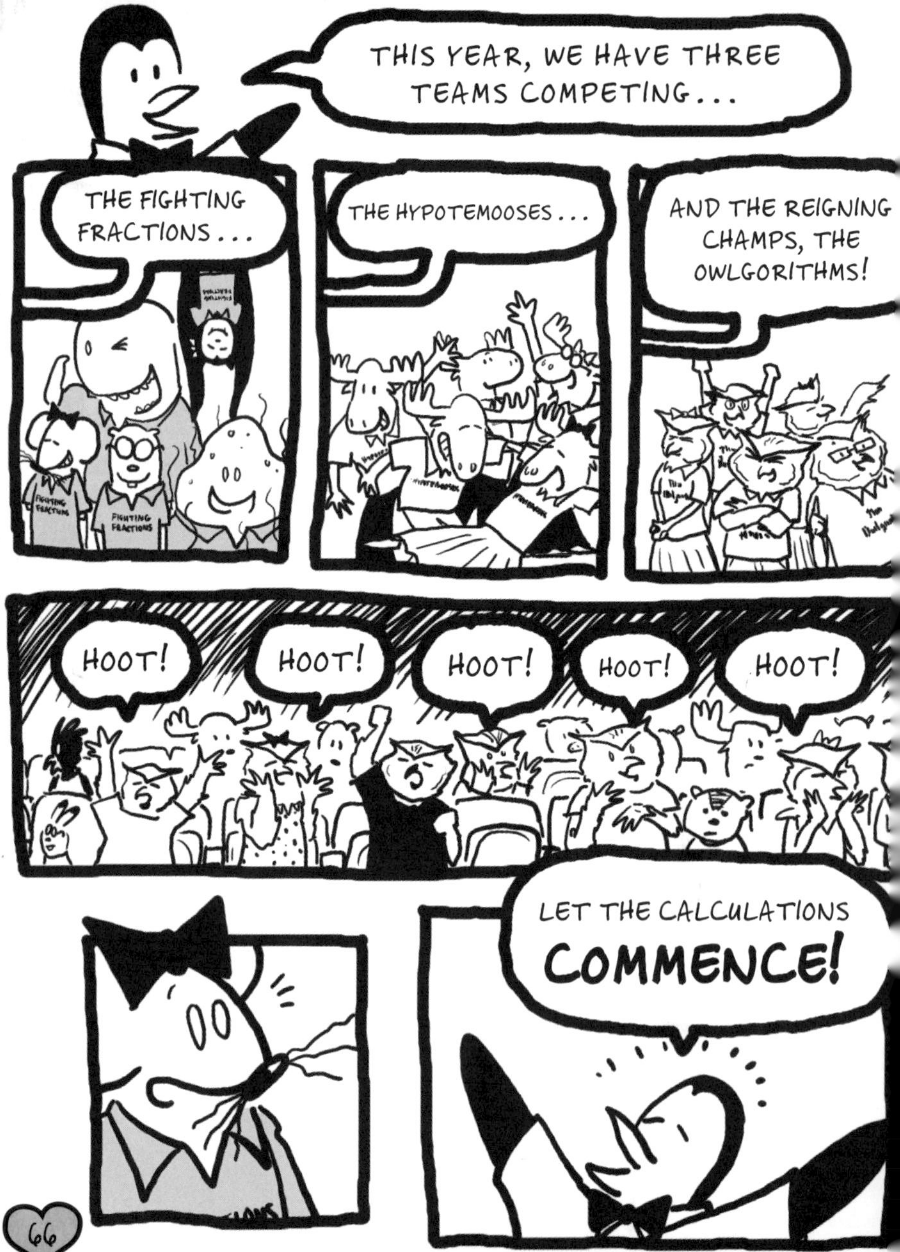

THIS YEAR, WE HAVE THREE TEAMS COMPETING...
THE FIGHTING FRACTIONS...
THE HYPOTEMOOSES...
AND THE REIGNING CHAMPS, THE OWLGORITHMS!
FIGHTING FRACTIONS
FIGHTING FRACTIONS
HOOT!
HOOT!
HOOT!
HOOT!
HOOT!
LET THE CALCULATIONS COMMENCE!

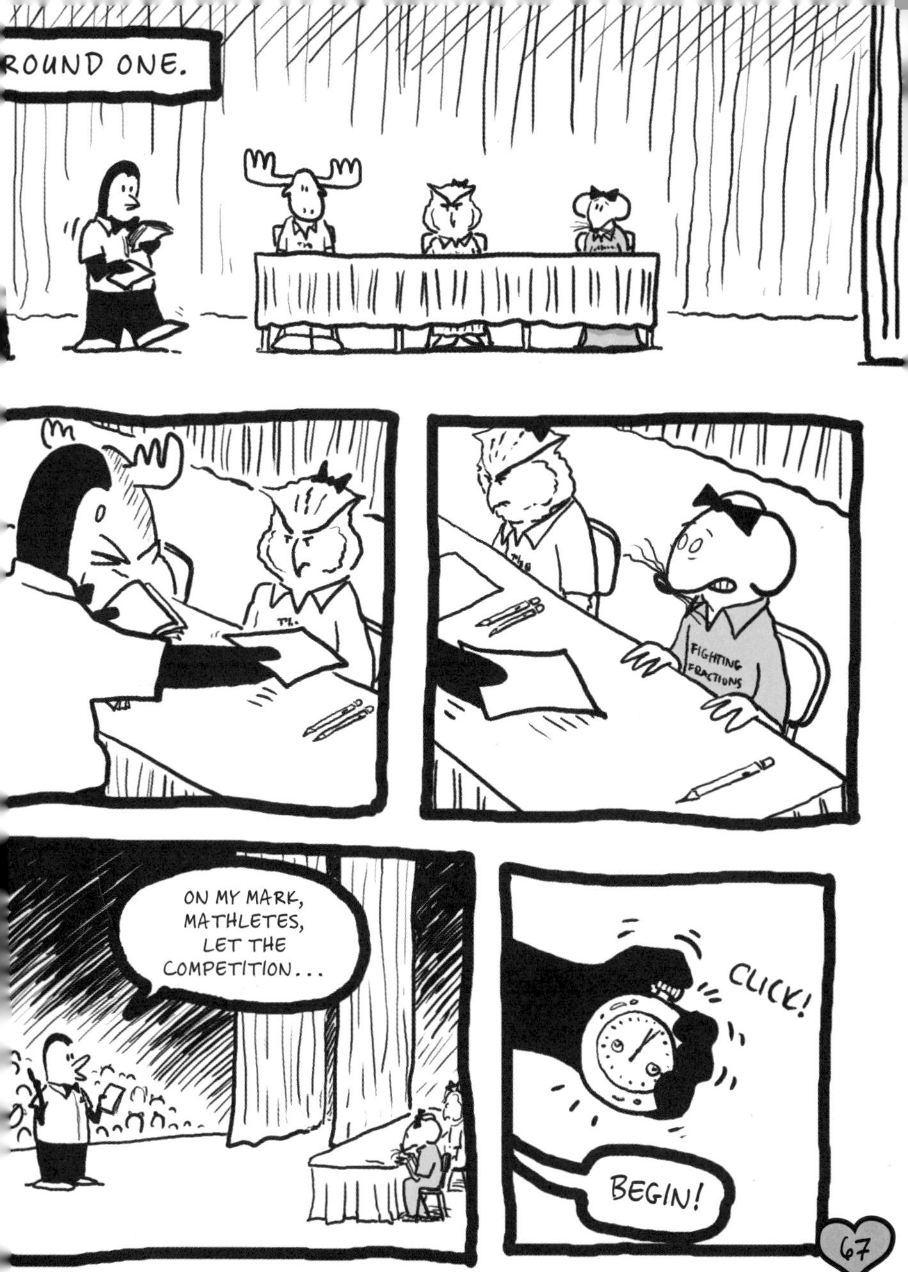
ROUND ONE.
FIGHTING FRACTIONS
ON MY MARK, MATHLETES, LET THE COMPETITION...
CLICK!
BEGIN!

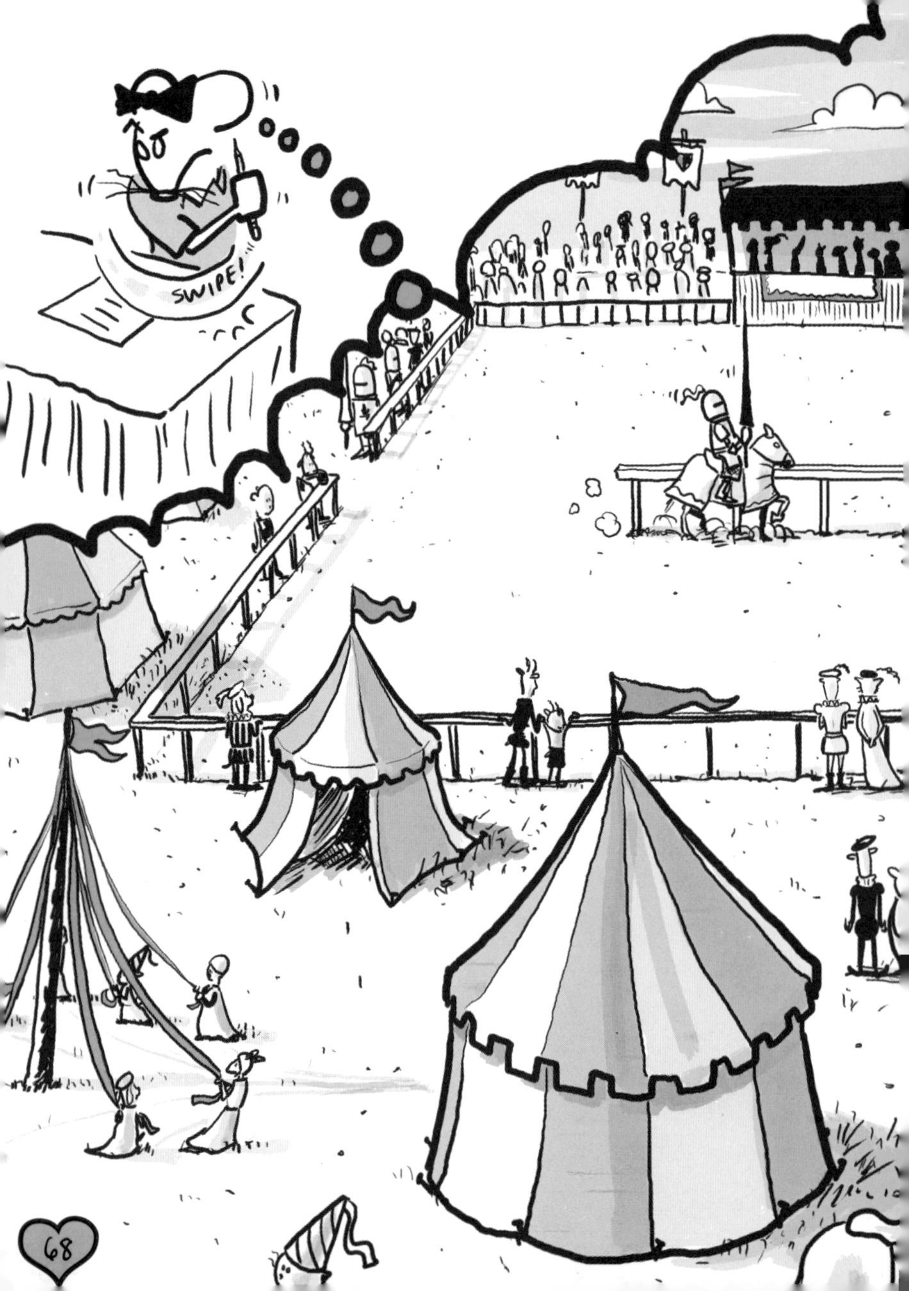
SWIPE!

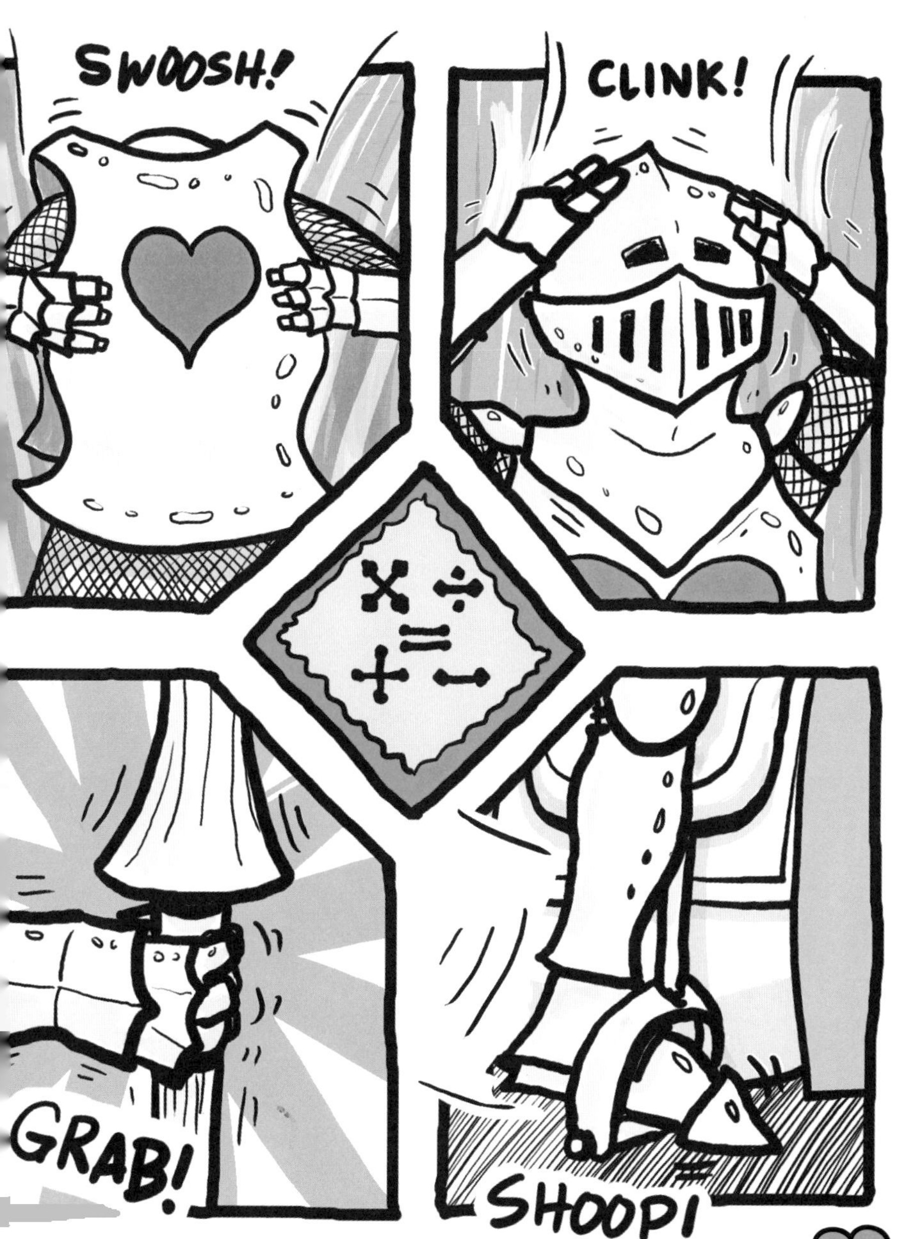
SWOOSH!
CLINK!
GRAB!
SHOOP!

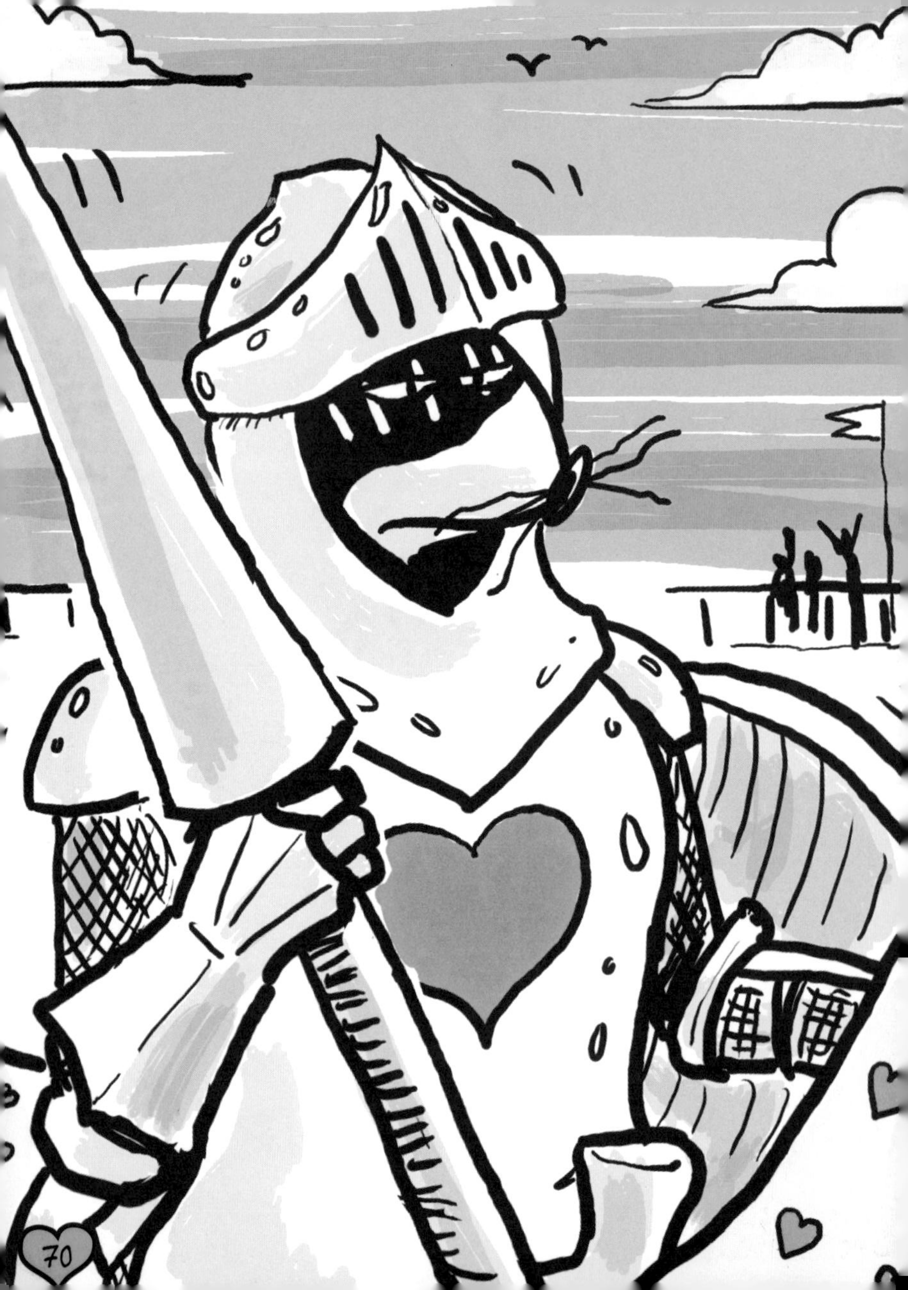

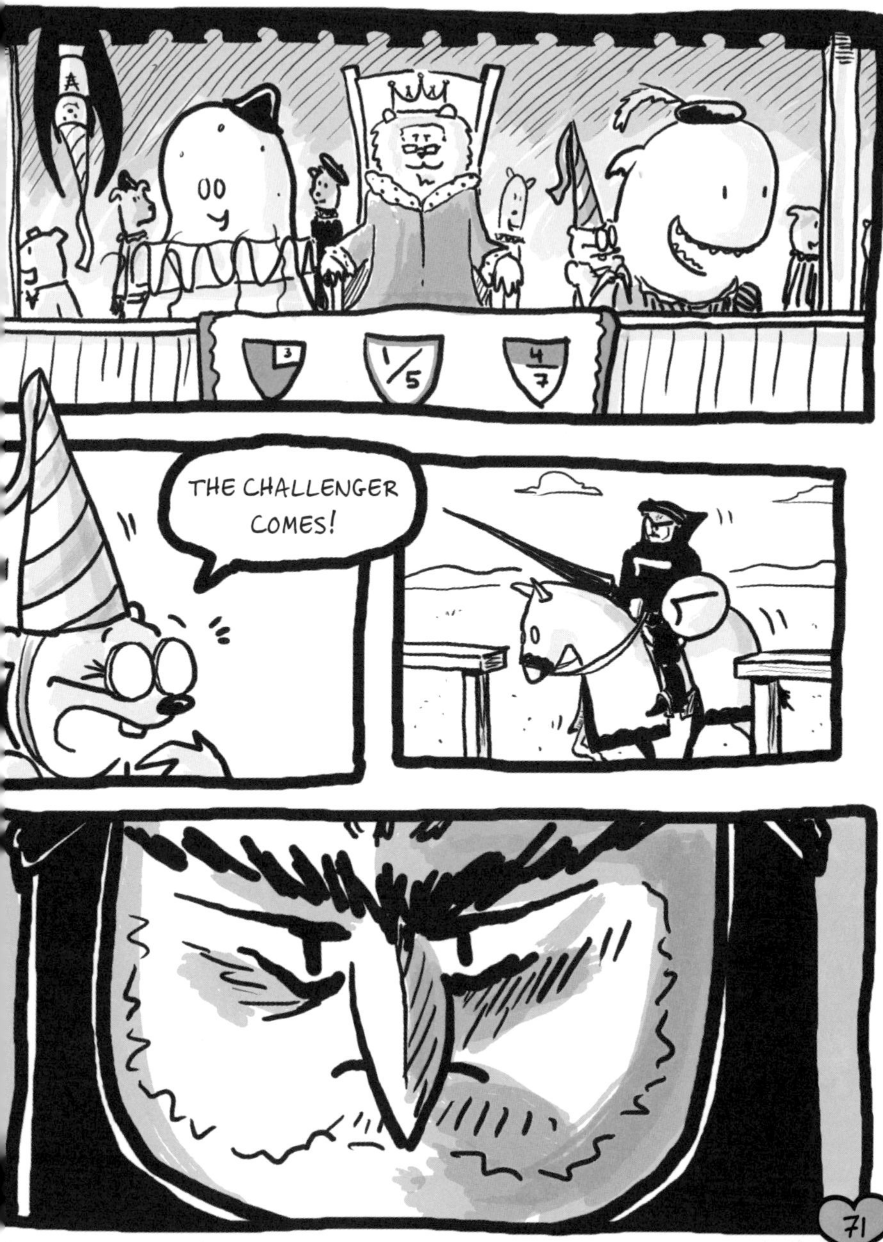
3
1/5
4/7
THE CHALLENGER COMES!

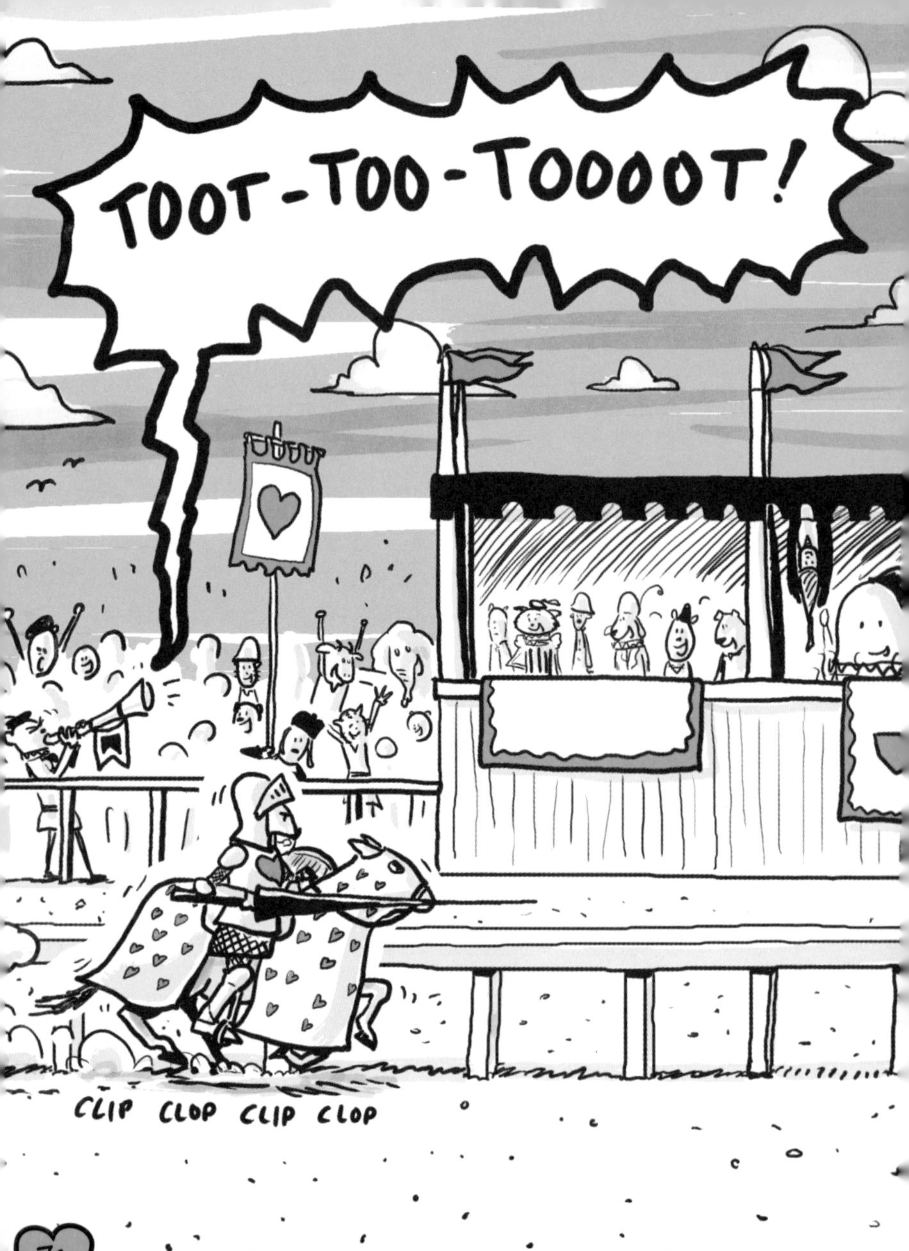
TOOT-TOO-TOOOOT!
CLIP CLOP CLIP CLOP

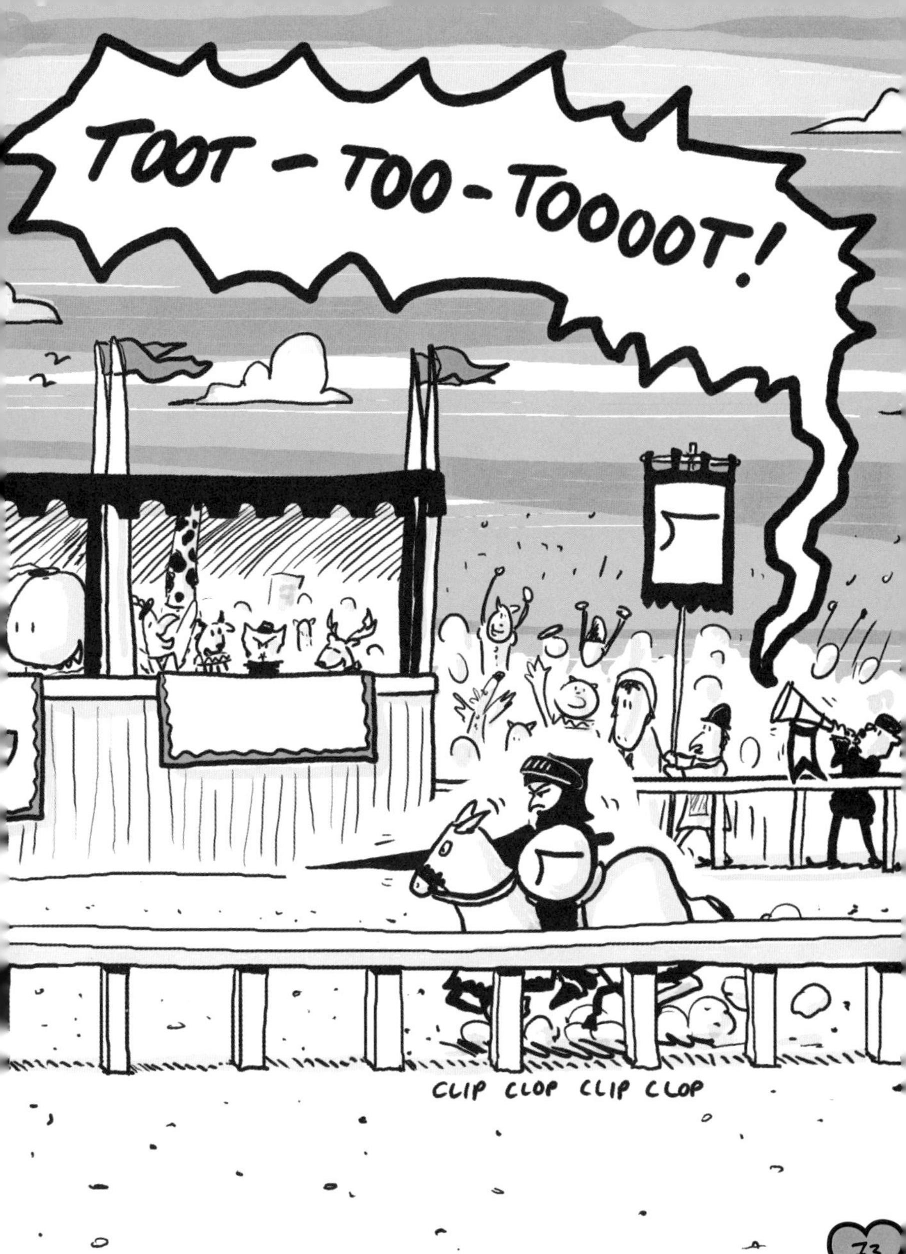
TOOT - TOO - TOOOOT!
CLIP CLOP CLIP CLOP

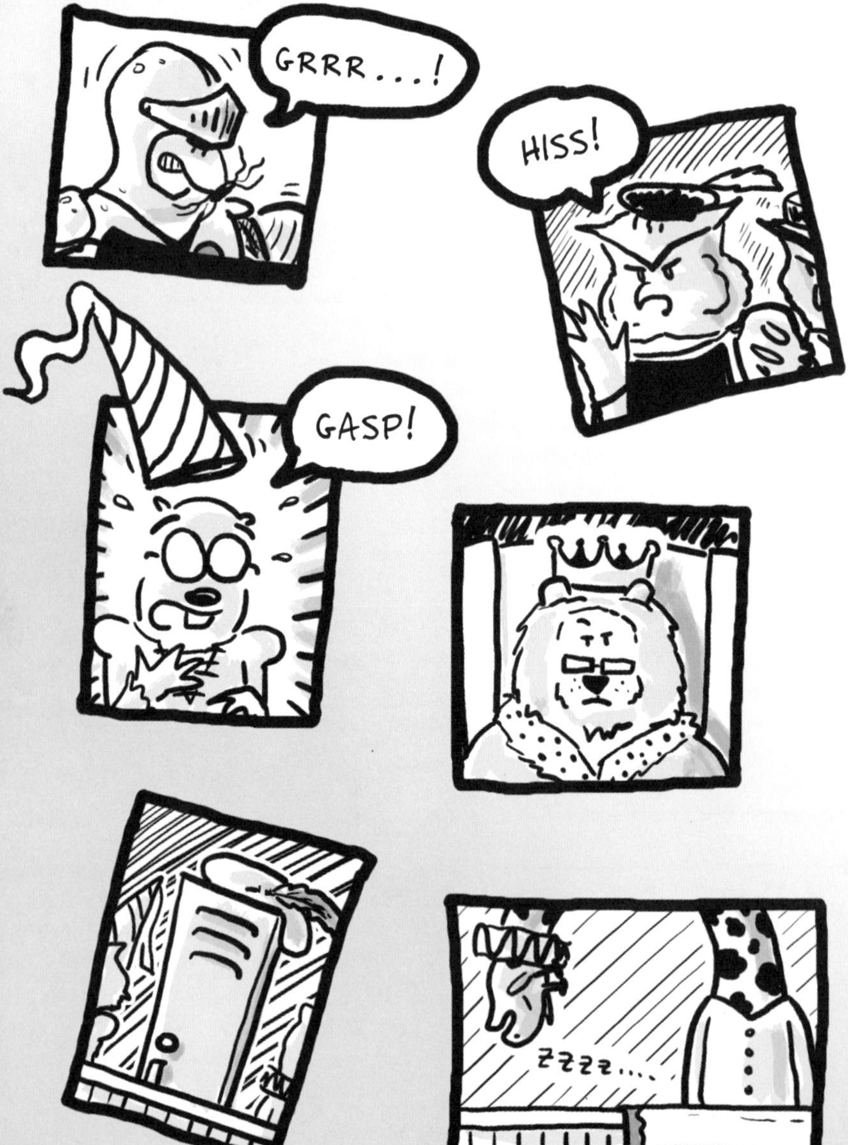
GRRR...!
HISS!
GASP!
ZZZZ....

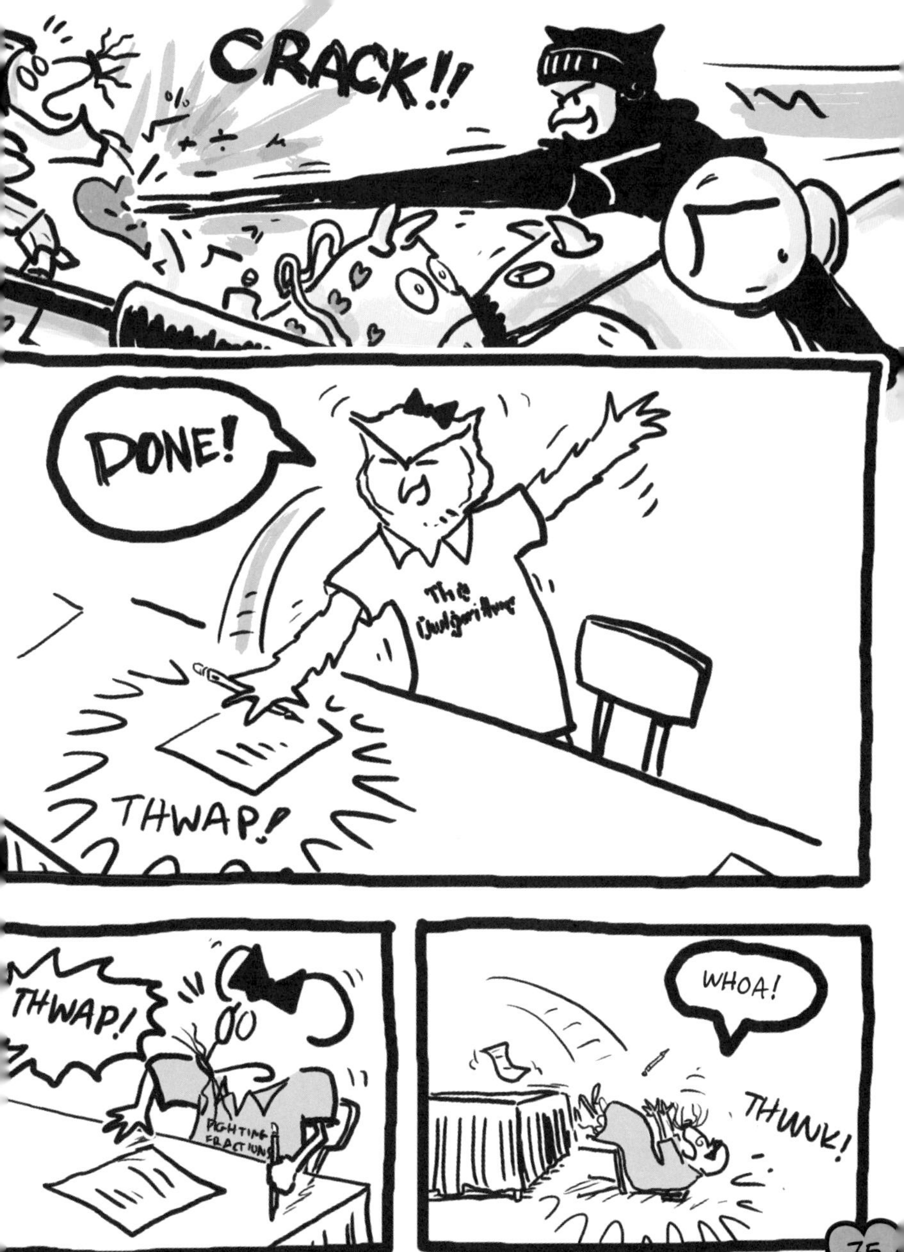
CRACK!!
DONE!
THWAP!
THWAP!
FIGHTING FRACTIONS
WHOA!
THUNK!

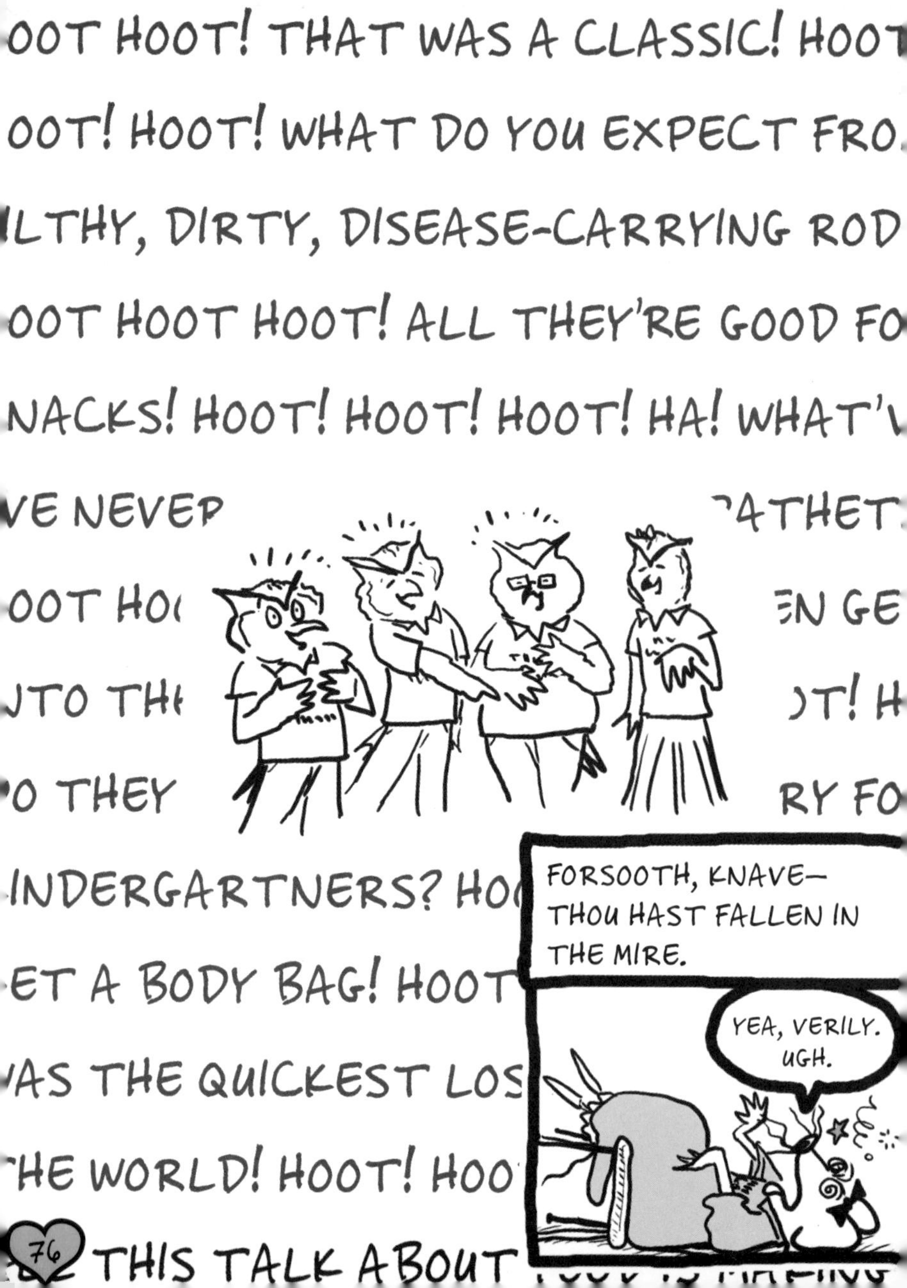
OOT HOOT! THAT WAS A CLASSIC! HOOT
OOT! HOOT! WHAT DO YOU EXPECT FRO
LTHY, DIRTY, DISEASE-CARRYING ROD
OOT HOOT HOOT! ALL THEY'RE GOOD FO
NACKS! HOOT! HOOT! HOOT! HA! WHAT'
VE NEVER
ATHET
OOT HO
EN GE
TO TH
T! H
O THEY
RY FO
INDERGARTNERS? HO
ET A BODY BAG! HOOT
AS THE QUICKEST LOS
HE WORLD! HOOT! HOO
THIS TALK ABOUT
FORSOOTH, KNAVE—
THOU HAST FALLEN IN
THE MIRE.
YEA, VERILY.
UGH.

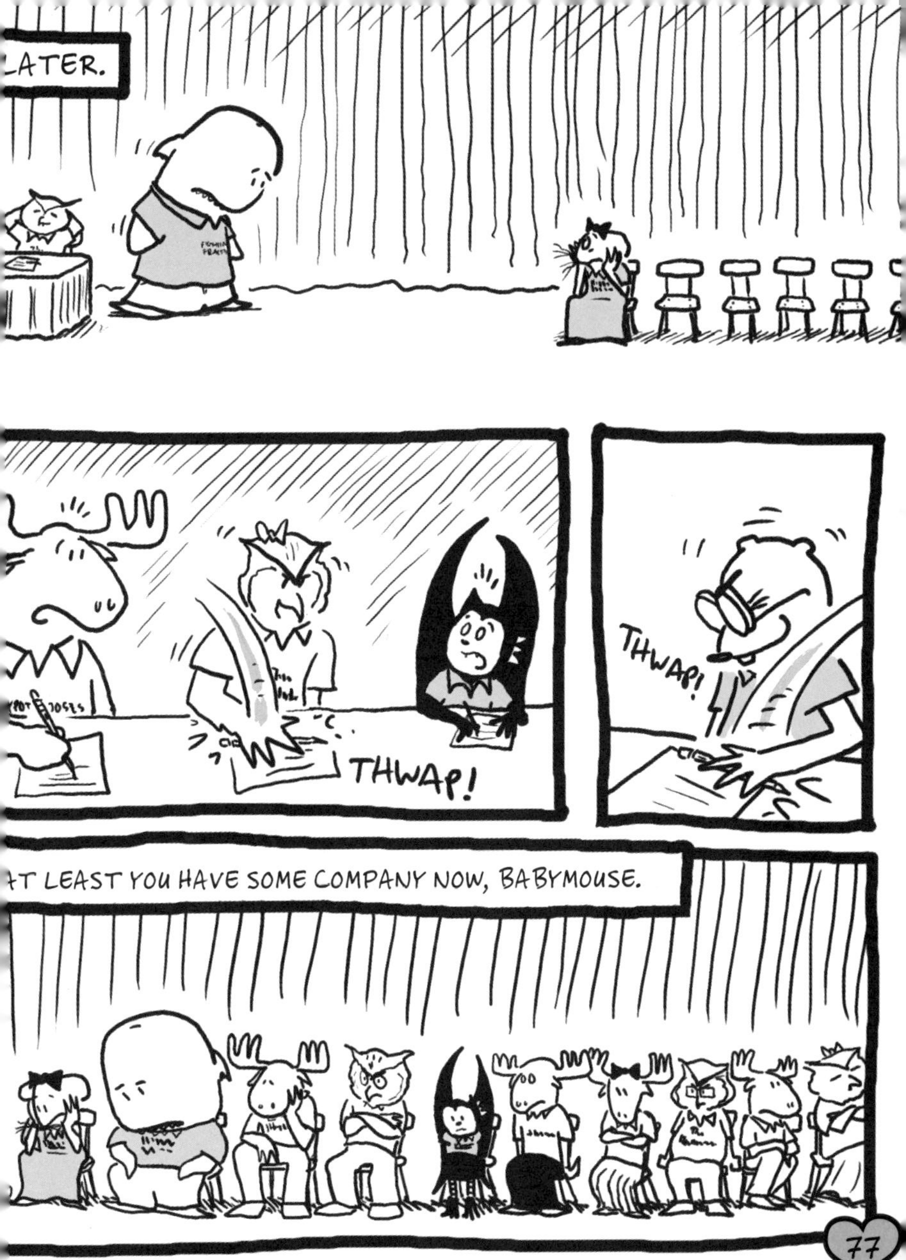
LATER.
THWAP!
THWAP!
AT LEAST YOU HAVE SOME COMPANY NOW, BABYMOUSE.

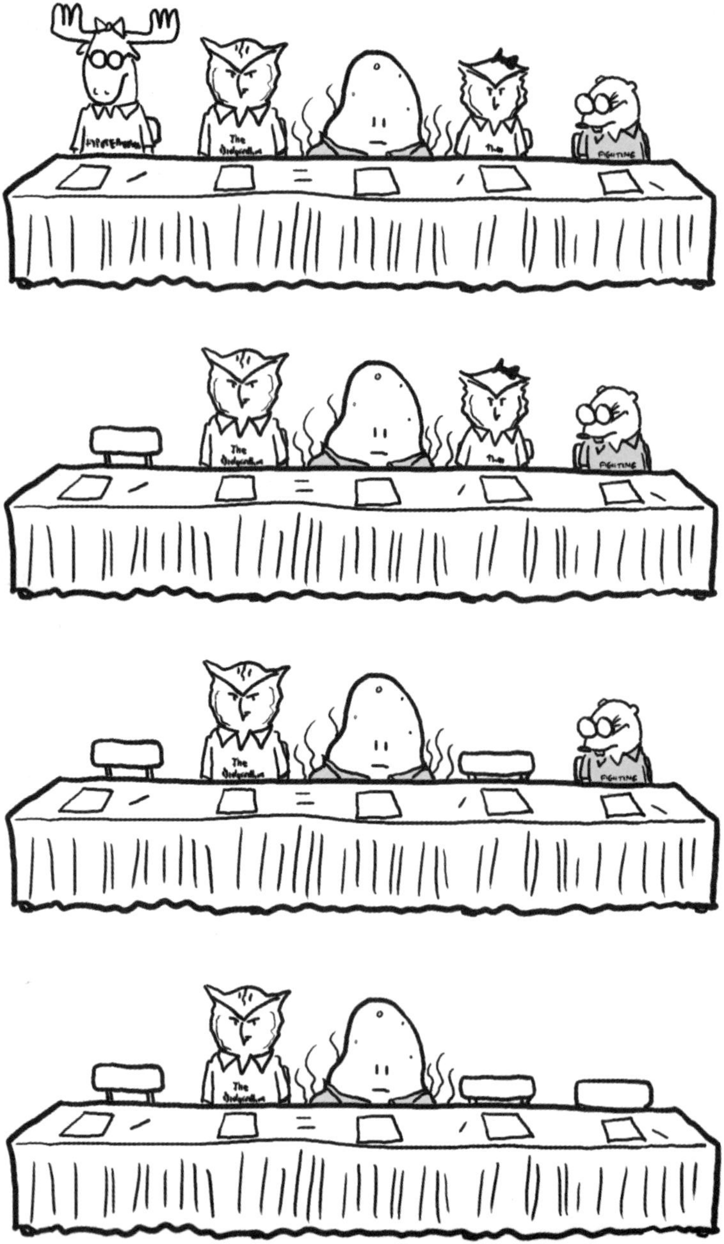

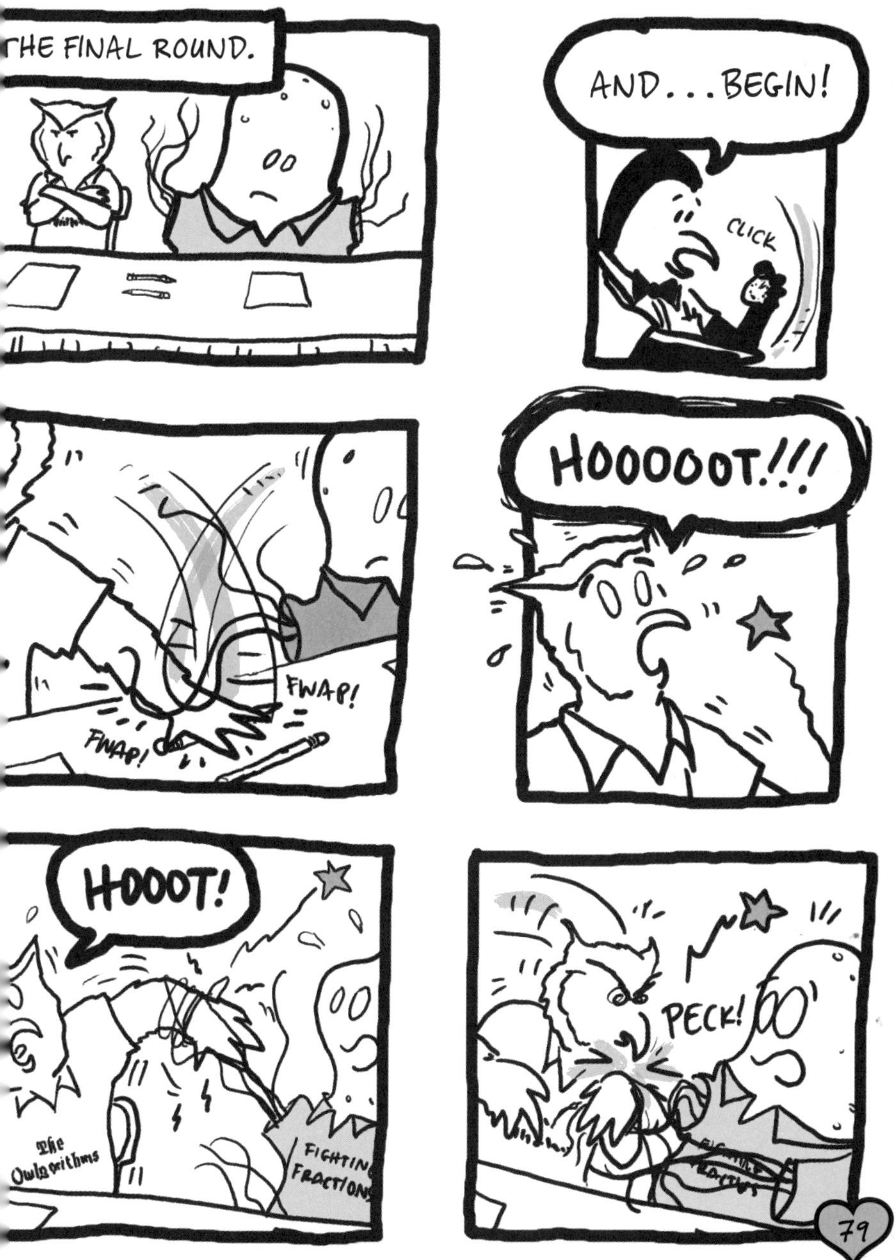
THE FINAL ROUND.
AND...BEGIN!
CLICK
FWAP!
FWAP!
HOOOOOT!!!
HOOOT!
The Owlgorithms
FIGHTING FRACTIONS
PECK!

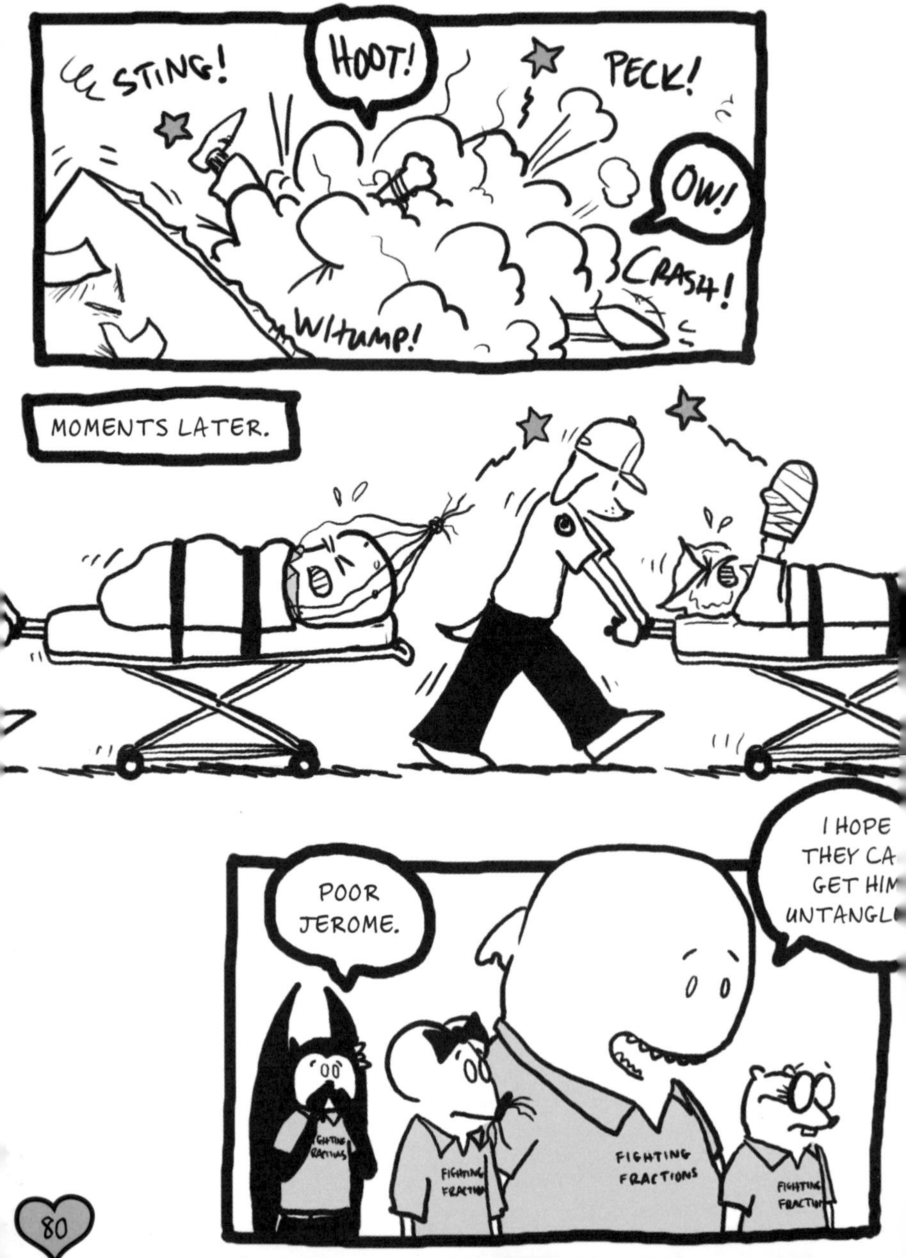
STING!
HOOT!
PECK!
OW!
CRASH!
WHUMP!
MOMENTS LATER.
POOR JEROME.
I HOPE THEY CA GET HIM UNTANGL
FIGHTING FRACTIONS
FIGHTING FRACTIONS
FIGHTING FRACTIONS
FIGHTING FRACTIONS

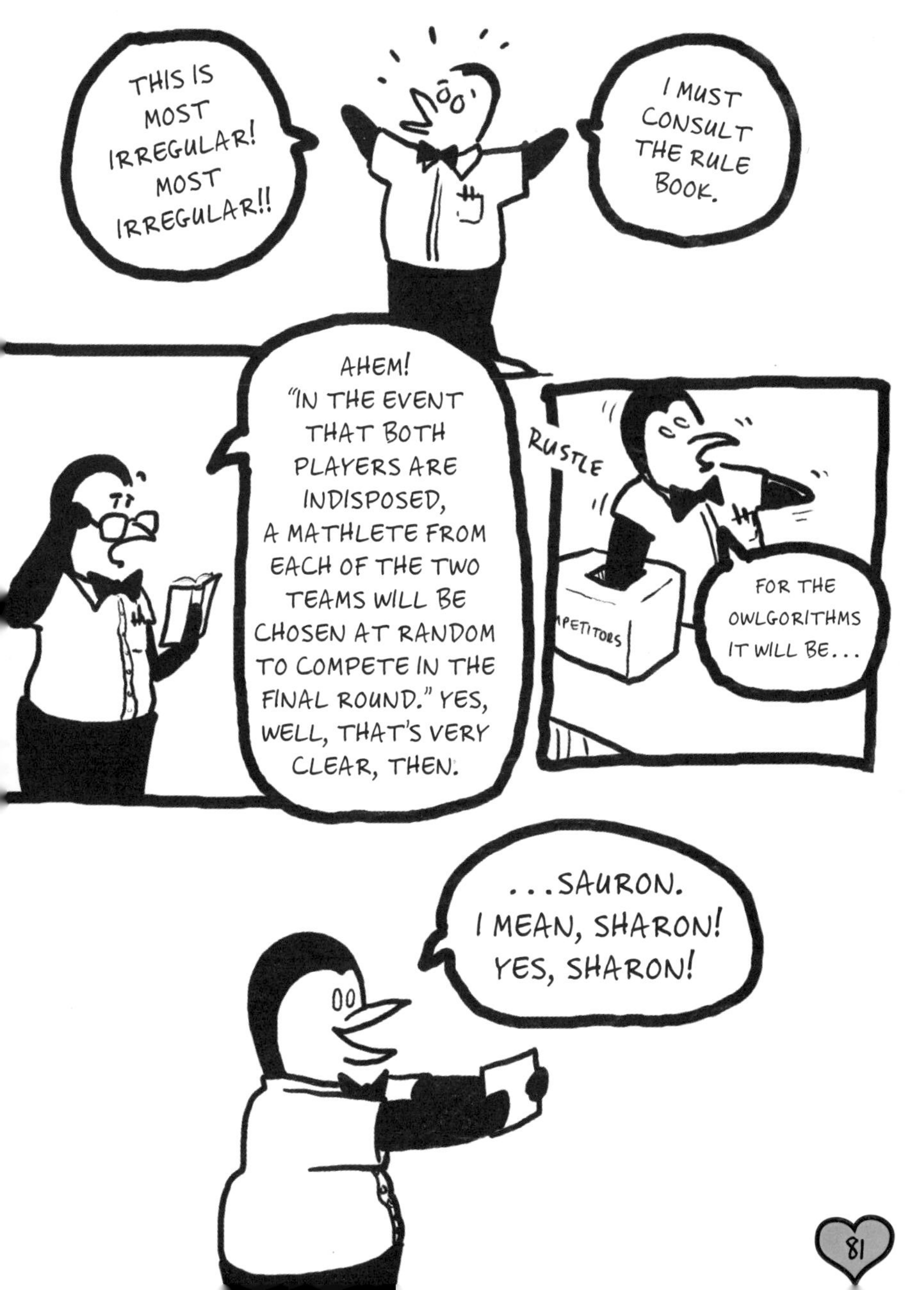
THIS IS MOST IRREGULAR! MOST IRREGULAR!!
I MUST CONSULT THE RULE BOOK.
AHEM! "IN THE EVENT THAT BOTH PLAYERS ARE INDISPOSED, A MATHLETE FROM EACH OF THE TWO TEAMS WILL BE CHOSEN AT RANDOM TO COMPETE IN THE FINAL ROUND." YES, WELL, THAT'S VERY CLEAR, THEN.
RUSTLE
PETITORS
FOR THE OWLGORITHMS IT WILL BE...
...SAURON. I MEAN, SHARON! YES, SHARON!

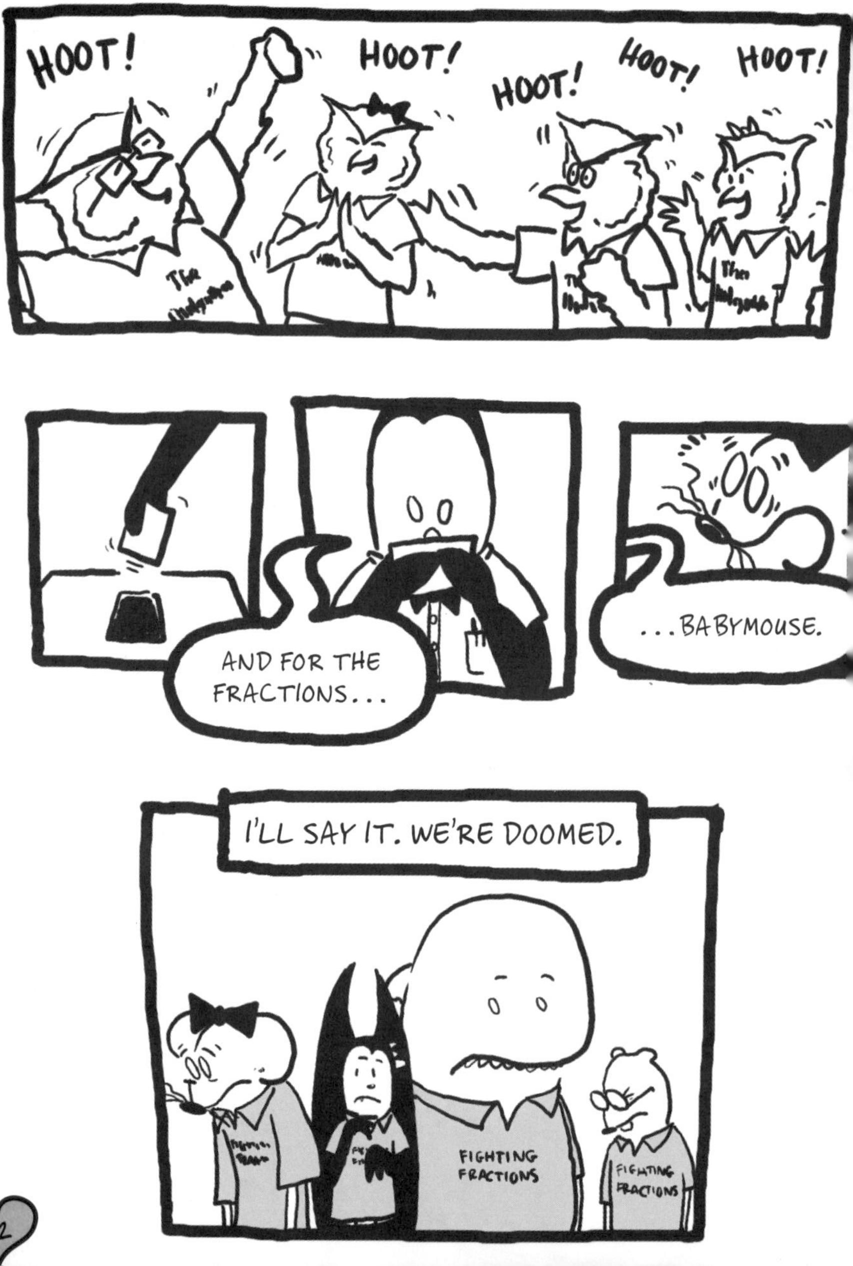
HOOT!
HOOT!
HOOT!
HOOT!
HOOT!
AND FOR THE FRACTIONS...
...BABYMOUSE.
I'LL SAY IT. WE'RE DOOMED.
FIGHTING FRACTIONS
FIGHTING FRACTIONS

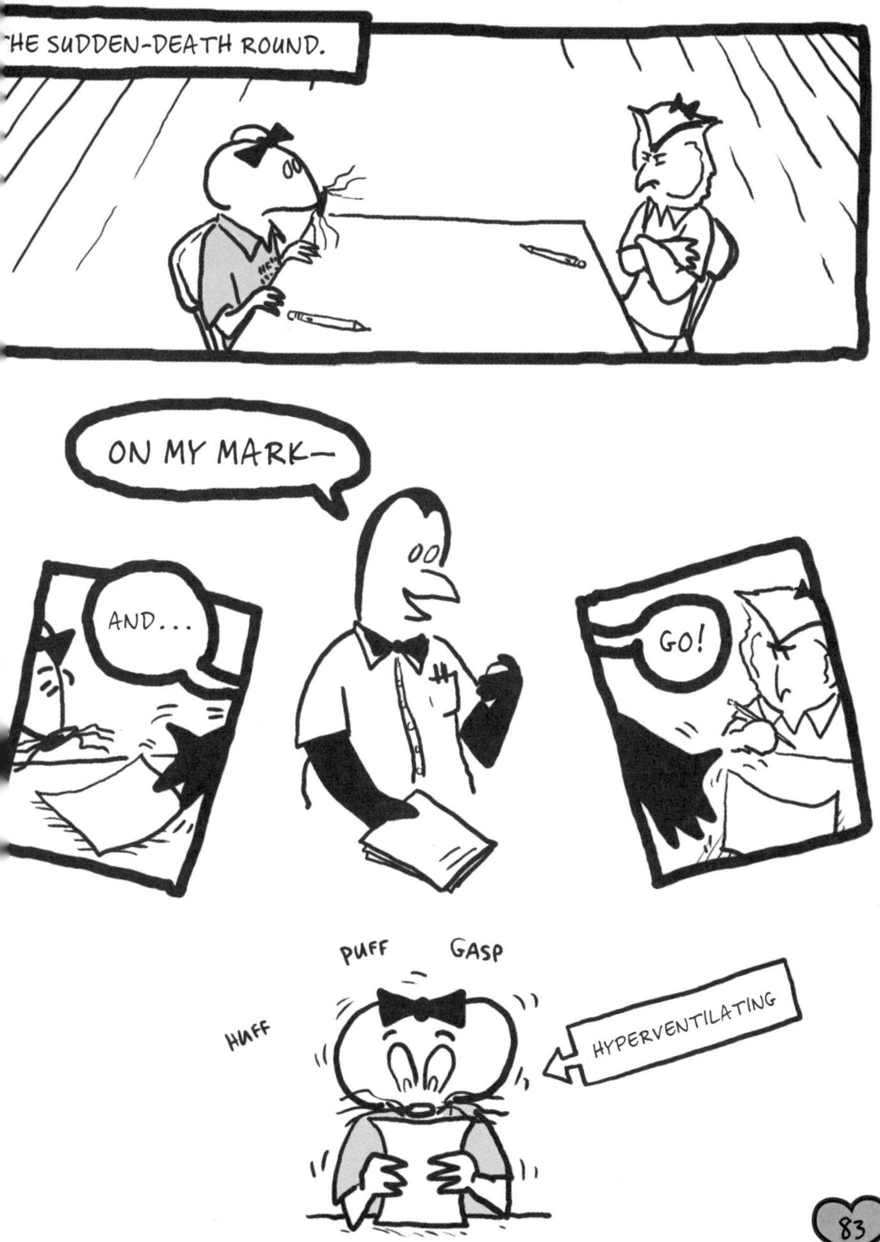
THE SUDDEN-DEATH ROUND.
ON MY MARK—
AND...
GO!
PUFF
GASP
HUFF
HYPERVENTILATING

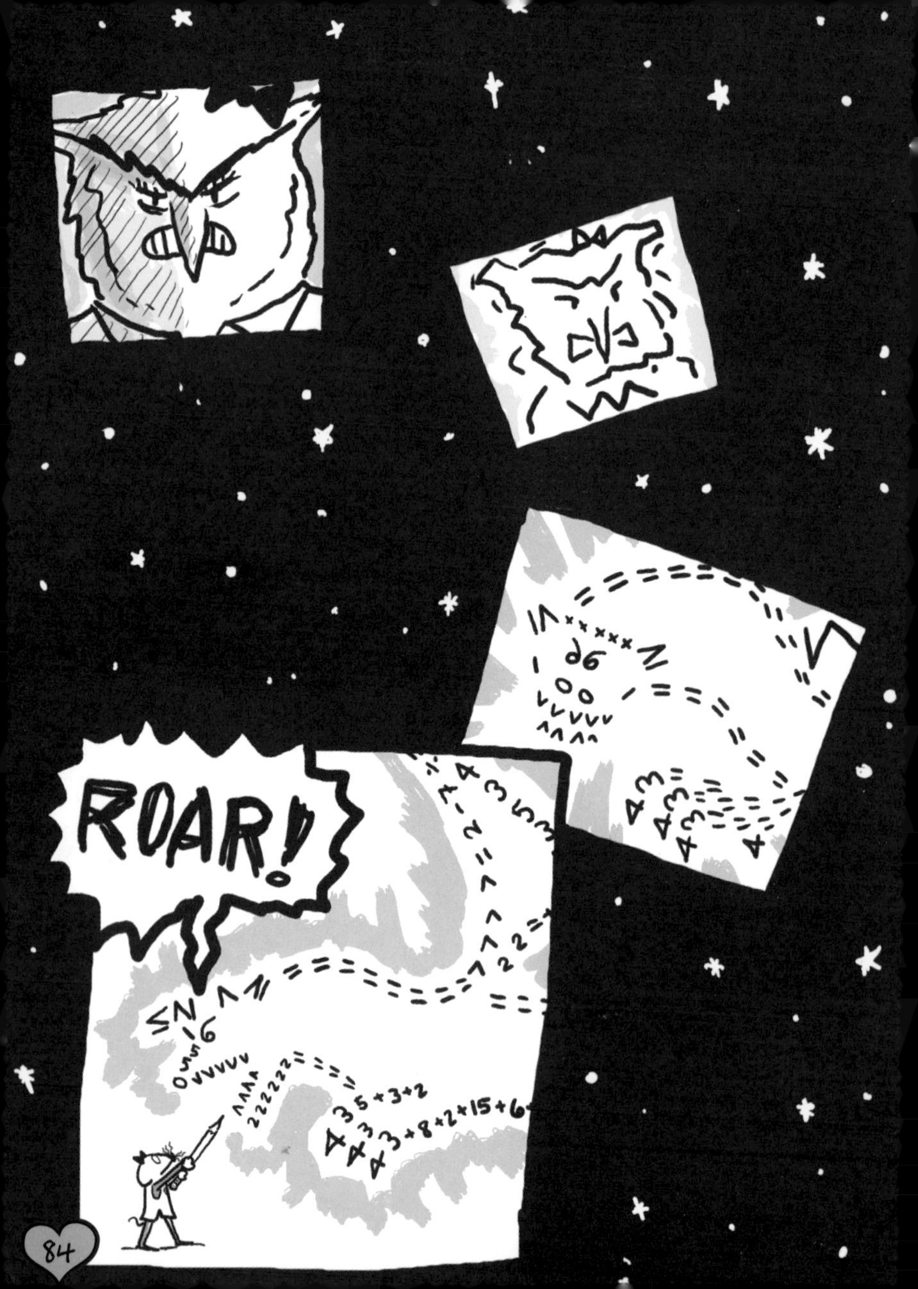
ROAR!

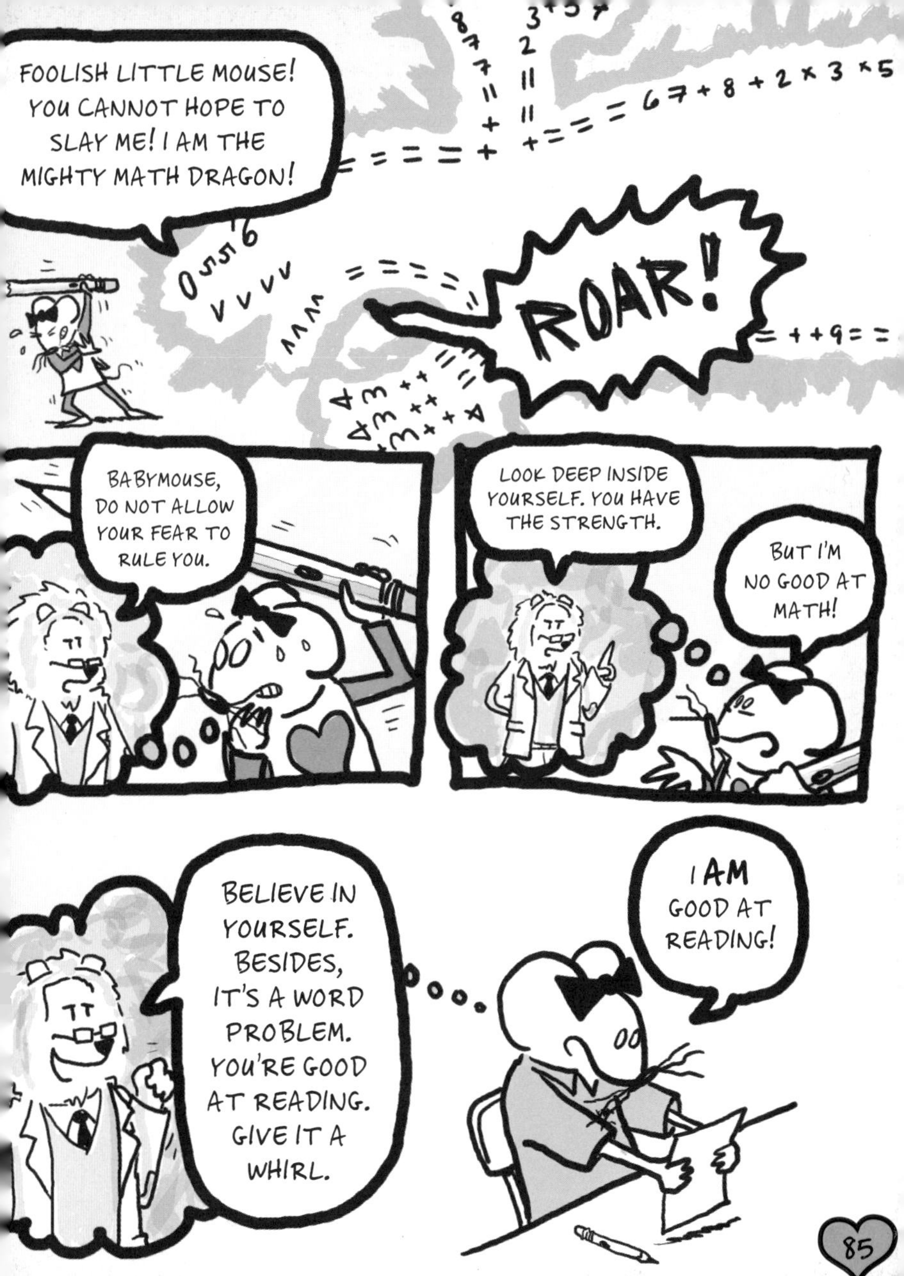
FOOLISH LITTLE MOUSE! YOU CANNOT HOPE TO SLAY ME! I AM THE MIGHTY MATH DRAGON!
ROAR!
BABYMOUSE, DO NOT ALLOW YOUR FEAR TO RULE YOU.
LOOK DEEP INSIDE YOURSELF. YOU HAVE THE STRENGTH.
BUT I'M NO GOOD AT MATH!
BELIEVE IN YOURSELF. BESIDES, IT'S A WORD PROBLEM. YOU'RE GOOD AT READING. GIVE IT A WHIRL.
I AM GOOD AT READING!

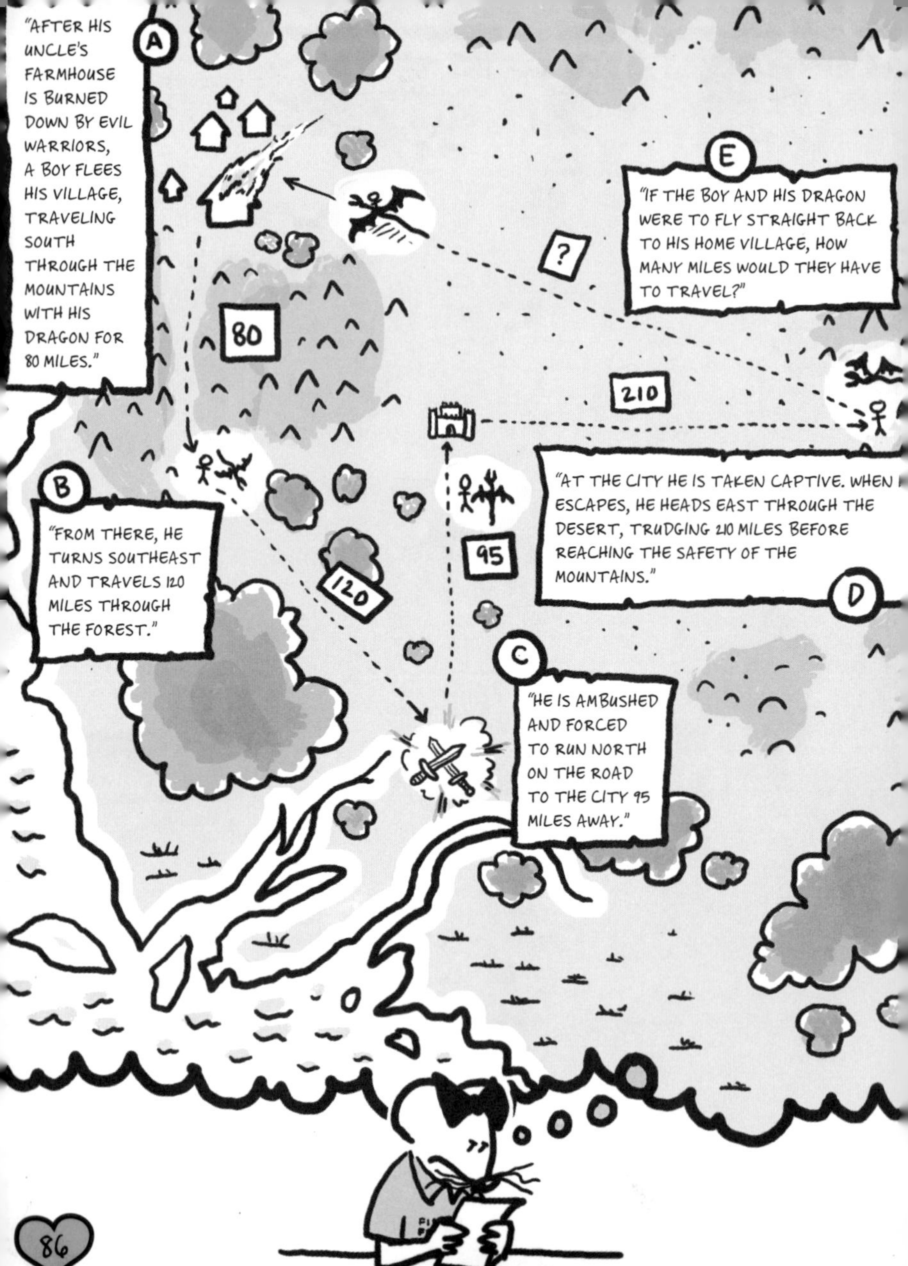
A
"AFTER HIS UNCLE'S FARMHOUSE IS BURNED DOWN BY EVIL WARRIORS, A BOY FLEES HIS VILLAGE, TRAVELING SOUTH THROUGH THE MOUNTAINS WITH HIS DRAGON FOR 80 MILES."
80
B
"FROM THERE, HE TURNS SOUTHEAST AND TRAVELS 120 MILES THROUGH THE FOREST."
120
C
"HE IS AMBUSHED AND FORCED TO RUN NORTH ON THE ROAD TO THE CITY 95 MILES AWAY."
95
D
"AT THE CITY HE IS TAKEN CAPTIVE. WHEN ESCAPES, HE HEADS EAST THROUGH THE DESERT, TRUDGING 210 MILES BEFORE REACHING THE SAFETY OF THE MOUNTAINS."
210
E
"IF THE BOY AND HIS DRAGON WERE TO FLY STRAIGHT BACK TO HIS HOME VILLAGE, HOW MANY MILES WOULD THEY HAVE TO TRAVEL?"
?

SCRIBBLE

FIGHTING FRACTIONS

SNAP!!

GASP!

FIGHTING FRACTIONS

FIGHTING FRACTIONS

FIGHTING FRACTIONS

RUSTLE

FIGHTING FRACTIONS

RUSTLE

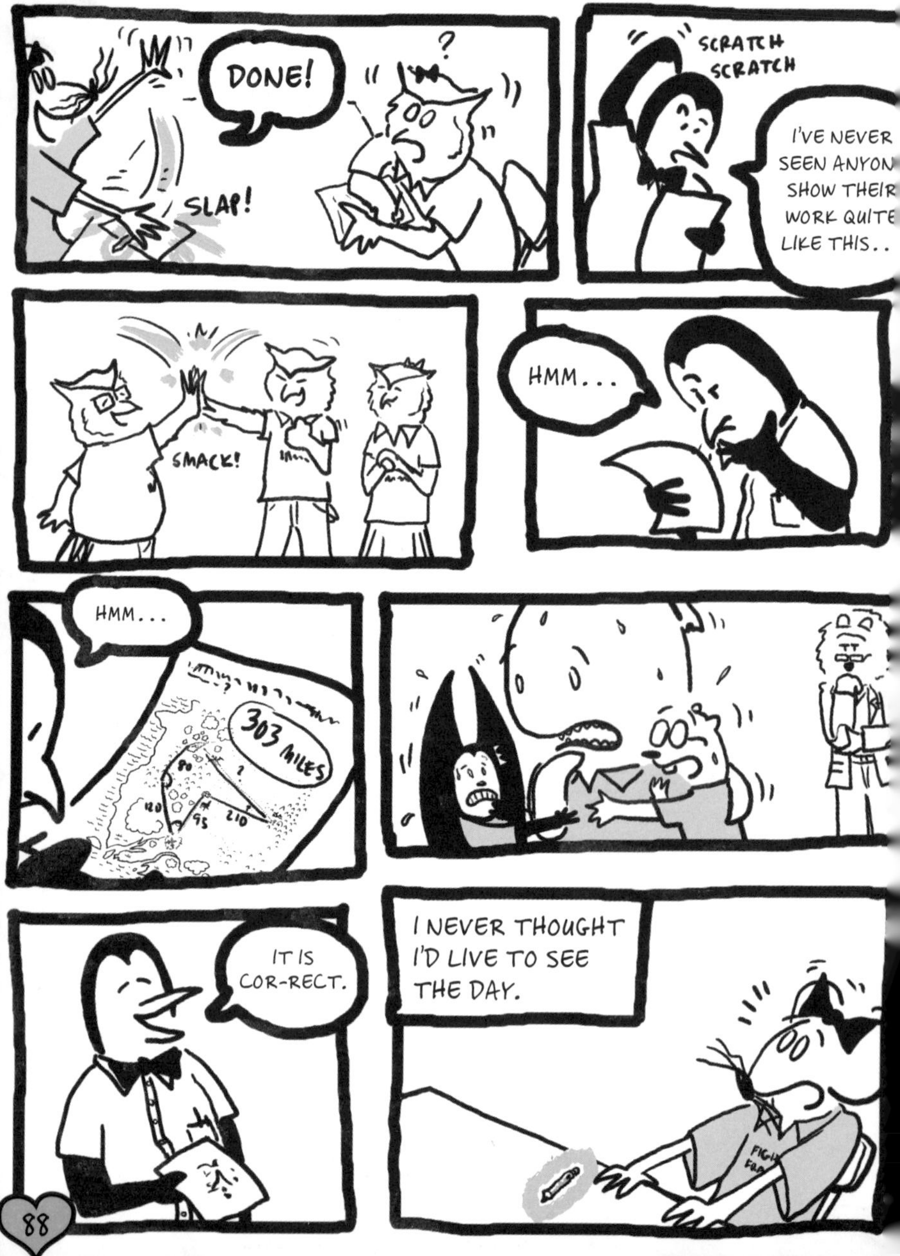
DONE!
SLAP!
SCRATCH SCRATCH
I'VE NEVER SEEN ANYON SHOW THEIR WORK QUITE LIKE THIS. .
SMACK!
HMM. . .
HMM. . .
303 MILES
80
120
95
210
IT IS COR-RECT.
I NEVER THOUGHT I'D LIVE TO SEE THE DAY.

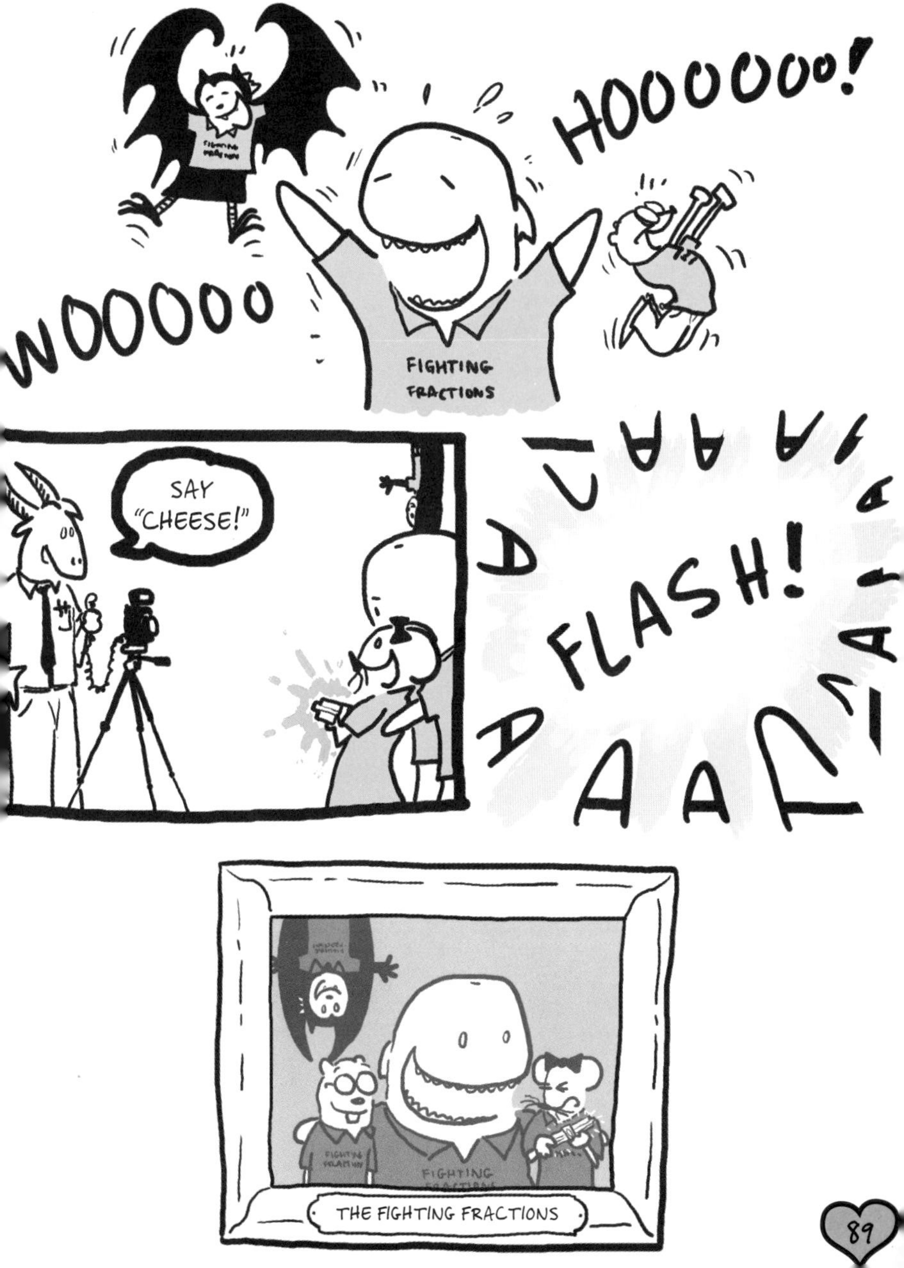
WOOOOO
HOOOOOO!
FIGHTING FRACTIONS
SAY "CHEESE!"
FLASH!
THE FIGHTING FRACTIONS

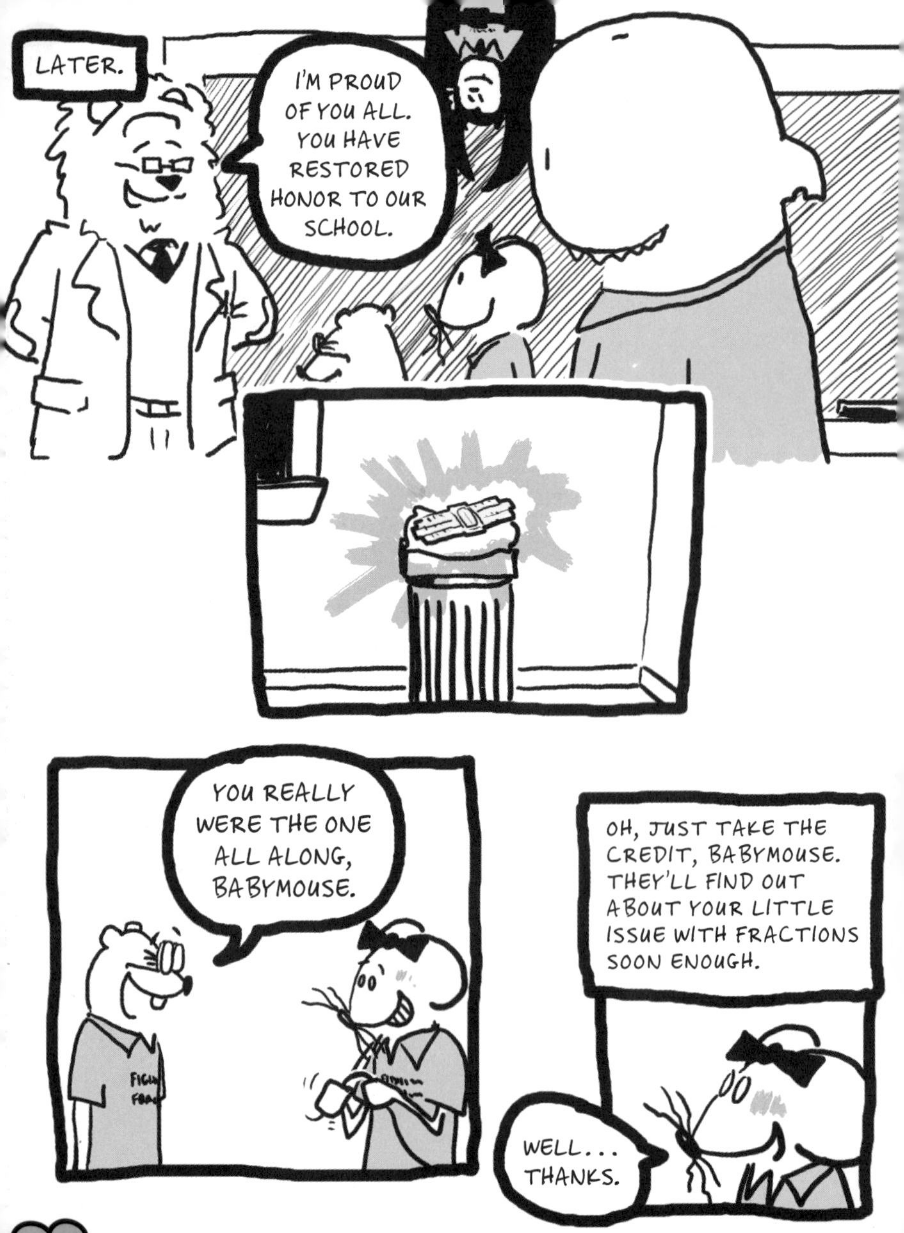
LATER.
I'M PROUD OF YOU ALL. YOU HAVE RESTORED HONOR TO OUR SCHOOL.
YOU REALLY WERE THE ONE ALL ALONG, BABYMOUSE.
OH, JUST TAKE THE CREDIT, BABYMOUSE. THEY'LL FIND OUT ABOUT YOUR LITTLE ISSUE WITH FRACTIONS SOON ENOUGH.
WELL... THANKS.

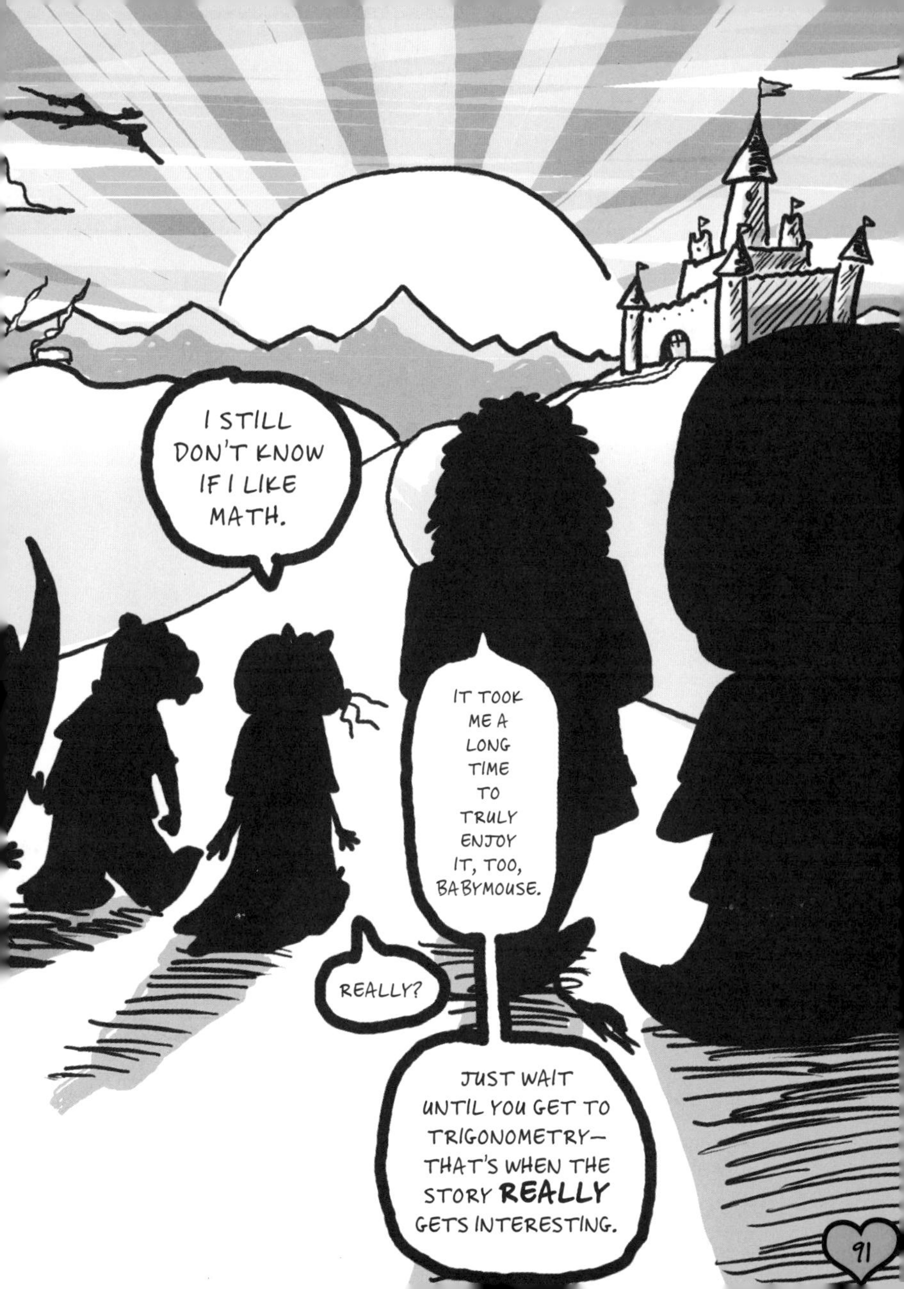
I STILL DON'T KNOW IF I LIKE MATH.
IT TOOK ME A LONG TIME TO TRULY ENJOY IT, TOO, BABYMOUSE.
REALLY?
JUST WAIT UNTIL YOU GET TO TRIGONOMETRY— THAT'S WHEN THE STORY **REALLY** GETS INTERESTING.

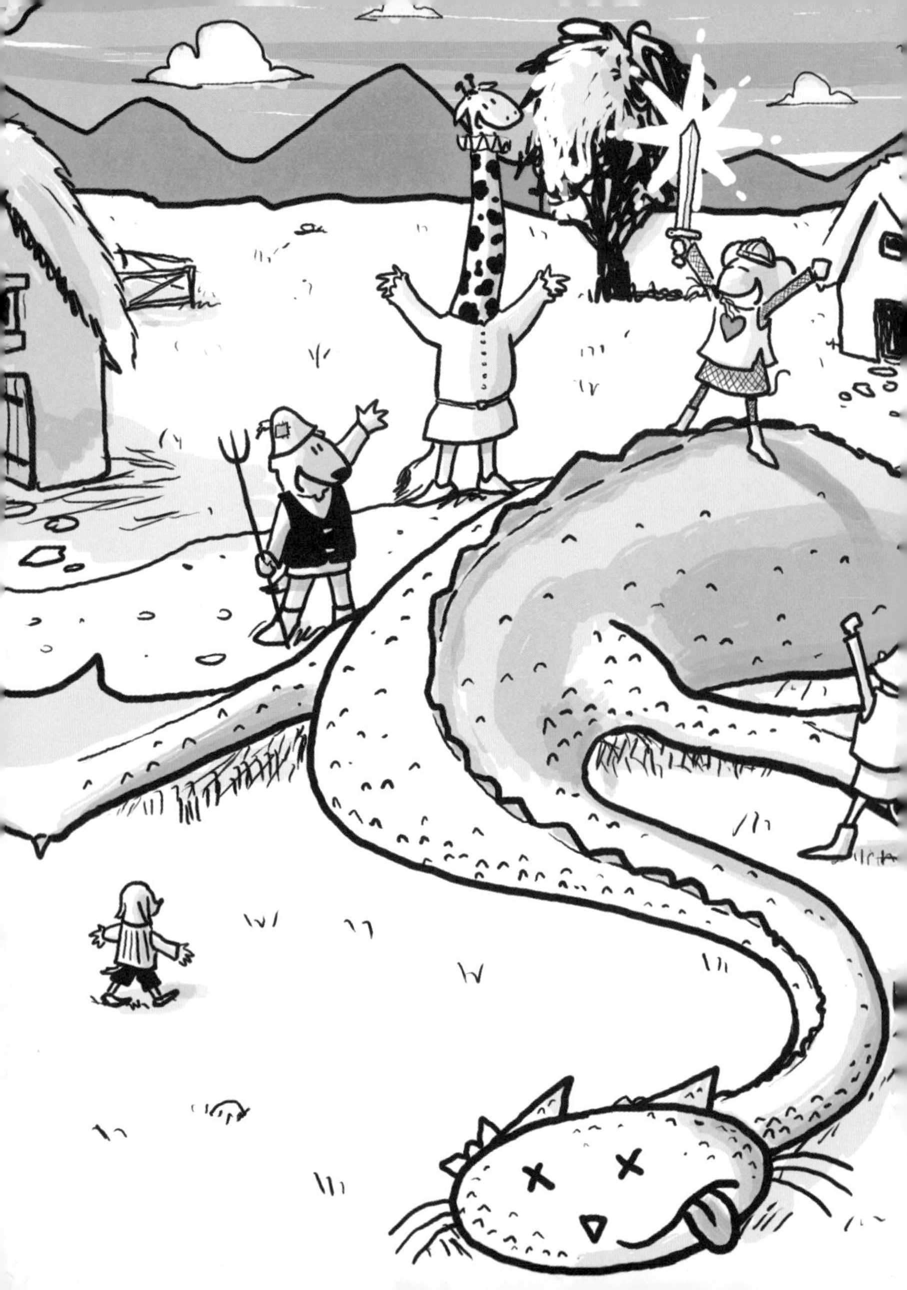

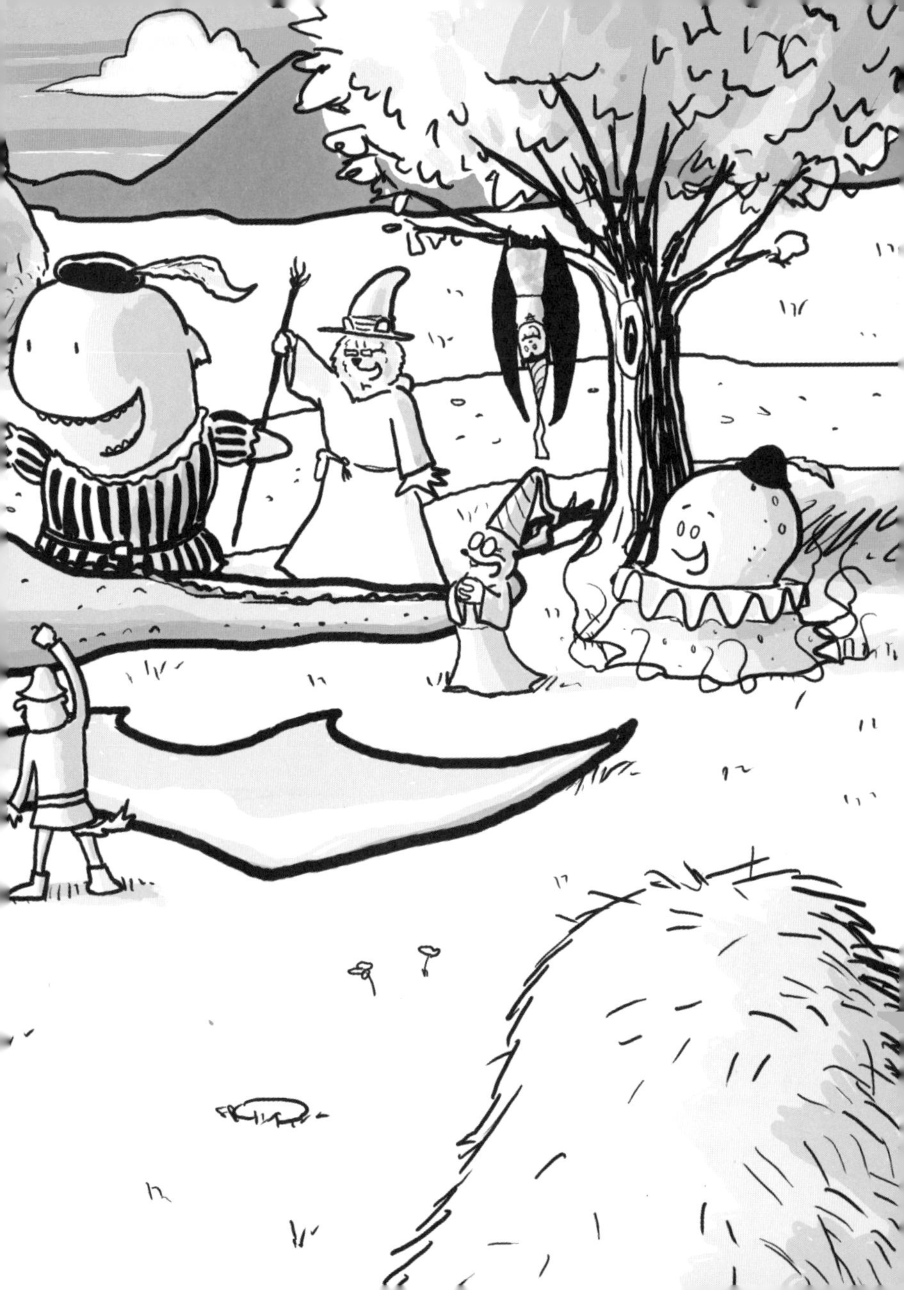

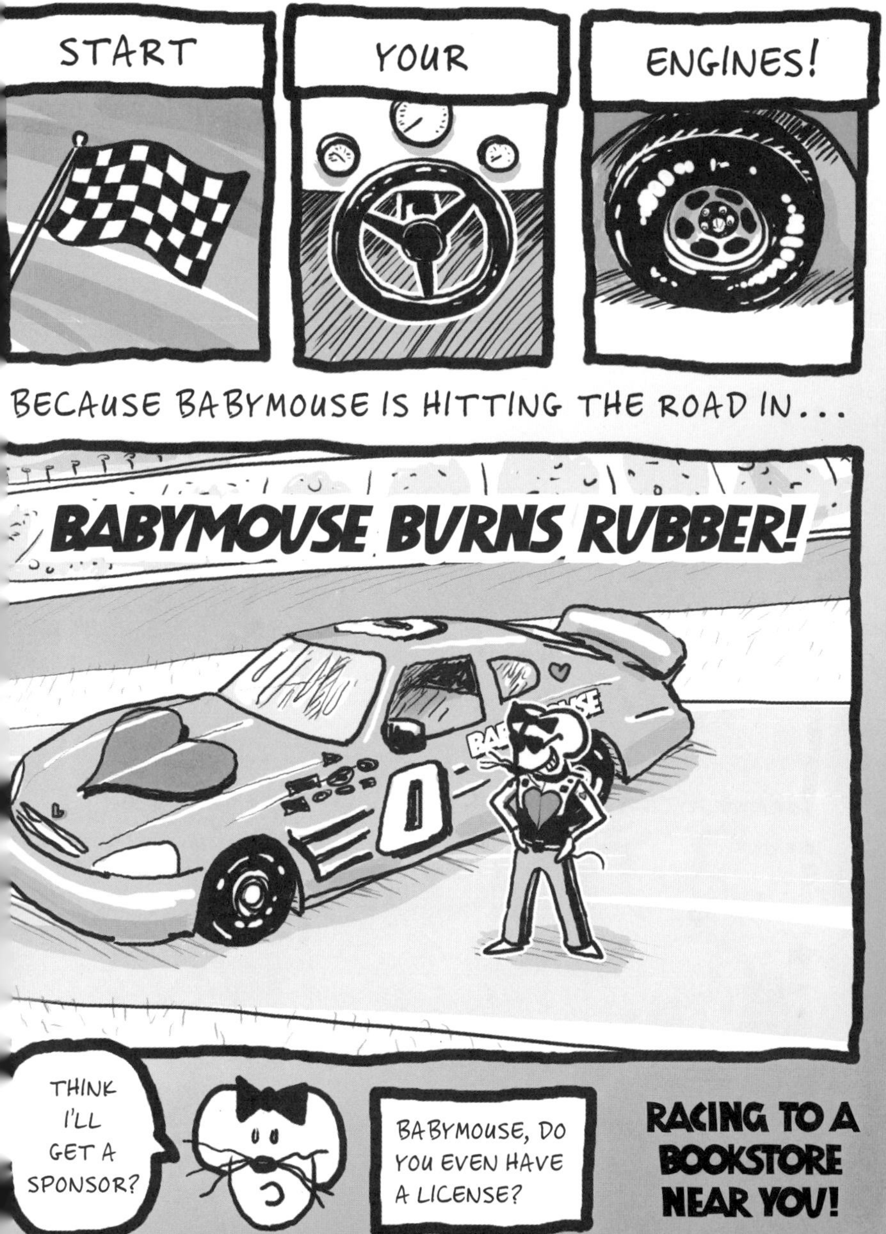
START
YOUR
ENGINES!
BECAUSE BABYMOUSE IS HITTING THE ROAD IN...
BABYMOUSE BURNS RUBBER!
THINK I'LL GET A SPONSOR?
BABYMOUSE, DO YOU EVEN HAVE A LICENSE?
RACING TO A BOOKSTORE NEAR YOU!

BABYMOUSE BONUS!

• TIPS ON BEING A DRAGONSLAYER •

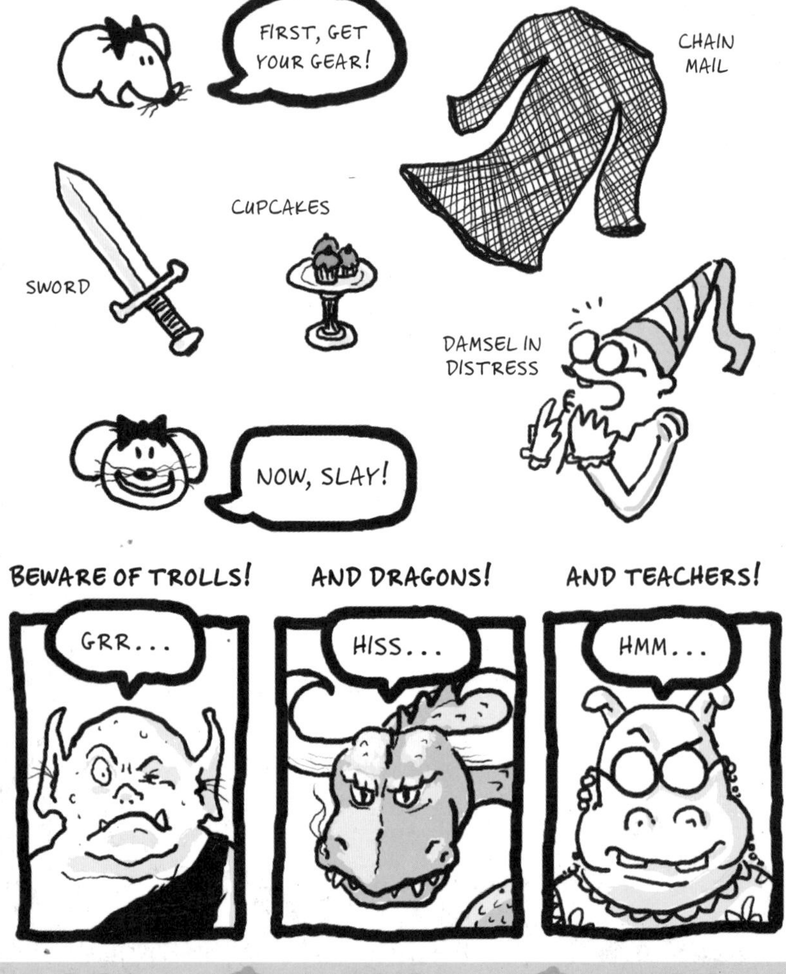

FIRST, GET YOUR GEAR!
CHAIN MAIL
CUPCAKES
SWORD
DAMSEL IN DISTRESS
NOW, SLAY!
BEWARE OF TROLLS!
GRR...
AND DRAGONS!
HISS...
AND TEACHERS!
HMM...

PRITHEE, WHEREFORE DOTH M'LORD AND LADY DON SUCH RAIMENT?

Brother-sister team **Matthew** and **Jennifer Holm** are neither wizards nor Hobbits, though they did play a lot of Dungeons & Dragons when they were kids. They have never discovered a door in the back of their closet, but as a child, Jennifer did once receive a personal phone call from Lloyd Alexander—and that was pretty magical. Today Jennifer is the author of several highly acclaimed novels, including two Newbery Honor winners, **Our Only May Amelia** and **Penny from Heaven**. Matthew Holm is a graphic designer and freelance writer.

You can visit the Babymouse Web site at www.babymouse.com.

Also available in Gibraltar Library Binding

PRAISE FOR BABYMOUSE!

★ "Nobody puts Babymouse in the corner!" —**The Horn Book Magazine**, Starred

"Move over, Superman. Here comes Babymouse!" —**Chicago Sun-Times**

"A new hero emerges in . . . Babymouse." —**The Bulletin**

"Emergent readers will cheer 'Babymouse!'" —**Kirkus Reviews**

"It is written that the Elvish Oracle Fessendyl foretold the coming of a young warrior-maid who would defeat the Great Dragon. Could this 'Babymouse' be the One?" —Gorzabal the Loremaster

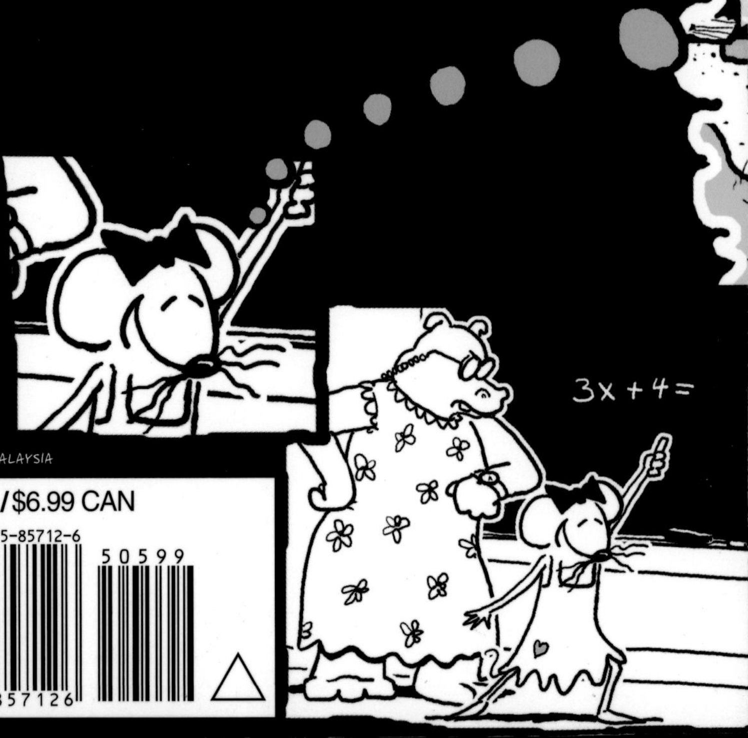
3x + 4 =

MANUFACTURED IN MALAYSIA

US $5.99 / $6.99 CAN

ISBN 978-0-375-85712-6

50599

9 780375 857126